Quench the Day
Red Wolf Trilogy
Book 1

Shari Branning

<u>Chapter 1</u>

"Curses? Good gracious!" Rowan was so startled she dropped her silk gloves onto the floor of the carriage and had to bend over to retrieve them.

Her cousin, Dustan, who was seated across from her, grinned in triumph at finally cracking her bored façade. He shrugged. "It's only a rumor," he said. He leaned forward, resting his forearms on his knees. "But aside from the 'accidental' deaths, there have been some things that people just can't explain." His sudden intensity testified that he wasn't just making up stories to shock her this time.

Rowan settled back into her seat and smoothed her skirts. "I had no idea the royal family had such violent tendencies." Secretly she was once again questioning her decision to move in with her uncle's household in West Talva. After two months, it was painfully obvious that the country out here was going to pieces. She frowned, afraid her next question might be another piece of common knowledge that easterners just weren't aware of.

She said it anyway. "I was under the impression that curses were..." she fished for something other than 'make-believe.' "That they were more a matter of legend."

Dustan didn't pounce on her ignorance this time, instead pressing his lips together and glancing out at the prairie as their carriage left the outskirts of Skybreak, jostling them when it hit the rutted country road. He fiddled with his string tie for a moment. "The Shonnowan people can do strange things," he said. "Sometimes their merchants will come to the city and sell magic items, for a high price. I don't believe cursing someone would be impossible."

"But who could think it a good idea to..." Rowan let her voice trail off. The thought of anyone placing a curse of some kind on another human being smacked of unnamable evil. She had a hard time envisioning such a thing, and it bothered her more than she cared to show her teasing cousin, though she couldn't hide the goosebumps that flashed up her arms.

"Our *Lesser* King Ormand is known to be a man without a conscience," Dustan said. "His face does spring to mind."

"I see. But if he's already killing off his personal enemies in contrived accidents..." *Why would he need to curse them?*

The carriage slowed, and she turned back to the window, catching a glimpse of half a dozen other carriages pulling up before they fell into line, and then the only thing she could see was a manicured lawn, flowering trellises, and a line of trees separating the estate's front yard from the open prairie.

Their driver stopped the horses long before they reached the front doors, waiting for the people in front of them to exit their carriages or buggies, and then for the drivers to move out of the way. They spent five minutes stopping and starting before they pulled up in front of the broad, shallow stairs leading to the mansion's double doors. Neither Rowan nor Dustan spoke again as they waited. Political discussions had no business at a coming-of-age celebration, unless they took place behind a potted plant or in a closed study.

Finally, their turn came, their carriage aligning with the entrance, and the Daws' footman opened their door, standing aside for Dustan to step down. Dustan, in turn, offered his hand to Rowan, who ignored him and jumped down on her own. It was their little ritual. He offered his arm next, which she also ignored, then grinned and followed her up the stairs to the open door, where a crowd was working its way inside. The evening sun shone at their backs as they entered, and Rowan thought ruefully that it would make her red hair look like a bonfire blaze on top of her head, no matter how skillfully her serving girl had arranged her curls.

She sighed as she stepped through the doors and directly into the ballroom. There were too many people pressed around them to be able to see much, so her gaze explored upward to the grand staircase that swept around the edge of the room in a flourish of curved brass railing. A few people stood talking on the lower steps to avoid the crowd, but her gaze caught on one man, and he was the only one she truly saw.

His icy blue eyes locked onto hers at the same time, and he fumbled his conversation, making his companion turn to look as well.

"Go on then," Dustan said from behind her.

She had paused just inside the doorway, with the crowd of young noblemen and women pressing in and flowing around her into the great open room. A young man bumped her elbow, and he turned to apologize, his gaze sweeping over her. His eyes lit appreciatively and he bowed.

"I don't believe I've had the pleasure, my lady. May I introduce mysel—"

Dustan brushed in front of him, interrupting his introduction as though he wasn't there, and again offered Rowan his arm. "We'll never make it past the entry at this rate, and I, for one, would like to find a beautiful woman who's *not* related to me to dance with."

Rowan whacked him on the arm with her gloves, even as her gaze returned to the staircase where the young man with the dangerous eyes had been standing. He was gone.

"Rowan!"

"Annalie!" She turned, smiling, and let go Dustan's arm, having to stoop a bit to return her friend's hug.

"That's my cue that I'm no longer needed." Dustan bowed in greeting to Rowan's friend, then sauntered off.

"I feared I wouldn't know a soul here tonight," Rowan said.

Annalie laughed. "Yes, I know how you hate introductions."

"Your men out here like starving puppies. Honestly. It's suffocating. Much worse here, in fact, than back east." She glanced at another man staring at them as they walked, arm-in-arm, toward a quieter corner of the room. "Woe to the girl cursed with red hair and long legs."

Her friend gasped, then giggled. But whatever she said next was lost to Rowan as she spotted the blue-eyed stranger again, this time standing along the wall by himself, arms folded across his chest. His gaze swept over the room, then rested on her.

He winked.

"Rowan?"

"Pardon?" She turned back to her friend.

"Are you well tonight? You were staring."

"Who is that?" She nodded to the man who still watched them.

"Oh. Him. Aaro D'Araines. Cousin to High King Heymish and King Ormand. Beautiful, isn't he? And he has the biggest ranch in the area. And he can afford to carry two—two! guns. And he's part of the royal family. Did I mention that?" She sighed. "He's notoriously disinterested in dancing though, so don't get your hopes up."

"*That's* Aaro D'Araines?" Rowan could feel the beginning of a blush warming her cheeks, at suddenly coming to the attention of the very person that Dustan had been prattling about for most of the carriage ride, before he got on the subject of curses. Her cousin seemed to be a little in awe of the other young man, who, as Annalie had pointed out, could afford to carry two expensive pistol and also the ammunition to practice with them until he was deadly.

"The man who should have been our king," Annalie said quietly, unaware of Rowan's discomfort. Then she jumped and looked around to see who might have heard her comment. They had the corner to themselves. Though there weren't any potted plants nearby.

"I expected—not him." Rowan said lamely.

Annalie went on, while across the room Aaro D'Araines pushed off the wall and wove his way through the crowd toward them. Rowan panicked and elbowed her friend in the ribs, afraid she'd still be talking about him when he made it over to their corner. He must already know they'd been whispering about him, and that was bad enough. Though she noticed he wore neither his guns or a sword tonight. So perhaps he wasn't quite the feral gunman Dustan made him out to be.

A delicate tinkle of crystal filtered through

the dozens of conversations going on in the ballroom. Mr. Daws, who was one of the noblemen whom Rowan's uncle was friends with, stood in the arched doorway leading to the dining hall, pinging a knife against a crystal goblet. Voices died into polite quiet.

"I want to thank you all for coming tonight to celebrate with us our twins' coming of age," Mr. Daws said.

Polite applause.

Rowan's eyes wandered from him back to Aaro D'Araines, who had paused in the center of the room, arms folded once again, as he leaned casually on one foot. His eyes flickered back in her direction as well, and a faint smile touched the corner of his mouth. He began edging toward them again as Mr. Daws continued his toast. Rowan didn't hear most of it. The closer those blue eyes came, the more they drew her. Chestnut hair curled wildly around his ears. He wore simple range clothes, though they looked new. A white shirt under a black vest, and black trousers. Somehow, he managed to look like a Western man and a nobleman at the same time.

"Are you coming?"

"I'm sorry?" She'd missed something.

"It's time to go to supper. Really, you mustn't stare so! And at Mr. D'Araines. You'll be the gossip of the town. Besides, as I told you, he doesn't dance. And we *are* here to dance."

Rowan let her friend tug her along with

the crowd filtering into the dining hall, until a hand on her arm stopped her. Work-roughened skin snagged on her lace sleeve. Her heart did a backflip even before she turned around.

Aaro tilted his head in greeting, rather than give her a full bow. "May I?" He offered his arm.

She felt heat flame into her face. She detested blushing. It made her look like a wretched tomato.

"I'm sorry, have we met?" She pinned him with a look.

His half smile tilted further upward. "No. But you already asked your friend my name. I have only to learn yours, but I'm not so stuck on formality." He offered his arm again. She glanced down. His sleeve was rolled up past his elbow, baring corded muscles wrapped in deeply tanned skin. No society-conscious gentleman would be so bold as to offer a lady his bare arm to escort her. She snapped her gaze back up to his eyes. They twinkled, daring her.

"Very well, Mr. D'Araines." She settled her hand gingerly on his arm, feeling the warmth of his skin against her suddenly cold fingers as he led her toward the dining room. Her gloves were still clenched in her other hand.

"What do you like to write?" He asked her.

"Write?" Rowan was taken aback. She had expected a comment about her appearance. How her eye color nearly matched her hair, or how he'd never seen such an intriguing shade of auburn before (even though it was closer to the color of copper). Or how she looked lovely this evening. They always commented on her looks.

"You have ink on your hands," he replied.

"Oh. Ah. I was writing to my father, back east, simply to let him know I will be continuing my stay here indefinitely. I have no great patience for writing, as a rule."

"I have a mother and a sister who wish I wrote more as well," he said. "But ranching bores them, and I don't practice needlepoint, so I don't have much news, generally." He cast her a sideways grin. They entered the dining hall, where a long table reached from one end of the room to the other. He pulled out a chair for her, and when she was seated, gave her a bow. "A pleasure to meet you, Red." He winked before walking away.

Annalie settled into the chair beside Rowan, her eyes all round with amazement. "Of all the... can you believe him? He didn't even introduce himself. And his shirtsleeves!" She tugged at one of her own sheer pink cuffs. "You would have had every right to turn him down."

"I didn't want to." Rowan grinned. "My dear, I think I'm in love."

Annalie looked at her askance. "You?"

She laughed. "No. But he's...refreshing."

She had never been enthusiastic about formal dinners. They seemed to drag on and on, one course after another, and always so polite and awkward. The Daws twins, Rebecca and Korr, looked uncomfortable, seated on either side of their father and mother at the head of the table.

"I wonder when King Ormand will arrive," Annalie said as they waited for their dishes to be cleared and the next course brought out.

"Is he coming, then? Dustan had mentioned it."

"Didn't you hear anything Mr. Daws said?"

"Honestly—no."

"It was very bold of him to invite both the lesser king—ah! I mean King Ormand—and Mr. D'Araines here tonight. Perfectly proper, of course, and exactly as it should be. I just hope it doesn't become awkward. Or dangerous! The poor twins!"

As Dustan had also already apprised her on the ongoing feud between Aaro D'Araines and his cousin, King Ormand, Rowan didn't ask, instead glancing toward the head of the table. Korr halfheartedly tried to make conversation with the young noble seated beside him. Even from her place near the foot of the table she could see his discomfort. Meanwhile, Rebecca stared down at her lap. Aaro was seated directly to her right, and she cast timid little glances at him. He said something to her, and she ducked her head, her face flaming.

Rowan bit her lips to keep from laughing.

"I pity them already. Is this their first ball, or are they always so shy? They really are sweet, if they would not be so terrified of talking to people."

"Not everyone is blessed with your bold wit, Rowan, nor your ability to draw people out."

"Whether those things are a blessing I've yet to decide. They more often get me into trouble."

After the dessert course, Mr. Daws stood and gave another short speech, inviting everyone into the ballroom, where there would be music, and the opportunity to dance, since, "Of course that is what the young people have come for." He smiled graciously.

Annalie leaned over. "I fear I must agree with you in this instance. Our country barn dances are much more fun than these formal balls. Though each has their own merits, and this *is* nice. I haven't had occasion to wear this gown in nearly a year!"

Rowan laughed. They stood, preparing to follow the stream of young people headed toward the open floor, when Aaro reappeared at her elbow. Again, he saluted her with a nod and offered his still-bare arm.

"May I? The musicians are starting."

Rowan rested her hand on his arm, hearing Annalie gasp quietly behind her. She steeled herself against further blushes, and met Aaro's icy, twinkling eyes. "I have it from a reliable source that you don't care to dance, Mr.

D'Araines.

He nodded, a sly smile stretching his mouth. "I've had no motivation to dance, until tonight."

"I see." She tilted her head, letting her own eyes match the twinkle in his. "I would have to conclude then, that you must be a very poor dancer, since you lack any sort of practice."

"You fear for you pride?"

"My toes, Mr. D'Araines. I'm a wild thing, and not used to wearing such flimsy footwear. A horse may step on my foot, and I care not, so long as I have my boots. But perchance a butterfly might bruise my toes, if it landed there now." She glanced meaningfully down at the beaded tips of her silk slippers, peeking out from beneath her skirt.

"Rest assured, your toes have as much regard from me as the rest of you."

"Ah good! So long as that's settled."

They were one of the first couples to step onto the dance floor, and Rowan could feel eyes turned in their direction. She willed herself not to blush again as Aaro rested a hand lightly on her waist, preparing for the first steps of the dance, where he would hold her hand and spin her away from him. She never truly expected him to dance badly. Somehow it didn't seem a part of his nature—what little she'd seen of it—to participate in anything that he couldn't do as well or better than everyone else. To her satisfaction, she was proved right.

"You haven't been in West Talva long," Aaro said as she twirled back to him.

"Two months."

"You started the journey during the winter, then?"

"Yes, sadly. Not one I would recommend in terms of comfort, though it was lovely."

Another series of turns and twirls cut off conversation for a moment. Then Aaro said, "Most would wait for spring to make the trip."

"I had several reasons for coming when I did." She smiled, but didn't elaborate. She had no wish to narrate the long year that had led up to her coming to stay with her uncle Lance and his three sons, nor was there time, as the dance ended, and another young man approached, heading right for them. She turned away, pretending not to see him, and tugged her little fan out of her sleeve, snapping it open to fan her face. "It is certainly warm enough now, and I do hate it when my face matches my hair. Perhaps I shall sit out this next dance."

Aaro glanced over her shoulder, presumably at the would-be intruder, as he gave her his hand, proper etiquette for leading a lady off the dance floor. "We can find the refreshment table, if you'd like."

"Perfect!" she cooed.

As soon as they were well away from the crowd seeking new dance partners she snapped the fan shut and tucked it away again. "And what's worse than having red hair and a red face is being set upon by puppies."

Aaro snickered. "Am I not a puppy, then?"

"I haven't decided yet what you are," she said as they reached the refreshment table, and he handed her a glass of water. She was flirting horribly, and he probably thought her completely shameless, but she couldn't bring herself to care. She was enjoying it too much.

"May I have the next dance then, while you decide?"

She raised an eyebrow at him as she sipped her water. "Certainly, if it saves me from the puppies."

He gave her that cocky half grin again, and they stood and talked while the music went on without them. They skipped the next song as well.

When the second song ended, they rejoined the mingling dancers and took their place on the floor. The musicians in their corner of the room had raised their arms to begin playing again, when a bugle sounded outside.

Mr. Daws hurried to throw the doors open, and two guards stepped through, positioning themselves on either side of the doorway. Mr. Daws bowed to the person standing outside and turned to the room. "May I present our noble lord, King Ormand D'Araines."

Rowan felt Aaro shift beside her. She

glanced at him. He had moved to rest his hand at his hip, a natural gesture for someone who usually wore a gun or a sword, who felt threatened. His brows were lowered in a frown, but when he turned and met her gaze, his expression cleared. He smiled and tugged her hand, drawing her further back into the crowd, away from the door.

"It seems my cousin has arrived," he said, "which means I shall be going soon. But perhaps we might make it through one more dance." He smiled, but all the relaxed assurance had gone out of him, and, while still appearing outwardly calm, she sensed his agitation. Even anger.

A thread of unease trailed through her. Not for herself, but for this young man with the ice-cold eyes and chestnut curls. She wished suddenly and intensely that she could run her fingers through that unruly hair, then nearly blushed again to catch herself with the thought.

Mr. Daws was making King Ormand welcome, sweeping his arms to encompass the ballroom in a gesture of welcome. She studied the king as he greeted several of the guests. He reminded her of his brother, High King Heymish, who ruled East Talva. Heymish had appointed Ormand to rule West Talva, since the sheer distance of the expanding country had made it cumbersome to be managed by a single ruler.

Of course, the two kings were twins, which would put Ormand's age at a bare thirty years. He was handsome, like his brother, though she found their younger cousin, Aaro, more to her liking. The king had a narrower build, his hair cut shorter, with a silver circlet around his head. He wore an embroidered black vest, and an ornate sword and dagger rode his hips. His blue eyes were a shade darker than Aaro's.

Already the musicians were picking their instruments back up. She returned her attention to Aaro as the song started. He seemed sober this time as he watched her. She could see the thoughts flickering behind his eyes, but they remained unspoken. The song was a slower one, more reflective, and the dance echoed the somber strains, pulling the partners close. Close enough that Aaro could rest his hand again on her waist as they turned.

"It's not my place to advise you," he said finally, bending his head close to her ear, "But beware the king. He seeks a wife."

"Some would seek the office of queen gladly," Rowan replied, her voice matching his for quietness, though she was somewhat taken aback.

"Not you though, unless I am mistaken. And unless I have misjudged you entirely, I think you would be no great match for my cousin, though you will draw his eye."

"As I've drawn yours?"

Shameless! She rebuked herself.

"Even so."

They parted in an elaborate series of steps and turns, and came back together again, closer than before. She with her hand on his shoulder, feeling the layers of muscle beneath his soft leather vest, he with both hands circled around her waist, prepared to lift and twirl with her. She caught the scent of leather and gunpowder on the air as he turned, and his breath brushed her cheek, his face so close he was within inches of kissing her.

"Might I interrupt?"

The voice came so suddenly and so close that Rowan gave a little yelp as she and Aaro separated, turning to the intruder. Couples continued to whirl around them, turning their heads to watch but too polite to stop the dance.

"Cousin," Aaro said, his voice devoid of emotion. He did not bow, or even incline his head to the king as he faced him.

"Will you introduce me to your charming friend?" Ormand said, his eyes on Rowan as he spoke to Aaro.

"Rowan Keir," she said, before Aaro had time to respond. She bobbed a curtsy. "An honor to finally meet you, sir."

"I assure you. The honor is all mine." He bent to kiss her hand, and her eyes met Aaro's for an instant over top of his head. The danger she'd seen lurking there earlier had taken place over merriment. The icy blue had turned to steel.

The king straightened and turned to Aaro.

"I'm certain you must have elsewhere that you need to be, my cousin."

Aaro's mouth pressed into a thin line, though a corner of it tilted slightly upward in a hard half smile at the king's dismissal. He bowed to Rowan. "Until we meet again."

Rowan's gaze followed him as he melded with the crowd beyond the dance floor. She caught a brief glimpse of him again as he turned around in the doorway and cast one more look back at her. He'd taken his wide-brimmed hat from the rack by the door, and he tipped it in farewell.

She turned back to the king, forcing her ire not to show, save in the fact that she didn't wait for him to speak first. "Sir, I fear we are hindering the dancers. Might we step aside?"

He smiled at her, a perfectly attractive smile which she found repulsive in light of his dismissal of Aaro. "Will you not finish the dance with me?"

She didn't dare refuse him, so she gave him a tight little smile and nodded. The lift and twirl that Ormand had interrupted when she danced with Aaro was about to repeat, and he put his hands around her waist. Where Aaro's grip had been gentle and respectful, the king's felt possessive. She fought the desire to slap him. Or at least to slap his hands away. She could feel herself blushing again, and resented it. In fact, she suddenly resented the whole situation.

People had watched in surprise before, when she danced with Aaro. Now they stared.

"Keir is an old name. There are not many of the Keir house out here on the frontier. You must belong to Lance somehow."

"My uncle, on my mother's side."

Rowan's father had taken her mother's family name, since hers was older, more respected, and dwindling in lineage. It was not an unheard-of practice, but had fallen out of favor more recently.

"Your family must be very devoted to the old ways. I had no idea Lance had such interesting and charming relations."

"Perhaps. Certainly more interesting than charming, though."

The song ended, and she excused herself.

"You would not dance again with your king?" Ormand said, still smiling.

"It would be an honor. But perhaps after this next round. I am thirsty, and my friend is there, waiting to speak with me. Forgive me." She bowed her head and curtsied before making her escape.

Annalie waited for her, her brows puckered into a frown as she tried to politely stave off a young noble set on dancing the next round with her. Her frown broke when she saw Rowan coming.

"My dear, are you well?" She took Rowan's hands. "You're flushed."

"Yes. Can you have missed all that?" Anger sharpened her tone, though she kept her voice low. Still, Annalie looked alarmed.

"Hush! Not here." Her eyes darted to the people surrounding them. "Keep your wit in check tonight. Tomorrow I will call on you. We must speak."

"That's all very well, but it doesn't keep me from having to dance again with that—with his *majesty* again tonight," Rowan hissed.

Annalies's eyes widened, and again she leaned up so she could whisper in Rowan's ear. "Go to your cousin Dustan and feign you are unwell. He has been enamored with a certain young lady all evening, and will not wish to leave, so I shall offer to take you home in my father's buggy."

Rowan looked at her friend with new appreciation, but with something close to unease. She remembered Aaro's warning, and now saw her friend's near panic. She shook her head, muttering, "I swear, everyone in this fool place has gone mad." But she sought out Dustan anyway, and began making her way over to him, aware that people's gazes still followed her.

Chapter 2

Aaro D'Araines stepped out into the night, shedding the stifling heat and crowded chatter of the ballroom like a soggy coat. Stars glittered in a black sky, only slightly dimmed by the light pouring from the windows. He could breathe out here.

A dark figure peeled away from the shadow of the flower bushes and strode toward him. He recognized the height and movement of the man before he could see his face, and relaxed.

"The horses are saddled and waiting," the man said. "I thought once Ormand arrived you wouldn't be staying long."

"So it seems." Aaro cast a look back to the blazing windows, hearing the faint murmur of music and conversation from inside, and thought again of the girl with the coppery red curls and the sharp wit. Her eyes, somewhere between copper-brown and hazel, had regarded him with playful interest, and for once, it irked him to be on the outside looking in. Especially when Ormand was at that moment dancing with the very same girl.

"'Raines?" Jake questioned.

"What?" Aaro still stared back at the house as though it would give him some special insight as he scowled in thought.

"Something happen?"

"Reckon so." He spun on his heel and headed toward the stables, talking as he went. "We're staying in town tonight. You're going to deliver a letter for me in the morning."

"Alright." If Jake was surprised, he didn't let on. "This about Ormand?"

"Partly."

They reached the stable, lit dimly by lanterns hung from a few of the rafters.

Ormand's soldiers played a game of cards on an upturned barrel near the door. They looked up as Aaro and Jake entered the stable. None of them spoke.

Aaro's hand went automatically to his belt, but the only weapon he wore tonight was the knife in his boot. He nodded to the king's men and followed Jake to the stalls where their horses waited. Moonlight streaked down through a high window, mingling with the lantern light outside the stall. He checked his saddle girth. The mare sidestepped, her ears pinned back, velvet nostrils wuffling as she twisted her neck around toward him, sidestepping again until her saddle scraped against the opposite wall.

"Take it easy," Aaro muttered, reaching for the saddlebags where his weapons belt waited. His hand paused on the buckle, and the horse moved away again, stomping nervously. Something felt wrong to him. Not any one thing, but dozens of little things that he hadn't even considered to be *things* until that instant. Ormand's dismissal. The soldiers' lack of greeting. The horse's unease. The dry whisper of movement, of something brushing against hard leather that he hadn't heard at first.

He heard Jake moving in the stall next to him, heard the door open and the horse's hooves thudding dully on the packed dirt floor as Jake led him out into the aisle.

"Waiting on you," Jake said.

"Come in here a minute," Aaro replied.

His friend swung the door out and stepped through, holding his gelding's reins loosely. The horse laid his ears back and tried to tug away.

"Listen," Aaro whispered. "Hear that?"

They stood listening. The horses huffed in and out. The king's soldiers talked in hushed voices back in the tack room. And again, there came a whispering scrape of movement.

Jake's hand dropped to his gun belt. "What is it?"

"I'm guessing another surprise from my cousin," Aaro whispered. "A man like him could consider himself fortunate, when his enemies keep dying in accidents."

Jake muttered a curse under his breath. "Like that brand-new saddle girth that turned up frayed a few weeks ago."

"*My* saddle girth," Aaro replied. He reached again for the saddlebag with his gun belt inside, and undid the buckle, then stepped back against the wall and threw the flap open. He jerked his hand back an instant before a forked tongue flicked into view above the lip of the leather bag, followed by a sleek yellow head and yellow eyes.

"Viper!" Jake hissed.

"And one that has no business being in this part of the world." Aaro bent and pulled the knife from his boot scabbard, using it to reach cautiously from the side and flip the saddlebag closed. The yellow head disappeared. He leaned forward, keeping as much distance as possible between himself and the saddlebag, and undid the buckle, slipping it away from the saddle. Jake drew back away from him as he carried the whole thing at arm's length out of the stall, then followed him back to the open tack room where they'd come in, and where the soldiers still sat around their barrel playing cards.

Without a word, Aaro upended the saddlebag, dumping its entire contents on the floor at the soldiers' feet. There were startled exclamations and curses as the yellow viper slid away from Aaro's canteen and gun belt. The men jumped to their feet, stumbling backward from the snake as it rippled over the straw-strewn floor. Aaro bent and plucked one of his guns from the holster. The shot clapped into them in the enclosed space, followed by the startled whinnies and stamping of the horses.

The slender yellow body convulsed for a

moment without its head, but that didn't interest Aaro so much as the fact that it lost its bright color almost immediately. The, poisonous yellow faded to dull gray-green along the back, and a pale cream color on the belly. Darker stripes ran along the length of its back. When it finally lay still, it was no longer a yellow viper, but a common garden snake.

"What...?" Jake murmured. "Was that...?"

"You boys might want to check your gear," Aaro drawled. "Seems like they've got a vermin infestation here." He nudged the body with his boot toe, despite the chill of revulsion that zinged through him. A viper that wasn't a viper?

People were pouring out of the house, the buzz of their questions loud in the still night as Aaro and Jake rode away. Neither bothered to stop and offer an explanation for the gunshot. Let the soldiers do that.

They turned onto the road that would take them back to the city and into New Town, where the buildings were built of pine rather than ancient stone and brick, and where there was a new hotel. Aaro's ranch lay three hours' ride to the north and east, and it would be nearly morning by the time they got there if they tried to go home now.

They walked the horses for several minutes in silence, and Aaro could feel the other man's unvoiced questions. They were loud in the squeak of leather as he shifted, the rustle of clothing as he repositioned his hat, and in his sigh. Soon he would break down and ask, but it was better to talk on the open road where no one was listening.

"Two reasons," Aaro said, knowing the first question would be why they were going to the hotel rather than riding for home, since Aaro had made it clear before the party that he had no intention of staying in town, no matter how late it was. He paused to be sure Jake was keeping up with his thought process.

"Go on," the other said.

"We're going to get some supplies. I'm riding east." Silence met this announcement, and after a pause he continued. "Ormand has gone too far, too many times. First Embur, now me. And that...whatever that snake was."

"Unnatural is what it was," Jake muttered. "You think those rumors are true?"

Until that night Aaro would have scoffed at the idea that Ormand was using magic. People liked to speculate, and if there was a mystery, they'd ascribe the most outlandish explanation they could to it. But now... he could think of at least one sudden death in the past year that had no explanation whatsoever. It was shrugged off as a sudden heart malady. But it could have been poison. Unlike a rattlesnake, a viper would never give away its presence, unless, like Aaro, you were already wary.

He sighed. "We can't prove any of that.

But Ormand's ruthlessness extends beyond murder, and that we *can* prove. If Heymish will listen to anyone, it'll be me."

"He won't think you're bidding for the throne?"

"He knows I've no interest in kingship. Let him appoint someone else, or let there at least be checks put in place. But Ormand must be stopped."

"So we get supplies tomorrow. When will you leave?"

"That depends on my other reason for staying in town tonight." He stopped, as much because he was questioning himself, making sure his resolution held, as because he enjoyed toying with his friend.

Jake let out a pained sigh. "Which is?"

"I'll be sending a marriage proposal to Lady Rowan Keir first thing in the morning."

Jake stopped his horse in the middle of the road, staring at him. "You sure that snake didn't get you?"

* * * * *

Rowan was alarmed, but also a little relieved to hear the gunshot that sent everyone crowding to the windows and doors. King Ormand had been headed in her direction, and she hadn't been able to speak with Dustan yet. The shot effectively stopped the party mid-dance, scattering the dancers, one of whom was her cousin. She grabbed his arm, stopping him from following the others, and pulled him aside.

"What is it?" He cast an anxious look to where everyone crowded around the door before turning his attention to her.

"I'm leaving. Annalie is going to take me home in her carriage. Please give my apologies to our host."

Dustan scanned her face. "Are you well?"

"I am. But say that I am not."

"What's wrong?"

She shook her head. "I can't say. But you needn't worry. Enjoy your evening. Annalie is saying her goodbyes now."

"Tell me what this is about when we get home?"

Rowan laughed shortly. "I will if I have it sorted out by then. Please, don't leave early for my sake. You must enjoy your young lady while opportunity smiles on you."

Dustan's face tinged red.

She found Annalie, and together they slipped back into the dining hall, where there was another door with only a single guard. They stepped out into the night, and Rowan breathed deep, feeling suddenly light and free and wanting to laugh with the joy of it. Annalie spoke to the guard, and he went to summon her carriage.

"Did you manage to find out what the gunshot was?" Rowan asked as they waited.

"Yes. Apparently, there was a snake in someone's saddlebag. They shot it dead." She shuddered.

"A snake?"

"A garden snake, is what King Ormand's guards said. The stable hand is saying it was a viper. No one knows where it could have come from." She went silent as the guard returned. Their carriage would be another few minutes before the horses were hitched.

"Whose saddlebag was it in?" Rowan asked.

"They didn't say." Annalie's gaze darted to the guard for an instant.

They waited in silence after that until the carriage drew up. The vehicle started with a jolt, swaying as they turned down the drive and onto the road.

Annalie lifted aside the little curtain across the window and peered out as though making sure they were alone, even though they were moving at a steady clip.

"Well?" Rowan said, leaning back and studying her friend in the fickle light of a lantern hung from a corner of the carriage roof.

Annalie turned back to her, her face worried, her little hands squeezing each other and plucking at their gloves. "My father says Ormand is seeking a new queen," she said.

"So I've heard," Rowan muttered. At her friend's startled look, she explained, "Aaro said as much when King Ormand arrived."

"He warned you already?"

Rowan shrugged. "I am not the only woman in West Talva. I don't see why you're so worried."

"As you said tonight, 'woe to the girl with red hair and long legs.' You're more beautiful than any of us. More—compelling, I suppose." She looked away, whether out of embarrassment or jealousy Rowan wasn't sure. "Any man would have to be blind not to notice you. And your wit is as compelling as your appearance."

"What are you trying to say?" Rowan felt impatience clamping around her chest.

"Forgive me if I speak bluntly. The lesser king will seek you out. Everything about you demands it. But you could never be controlled, and submission is one thing Ormand demands of his subjects—and especially his queen."

Rowan strangled on her anger. The tiny carriage felt like it was closing in on her, smothering her. "This is ridiculous!" She wanted to laugh or to scream, but the closeness of the carriage forbade it.

"Ormand was married before. For a year. His wife, Queen Embur, died shortly before you came here. Her saddle girth broke as she was riding, and she fell and was trampled. No one believes it was an accident. And she, too, had red hair."

"Please! I danced half a song with him, and you'd already have me married and murdered."

"Does it not make you pause that Mr.

D'Araines, the king's own cousin, also warned you?"

For a moment, Rowan didn't reply. The image of Aaro's dangerous blue eyes, his unruly hair and rolled-up shirtsleeves flashed in her mind. "Whose saddlebag was the viper in?" she asked again.

Annalie looked down at her hands. "They didn't say."

"But you guessed."

"Yes," she replied. "Aaro D'Araines doesn't speak openly against his cousin, but he cannot be swayed, or cowed, or bribed. And he attracts loyalty where he does not seek it. Ormand has always treated him like a threat."

"I see."

They rode for a long time in silence before the carriage finally rolled to a stop. One of Uncle Lance's men opened the door, offering his hand to Rowan. She flashed him a smile, but ignored his hand, stepping down lightly on her own. She turned back to the carriage.

"Thank you. I'll see you again soon, I'm sure."

Annalie reached and grabbed her hand before she could turn. "Please. Even if you don't believe me, pretend that you do, and be cautious."

Rowan looked into her friend's worried eyes and smiled. "Of course. I'm not such a fool as to toss out a friend's words when they're so earnestly given."

The carriage pulled away again, and Rowan took herself up to her room, though she didn't stay long. She shed the gown with its suffocating corset, and the little cloth slippers, and instead slipped into a pair of trousers she'd stolen from Dustan, and her boots. She crept out the kitchen door into the garden, and beyond, climbing the short dike that separated her uncle's land from the open prairie. Darkness robbed the world of color, while moonlight washed it in silver. Mist hung above the hollows of the land, and far, far away came the lonesome cry of a wolf.

For a little while she brooded on the evening. Letting her anger boil to the surface, and then subside. Remembering Aaro's eyes, and the feel of his hands, then laughing them away. Feeling the chill from Dustan's talk of magic and curses. She loosened her hair from its coil and tossed it into a mess in the moonlight, walked along the top of the dike and sang a song to herself. Then, satisfied that she'd shaken off the whole, foolish, maddening evening, and the worries that had come with it, she went back in and went to bed. But not to sleep.

Chapter 3

A *marriage* proposal?!" Rowan spun from the window on her boot heel and glared at her uncle. She wore Dustan's trousers again that morning instead of a skirt, a small act of rebellion against last evening's stress.

"One offer of marriage, and several others who seek permission to come courting," he answered, peering at her across the desk and over top of his wire-rimmed spectacles. His moustache twitched, and he rubbed the corner of his mouth. His eyes twinkled. "I have to admit, I'm a little surprised at the proposal. But considering the source..."

"Who?" She stomped across the room and snatched the letter out of his hand. "And for the love of creation, why do they send such things in letters, when not a one of them has said a single, solitary thing to my face? Have I no will of my own? No *mind* of my own?! For the sake of all reason, do they think me incapable of forming an opinion? And if I were such a drudge, what could possibly endear me to any of them?"

Despite her walk in the moonlight, and all her attempts to shake off the events of the party, she hadn't slept well, her mind refusing to slow down. She felt irritable and high-strung.

She returned to the big bay window

overlooking the line of cottonwoods and the slender ribbon of creek that separated Old Town from New Town, the proposal still gripped in one hand, while she tugged furiously at the end of her long braid with the other. Already a haze of heat and dust hovered above the road that crossed the creek near the house. As she watched, a lone rider crossed from New Town, pausing just this side of the creek and glancing up at the window where she stood. Even from a distance she could see the icy blue of his eyes.

Aaro smiled up at her. He raised a hand and tipped his wide-brimmed hat before urging his horse on out of sight. Her heart stuttered. Suddenly she had no doubt whose proposal she still clutched in her hand. She held it up to the light from the window and read.

Sir,

With due respect toward the convention of offering pleasantries, let me get right to the point. I intend to marry your niece. Take this as a proposal, if you will, and consider me one step ahead of the others who will shortly be seeking to court the lady Rowan. I expect she will not be easily convinced, but I consider this a reasonable obstacle. There is no need to pressure her, as is common toward daughters of noble families, and I have no need of a dowry from her. Please consider yourself free of any responsibility beyond allowing me to carry out my intentions, which, I assure you,

*are honorable, both to the lady and her reputation.
Also, please advise if there is anyone else to whom
I must apply for blessing. The lady mentioned a
father in Heymish's East Talva.*

> *Yours,*
> *Aaro D'Araines.*

The seal following the signature was a
modified version of the royal crest, proclaiming
its bearer to be a member of the extended royal
family.

"Of all the—" She stood frozen for a
moment, then let out a snort, which turned into a
giggle. In a moment she was doubled over, eyes
watering, hiccupping with laughter. "Of all the—"
she tried again, but the attempt only made her
laugh harder. "By all that's unreasonable. I
already love him for his audacity."

She wiped her eyes and turned back to her
uncle. "You see? You can tell your dear Miss
Gisela that she needn't pressure me any longer.
The problem of what to do with your pesky niece
has been all straightened out, and she is free to
win your heart once again."

Uncle Lance snorted. "That woman. But,
my dear, you are a very beautiful problem that I
don't mind in the least having around. Though
why you agreed to move to this uncivilized
wilderness is beyond me." He leaned back in his
chair and mopped sweat off his face with a hanky.

"Hmm. You can be sure that when I did, I

had no idea that women were such a commodity here. Or that they could be so... smothered." She sat down on the corner of the desk and tossed the letter back onto the pile, rubbing her forehead. If she didn't end up with a headache by the end of the day, it'd be some kind of miracle.

"West Talva can be a bit old fashioned, I supposed, despite being the newer frontier." He took off his spectacles to clean them. "But about this proposal. I'm not well acquainted with the young man in question, only his reputation. If you wish, I can warn him off. Or if you'd rather handle it on your own. I know you prefer not having people meddle."

"Oh Uncle, *you* don't meddle, so I don't mind. But perhaps... oh I don't know."

"You have an interest in the young man?"

She rubbed her head again. "Interest? I don't know. We only just met last night."

"Well. I know he speaks his mind, if nothing else. Diplomacy seems to have skipped that branch of the royal family. Regardless of that, he seems to attract an inordinate amount of loyalty."

"So I've heard," Rowan muttered, remembering Dustan's lengthy monologue on the subject during last evening's carriage ride. She shoved away from the desk and paced. "Please! It makes me squirm to speak of it! I've no intention of marrying him or anyone else before the year is out, at least. And I'm not completely incapable of looking after myself. I have two hands, the same as any man, and if it came to danger, I don't think any would try to lay a hand on me twice."

A new voice spoke from the doorway. "Pity the man who tried the first time."

Rowan spun toward the door as Dustan strolled in, thumbs hooked in his belt.

"Honestly, I pity the man who must woo our Red Wolf at all. *I* can't even keep her from stealing and wearing my clothes." His eyes twinkled as he claimed Rowan's deserted perch on the corner of the desk. "I imagine we have a veritable flood of the poor schmucks after the dance. If they weren't all scared off by the D'Araines rivalry. Speaking of which..." he turned to Rowan. "I told you there would be a shooting last night. It just involved a snake."

"Rivalry?" Uncle Lance frowned.

Rowan snorted.

"Everyone knows the saying 'red hair draws danger.'" Dustan yawned affectedly. "That must be twice as true when it's accompanied by such ferocious wit." He picked up Aaro's proposal and scanned it, and his face grew more serious. He folded the paper up and tapped it against his leg, frowning.

"*Now* what's wrong?" Rowan could feel her irritation setting in again like a physical itch.

Dustan's gaze rested on her, studying her, but he spoke to his father. "There was a messenger this morning. I was coming to tell you.

The lesser king is making his rounds, visiting some of the nobles today, and he expects to dine here with us at noon meal."

"Delightful." Uncle Lance's moustache drooped, and his brows puckered. "Lovely of him to give so much notice. And I wish you would not let yourself fall into the habit of calling him the 'lesser king.' It's liable to slip out in front of him when you're not intending."

Dustan shrugged, glancing from his father to Rowan. "I'd be more worried about other things. Like the length of time our *King Ormand* has been without a queen, since the last one so conveniently died."

"And now let's go 'round again!" Rowan scowled. She owned a razor-edged dagger that she carried on her person more often than not. At the moment, she had it strapped to her forearm under her sleeve, and as she spoke she pulled it out, contemplating what she could throw it at without causing damage.

Dustan and Uncle Lance both raised their eyebrows.

"It's not even been a full day, and I've been warned about your noble king twice already. And now you both must take it up. So I danced half a dance with him. It's no reason to make the leap into full panic."

Uncle Lance sighed. "There *is* a reason he's called the 'lesser king,' besides that he rules beneath his brother's authority. Unfortunately, his quality of character is rather less than his brother's as well." He pushed his spectacles up his nose and shuffled the papers together on his desk. "His cunning, on the other hand, is not lacking. You say he danced with you last night?"

"A dance he interrupted from Aaro," Dustan cut in. "The whole party was talking of it afterward. Rowan snuck out after the dance, and Ormand was obnoxious in trying to seek her out. I don't know why I didn't make the connection before." He looked downright worried now.

"*I* know why," Rowan said. "Since last night your head has been too filled with your young lady to leave room for less important matters..."

Dustan turned red.

"...Which this truly is," she finished, glaring.

"My dear, I know you have no patience for anything you deem unreasonable, or trite," Uncle Lance said. "But in this instance, listen to those of us who've been under Ormand's rule longer. Pick one of these young men that have shown an interest in you, and spend the day in New Town at the market. I'm sure any of them would jump at the chance. And you might find it enjoyable, if you let yourself."

"Dustan can go with me."

"If King Ormand is coming, he will expect my sons to be in attendance. There would be fewer questions that way, and fewer questions from our king is entirely a good thing. I will merely tell him you had made plans with one of the young men who showed interest last evening." Uncle Lance peered at her, waiting.

Rowan met Dustan's eyes briefly. He gave a tentative half shrug, and she wondered if he was thinking the same thing she was. That the king might take it worse, rather than better.

She walked back to the window. None of this was the fault of her uncle or her cousins. They weren't overbearing, the trait she found so intolerable, and the one thing that had ultimately sent her from her home in the east, not realizing that the attitude was even worse on the frontier. Always cloaked in the guise of protectiveness, of course, and of social ritual. Still, she had to smother the urge to lash out. She huffed a sigh through her nose.

"Very well. You may send for Aaro D'Araines, if he is still in town, and inquire if he would be my escort to the market this noon. If he isn't to my liking after a day's tedium shopping, then all's well. He'll have served his purpose." She strode for the door, more than ready to dismiss the conversation, but turned back to them in the doorway, raising a saucy eyebrow. "Will you send him the message, or shall I?"

* * * * *

Unlike many of the nobles back east, Uncle Lance and his household were typically up with the sun each morning, so even with an hour's debate after breakfast, several hours remained until she could expect to see Aaro D'Araines. She wasn't about to wait around for him, especially since she couldn't get him out of her mind, and she'd go crazy if she didn't find something to do. So she went out and fed and watered the chickens before the kitchen staff could get to it, and hunted for eggs. Then she strolled the edge of the property.

Her uncle's estate was part of what must once have been the city's outer defenses, back when Old Town had been built by the ancients. The dike she'd walked the night before had been a sod wall at one time, though now it was sunken down and covered by long grass, an embankment between them and the open prairie. No one seemed to know much about the original people who had hauled stone and dug wells and built the ancient cities out here on the frontier. Perhaps the Shonnowa people knew. Or perhaps it was one of their races that had built the stone castles and foundations, though now most of them were nomads.

Thinking of the Shonnowa put Rowan in mind of her conversation with Dustan the previous day, before all the muddle with the king and Aaro happened, and those chilling rumors about magic and curses. She scoffed to herself, trying to drown out her secret childish desire to meet one of the Shonnowa. Ridiculous notion.

Wind whipped around her, blasting hair

across her face and pressing her blouse and
trousers against her body. She had put off getting
changed, another small act of rebellion she could
throw in the face of all the ludicrous conventions
and worries that were constantly forced upon
her. Today, of all days, she hadn't the patience for
them. And she didn't expect Aaro for another
hour—at least she didn't until the moment when
he spoke from behind her.

"Looks like I might be a bit early."

She'd been trying to get a strand of hair
out of her mouth, while the wind kept blowing
the rest of her mane across her face. She whirled
blindly at the sound of his voice, tottering on top
of the dike, tipping precariously and flapping like
a stork.

He caught her around the waist and
lowered her to the ground in front of him. She
still couldn't see, thanks to her mass of curls,
until he swiped them back from her face, using
both hands to pin her hair behind her head. She
found her view suddenly unobstructed, looking
right into his laughing blue eyes.

"May I?"

His face was only inches away, and she
wondered if he was asking permission to go on
holding her hair, or to kiss her.

"No, you may not!" She sputtered. "And
yes, you are. Early!" She swatted his hands out of
her hair and spun toward the house. "Excuse me."

She stalked through the back hallway and

upstairs to her room. "The only thing worse than eating a tomato is looking like one!" She slammed the door and scowled fiercely at her mirror reflection. "Tomato!"

She was red from hair to neck, and she turned even redder still as she realized her blouse was scandalously unbuttoned halfway down her chest, revealing the lace of her undergarment, and some softly curved skin she would rather not have shown anyone.

"Aaagh!" The loose buttonholes must have slipped as she was feeding chickens and battling the prairie wind. And of course it hadn't mattered when she was alone with an hour—so she thought—yet to wait.

"Jackass!" She didn't know if she was insulting Aaro for showing up early, or herself for being so careless. She tore through her closet, looking for something, *anything* appropriate to wear.

A soft knock came at her door. "Lady?" It was her serving girl. "Can I help?"

"Yes!" Rowan flung the door open, holding a gown up to herself. "Buttons!"

The girl, only a couple years younger than Rowan herself, came in and helped her finish climbing into the gown, a deep blue eyelet lace with a modest V neckline, then did up the fifty or so little buttons at the back.

"Your hair?" she asked.

"Just get it up so it doesn't blow in my

face. Serve the idiot right for arriving that fast, if it looks like a bird's nest."

Despite Rowan's grousing, the girl had her hair twisted up into an attractive knot at the side, just behind her right ear, within a few minutes.

"You look very handsome, lady." She tucked one last pin into place and stepped back.

"Handsome? My mother was a handsome woman. I'm just..." Rowan looking into the mirror and snorted. "Well, not freckled at least. That's one small comfort." She leaned closer. "Ugh. Never mind. There they are. Hiding under all that tomato color."

The girl tried to cover her giggle, and Rowan winked at her.

"Not so very freckled, my lady. Only enough to be charming."

Downstairs, Aaro had been welcomed into the house, and stood talking with Uncle Lance in the front room. He raised his eyes as she descended the stairs, and their gazes met. Rowan could feel her face burning, but she lifted her head high and descended the stairs like a queen.

"Mr. D'Araines."

"Miss Keir." He bowed ever so slightly from the waist, holding his wide-brimmed hat in his hands. He wore a brown leather gun belt today, slung low across his hips, with a dagger sheath behind each gun holster. His chestnut hair had been pressed down in a circle by the hat, but his eyes still snapped with their mix of laughter and danger. "I'm sorry you felt you had to change on my account. You looked as lovely before as you do now."

Rowan felt a growl building in her chest. If there was one thing in the world she both hated and loved, it was someone who could match her wit-for-wit and knock her off balance. But he certainly had the advantage in this instance. He'd caught her by surprise. And all the retorts that sprang to mind would be deemed inappropriate.

He offered his arm, this time with his sleeves rolled down. "Shall we?"

"Certainly." She stuck her nose in the air and walked past him, ignoring his arm. Behind her she heard her uncle cough as Aaro bid him good day and followed her out the door. She stopped in the courtyard. Not a horse or carriage of any kind was in sight.

"Forgive me," Aaro said. "I already stabled my horse. I hadn't brought a buggy into town, and besides, I thought perhaps you were the kind of girl who'd rather walk. It's a short distance into New Town, and the day's heat hasn't set in yet."

Rowan snapped open the fan at her wrist. "Walking I don't mind. As for the heat—being from the East, I have to disagree. It would be this warm at the peak of the day, and most ladies would be languishing indoors."

Aaro grinned as he plopped the hat back onto his head. He stuck his thumbs into his belt and cast sidelong glances at her as they walked.

"Truly, you cut a fine figure in those trousers," he said after a little while. His eyes twinkled. "And I do believe I prefer your hair down."

"Perhaps not the most appropriate style for a windy day amongst people, though." Not to mention she'd be the gossiped horror of the town if she showed her face in public with loose hair.

After another long pause, he said, "I've been right on two counts so far today. That you would like to walk, and that I'd find you outside, rather than waiting indoors. I'd like to know if I'm correct on a third, as well." He waited until she looked over at him, eyebrows raised, then continued. "That you're the kind of girl who's more likely to ignore a man you fancy than to throw yourself at him. Which leads me to think you must have another motive for your invitation this morning."

She squinted at him. "I am, in fact, attempting to avoid your cousin, who is coming to lunch today. But since you intend to try to marry me, I thought it would be no great loss on your part."

Aaro threw back his head and hooted with laughter.

"To answer your other insinuation though," Rowan went on, "that I 'fancy' you—I refute that as arrogant, assuming, and ungentlemanly."

"But not untrue?"

"*That* is a moot point."

He offered his arm again, and this time she rested her hand lightly on it. They had crossed the creek and were coming into New Town, the portion of the city that had been built within the last generation, where the buildings were pine and man-made brick, rather than old oak and stone. It felt like stepping from one world into another.

"So you would risk the king's anger by not being present when he comes to call on you today?" They were walking past the hotel, with its wide front porch rimmed by wilting flowerbeds.

"He did not specify that he was calling on me."

"But he is."

She shrugged.

Aaro gestured to the hotel. "Will you come into the dining room with me and have at least a glass of water before we go to the market? Your invitation this morning caught me in the midst of some business, and I never filled my canteen."

Rowan nodded, suppressing the uncomfortable notion that they must look quite like a couple going to lunch. Several ladies on the street watched them, whispering behind their fans until she and Aaro entered the still-cool dining room. There weren't as many people about at that hour, being too late for breakfast and too early for lunch. Another couple sat in the corner sipping coffee. Beyond that they had the room to themselves.

Aaro pulled out a chair for her, then sat down with his back to the wall so that he faced the empty room. He took his hat off and set it on the table at his elbow. A serving girl brought them glasses of water without being asked, paused to see if they would order anything, then left.

"You were watching me last night," he said once they were alone.

Rowan pressed her lips together and held his gaze. Meeting those eyes, intensely blue and penetrating, made something inside her jump. They were both exhilarating and unnerving. "You certainly have a gift for belting out whatever's on your mind, Mr. D'Araines."

A flicker of a smile touched his face. "When I wish."

She folded her arms across the table and leaned forward, studying him. She didn't doubt that more stayed hidden behind those blue depths than what he so bluntly voiced. "I remember you watching me more than once as well," she said. "It's common, I believe, for people to look at one another when gathered in social settings, such as last evening's ball."

"Some people draw the eye more than others, though," he replied, running a finger around the rim of his water glass and never moving his eyes from her face. Perhaps it should have made her uncomfortable, but Rowan wasn't in the habit of backing down from anyone.

"Sir, for all your bluntness, I don't see your point."

Again with the almost smile. This time it reached the corners of his eyes. "What did your uncle think of my proposal?"

Rowan laughed and leaned back. "I think even he couldn't tell you that. Since you're in the business of speaking your mind, I'll tell you that he wonders which of your cousins you most take after. King Heymish, or King Ormand."

"I see. And you?"

"I could hardly say. You don't resemble a king." She quirked an eyebrow at him, with his weapons belt, wide-brimmed hat, and riding boots. "If I must say anything, I'd say you're your own man. What kind of man, I don't know."

"You think me arrogant?"

"Audacious."

"Dangerous?"

"It's not my custom to be intimidated by men."

He half stood from the table to give her a bow. "It's true, I spent the whole of last evening watching you, as did every other gentleman in the house. But they will not have the final honor of making you their bride."

Rowan squinted at him and took a sip of her water as he sat back down. "Probably not."

The conversation turned to other things. She asked him about his family, and he explained that his father had died—supposedly in an accident—right after Ormand came into power, leaving the ranch in Aaro's hands. His mother had gone back east to stay with Aaro's married sister.

Rowan had no idea that a large chunk of time had passed until the serving girl came back and asked if they were having lunch. The dining room had filled while they sat and talked. They ordered lunch, then sat back, silent for the moment as the comfortable buzz of conversation circulated around them. The room was beginning to be warm and stuffy, though not uncomfortably so.

It was good to know, Rowan thought, that the man across from her could hold an intelligent conversation, and not just flirt. Though he had done plenty of that as well.

"Why did you come west?" Aaro asked the inevitable question.

She touched the knot of hair at her neck and looked away for a moment. People were always eager to judge. Especially there seemed to be a deplorable double standard for women. She didn't want Aaro to be one of the ones looking appalled at her independent streak, telling her what she *should* have done. On the other hand, if he was one of those people, then she would have no further use for him, and she'd know it instantly.

"I came because I didn't fancy my aunt's matchmaking, nor my father's insistence on marriage, nor both of their overbearing, suffocating plans for my life. As though being unmarried and independent at nineteen were a horrendous blight on the family name."

Aaro looked at her in silence for a moment, his eyebrows raised, and she steeled herself for the disappointment that was to come.

He started to chuckle, and then he laughed out loud, drawing several people's attention from the neighboring tables. Rowan watched him, waiting.

"You came west because you didn't want to get married?"

"Exactly so. They might not have forced me, in so many words, but you have no idea the pressure put on noblewomen. If I was a man, it would be perfectly acceptable to put off all that family business, to travel, or do whatever I pleased. But the most I could get my father to agree to was giving me the funds to come stay with Uncle Lance. A compromise, but still a victory, for I'm no longer under father or Aunt Rose Marie's thumb."

"And what do you plan to do with your independence, now that you have it?" Aaro said, still chuckling.

"I don't know." She let her gaze wander past him to the window and the brassy noon light outdoors. "My mother was Uncle Lance's sister, and he's much more tolerant of a free spirit. My father... has not been quite right since she died.

He made it clear that I was not to come back until I saw things his way. Mother could always talk him out of his straight-laced notions, but I fear I do not have that power over him." She paused. "I like horses. I fancy my cousin Dyllan would let me come and work for him, once he gets his ranch established. Or perhaps I will find someone I fancy and get married after all. Not any time soon, though. And not the boy they had chosen for me." She laughed. "The puppy."

Aaro sat back, arms folded across his chest, smiling. "I consider myself fortunate then. Your escape from him brought you to me. And if you still want to work with horses, I have those as well."

"Well! I'll certainly keep that in mind." She laughed.

* * * * *

After a long lunch they returned to the street, strolling around the town square, past the turnoff leading to the livery stable and the messenger service headquarters. Vendors sat under awnings, fanning themselves and watching passerby. Few of them were ambitious enough to stand and call out their wares in the growing afternoon heat, unless someone showed an interest.

They walked slowly, staying in the shade of the vendors' awnings as much as possible. Rowan had her fan on its little string around her wrist, and occasionally she fluttered it at her face, though even that seemed like more effort than it was worth. She imagined her face must be a brighter red than her hair by this point.

"Is it always so hot here, or are we in some sort of a drought?" she asked.

Aaro seemed undisturbed by the heat, despite a trickle of sweat working its way down his neck. "Pretty normal for this month," he replied. "Mostly high summer is drought season. Just hope we don't get tornadoes."

Rowan paused at a stand selling jewelry and other trifles. It was a mask that caught her eye, made of leather and silver mysteriously fused together in a strange, fierce pattern. Curious, she put out a finger to touch it, and a tingle ran up her arm, and down her spine, making her blink. She raised her eyes from the mask to the merchant. *Magic?* With all the talk lately, it was the first thought that sprang to mind. Was magic something a person could feel? She shivered, and resisted the urge to wipe her hand on her skirt.

The merchant rose slowly to stand behind the table. Age bent her back, her face darkened and weathered by the sun, more than anyone Rowan had ever seen, and suddenly another question was gnawing at her tongue. *Shonnowa?*

"It is a masterpiece, no?" the old woman said.

"It's truly amazing."

"But perhaps not suitable for a young noblewoman." The old lady reached into a box behind the table and brought out a copper pendant on a braided black leather thong. It was hammered into the image of a wolf.

Rowan laughed in delight.

"You like it?" Aaro asked from behind her.

"It's my emblem," she said, picking up the necklace and gazing at it in the sunlight. "My cousins call me the Red Wolf. Usually when I've done something ridiculous and unladylike."

"You must have it then," he said, drawing out a handful of coins from his pocket.

Rowan looked from him to the gleaming copper wolf. "Principle demands I should refuse, since I've not accepted your proposal. But..."

"All in good time." Aaro winked at her. "I'm a patient man, and I don't mind investing in a sure thing."

"You're really so insufferable that it almost makes you charming."

He gave the woman her money and took the necklace out of Rowan's hands. "May I?"

She turned her back, and felt the gentle brush of his fingers on the back of her neck as he tied the leather cord. Goosebumps raced up her arms, and his hands lingered for just a second before pulling away. He turned her around to face him, the wolf pendant now resting in the hollow of her throat above the V neckline of her dress.

"Perfect." He looked pleased with himself.

The merchant woman, all but forgotten

for a moment, spoke again. "Perhaps the mask is more to the gentleman's taste." She watched them with piercing, almost black eyes, and a look that Rowan couldn't decipher. "It has far more worth than what is in the craftsmanship alone. Try it, if you like."

Aaro tipped his hat to the old woman. "Perhaps on a different day."

"Perhaps." She smiled, showing missing teeth.

They had moved on down the street to the next vendor when someone called out from behind them. They both turned, and Aaro greeted the other man, who looked to be around the same age, dressed similarly to Aaro with tan trousers, a black leather vest over his shirt, and a gun belt. He didn't wear knives behind his gun holsters as Aaro did though.

"Jake, may I introduce Miss Rowan Keir. Rowan, my foreman, Jake."

Jake tipped his hat, his eyes sparkling as he glanced between her and Aaro. "Ma'am."

Aaro turned back to her. "Forgive me. This should only be a moment."

Rowan wandered away as they spoke, looking for something to catch her interest. The dull clatter of horses' hooves approached up the street, and she glanced up to see a dozen men, dressed in King Ormand's blue and gray livery. All except for the man in the middle, who wore a silver circlet in his dark hair that flashed in the sunlight.

Rowan's pulse spiked, and she turned away, feigning interest in a length of crocheted lace. The horses slowed. She forced herself not to turn around.

"Pardon, my lady." The king's voice was as she remembered it—low and smooth like Aaro's, but without his hint of a drawl.

She moved on, pretending she hadn't heard, and spoke to one of the merchants. Behind her, she heard the creak of saddle leather, and the soft thud of boots hitting the ground.

"Of all the—" she muttered under her breath.

"Miss Keir?" Ormand said, directly behind her now. She couldn't very well ignore him any longer, so she faked a little jump as though just realizing he was there, and turned.

"Sire!" She curtsied, still acting surprised. "I beg your pardon."

His gaze felt cold and somehow slimy as it flickered up and down, covering her entire figure. "You are even more ravishing in the sunlight than you were last evening in the lamplight. I trust you are well today?"

"Much better! Thank you." She snapped her fan open. "It was incredibly warm last night, was it not? I'm afraid I'm not used to dancing in such stifling heat."

He nodded politely. "I have just come from your uncle Lance, where, I confess, I had assumed I would have been able to dine with you this noon. And here I find you in the market without an escort. Surely your people don't often let you wander town alone. Although, now that I think on it, they mentioned that you were out with a young man."

Sweat trickled down the middle of Rowan's chest, making her want to rub the tickle away. She shifted and touched the copper wolf at her throat instead. Down the street, she could see Aaro and Jake, no longer talking, watching them, unnoticed by the king or his men. A misgiving, vague enough that it couldn't be defined as anything but intuition, warned her not to point out who her escort was. Suppose Ormand should somehow use it against Aaro?

She touched the pendant again, forcing a breath in and out, cleansing the distain from her voice before she spoke. "You are kind sir. The young man was called away, unfortunately, at the last moment, but my shopping trip could not be delayed, and since none of my cousins could be spared to come with me—here I am."

"And I am to blame! But still, I must insist you should have at least brought a servant with you, to carry your packages." His gaze passed over her again, obviously noting the lack of purchases.

She flashed her most charming smile. "Not all of a girl's needs require bulky bundles. I assure you, I am quite safe and comfortable, though I thank you for your concern."

Where Aaro's look held intensity and laughter, with the hint of danger, King Ormand's eyes were cunning, masked with shallow charm. Impatience pressed on Rowan to be away from him.

"Nonetheless, I won't have a young noble woman as beautiful as yourself walking the streets of my city alone. I shall escort you home."

Rowan laughed inwardly. The comment was just too tempting to pass up. She widened her eyes slightly, then dropped her gaze in a look both shy and coy. "Sir! You should not worry so! Since this *is* your city, I have perfect confidence that your streets here in West Talva are just as safe as East Talva. You mustn't be so modest." She raised her eyes and flashed him a smile, fighting to keep back a snort of laughter.

Ormand blinked at her, and cleared his throat. "Ah, well thank you, my dear. But I still must insist on taking you home. There's a matter I would like to talk to your uncle about." He offered his arm. "I trust you've found everything you need."

Rowan glanced back to where Aaro and Jake stood in the shadow of the tack shop, watching, as she put her hand on the king's arm. Aaro's face had gone hard.

"Smith, give the lady your horse," Ormand ordered as they approached the group of guards. One of them dismounted instantly, linking his fingers to give Rowan a boost. This time she didn't bother to protest, despite that her skirts bunched up around her knees as she swung into the saddle. She seethed inwardly. No one who considered himself a gentleman would suggest, much less insist, that she ride astride a horse in a dress meant for walking.

They started back toward her uncle's, the horses stirring up a cloud of dust that stuck in her throat. Sweat plastered her dress to her back, and she could feel tendrils of escaped hair sticking to her neck. If she were walking, she could at least *act* cool and composed, fluttering her fan in that way that people found so charming. Truly, all it did was draw attention away from the sweat and dust.

Ormand glanced over at her, his eyes flickering to her bared lower leg. She clamped her mouth shut and made a list of all the ways she could kill him.

Chapter 4

By the time Aaro saw the king coming up the street, he had already spotted Rowan, so it was too late to get her out of sight. He itched to walk up to his cousin and hit him across his pretty face, or better yet, put a bullet through that fancy red vest. But there were too many men with him. And Ormand was too good at twisting a situation to his favor. Aaro could think of half a dozen ways that things could turn ugly. Ormand could try to provoke him, then claim that Aaro had pulled a gun, and have his men cut him down then and there. Or in his anger he might take Rowan back to the castle and force a priest to marry them immediately. No doubt he had someone who would agree to perform the ceremony without Rowan's consent.

He slouched closer so he could hear their conversation, staying as inconspicuous as possible, with Jake following him. He would jump in if he had to, but he'd see how things played out first.

Ormand was talking, and Rowan was acting. Her gaze flickered in his direction from time to time, but she said nothing about him being there. Ormand was insisting on taking her home, blustering about a woman being on the streets alone. Aaro's heart lodged in his throat at her cutting response. But she pulled it off flawlessly, the embodiment of poise, allure, and innocence. Something else shifted in his chest. Something much more powerful than fear for her safety. An admiration so deep it bordered on worship. Ormand was rendered speechless for a moment, and for that Aaro silently vowed his loyalty to this girl for the rest of his days.

Even Jake, standing at his shoulder, swore softy in appreciation. Aaro put up a hand for him to be quiet, but couldn't help flashing him a grin.

"There's a matter I would like to talk to your uncle about," Ormand was saying. He ordered one of his men to dismount, and led Rowan to the horse. His gaze never left her as she swung up. She remained graceful and relaxed, though her lips thinned out as Ormand's gaze rested another instant on her, with her dress hiked up almost to her knees.

"Bastard," Jake swore again. "Can't blame him for staring, though."

Aaro swiped a trickle of sweat off his face as he watched them ride out.

"If you let your swamp adder of a cousin get that girl, I'll whip you myself," Jake said. "And if you ain't going to do anything about it, then you just let me know, and I will."

"Count on it. I'm going after them. Better get a hustle on those supplies. We might both have to travel in a hurry. Maybe you should get some girl stuff, too."

"Girl stuff? Like what?"

Aaro threw a hand in the air. "How should I know?"

Jake looked at him askance. "She's a girl. I'm sure she's got her own stuff. It's not like there aren't towns between here and the capital."

"Right." Aaro took his hat off and ran a hand through his sweat-damp hair, blowing a breath. "Right."

"Get going, you big donkey butt."

Since Aaro's horse was in Lance's stable, he had to follow the king's company on foot. Short walk though it was, he chafed at the time. Not that he could have gone any faster anyway. He didn't want to actually catch up with the king, but rather stayed back far enough not to be seen. By the time he slipped around to the back of the house, Ormand and Rowan had already gone inside, leaving the guards to wait in the courtyard.

He stationed himself next to the back door that Rowan had used that morning, and paced. In another moment the door opened, and Rowan was there beside him. She grabbed him by the front of his shirt before he could speak and dragged him into the shrubbery

"Where were you?" she hissed.

"Following you. Making sure my cousin acted like a gentleman."

She huffed and spat out a few unladylike words, then, "Some gentleman."

"Why didn't you tell him you were with me?" he asked, though he was glad she hadn't.

"Why didn't you come claim me?"

"Oh? You're mine for the claiming now?"

She smacked his chest with her fan, which Aaro figured was about the next best thing to a kiss. "You know what I meant."

"If I'd had to, I would've. If I had been with you when he first came up... But the whole thing was all wrong. The soldiers, the public square—he's already tried to kill me twice and make it look like an accident."

She eyed him for a moment. He could almost feel the force of her thoughts, piecing together the situation. Her copper-brown eyes set his heart racing. She didn't act coy or innocent with him, as she had with Ormand. Nor was she flirting, bantering wits as she had last night.

Finally she said, "Which was why I didn't tell him you were there. That viper last night was meant for you."

He nodded. The viper/garden snake still raised questions in his mind, but they had no power to keep his attention today. He couldn't take his eyes off her. Hadn't been able to since his first glimpse last evening, but now that she was herself, fierce and independent and burning bright in the sunlight, he figured he'd be blind if he even tried to look elsewhere.

"Well this is a pretty situation," she said, half smiling, though her eyebrows puckered together. "The king is trying to kill you, and, I've an idea, trying to marry me. Although now that I say it out loud, it sounds even more ridiculous than it did when I merely thought it." She laughed a little. "And if I'm forced to marry that swine—beg your pardon—there might be another 'accidental' death."

Aaro didn't return her smile. "Make no mistake. He's asking your uncle for your hand even now. If you tried to kill him and failed, he would have you tortured to death. If you succeeded, you would he killed by the guards before you could escape."

"You have no confidence in me," she said lightly.

He clenched his fists to keep from grabbing her shoulders and shaking her, feeling his chest tighten. "I have every confidence in you, Red. But it's a game you'd be playing with death, and that's always left until all other hope proves false. Besides. What if you didn't have an opportunity right away? Do you fancy enduring a marriage of any length with Ormand?"

She looked away, her cheeks tinging red.

Aaro anticipated her next question and countered it. "He would have you followed if you went back east. He is spiteful, obsessive, and controlling, and that would be the worst move of all."

"I'm hardly worth all that trouble."

"*I* would follow you." This time he did put

his hands on her shoulders, squeezing them gently. "I would have followed you after the first time I met you."

"Last night, you mean?" She arched and eyebrow at him. "Truly, this is ridiculous. We don't even know for sure that's what's going on in there."

"I know for sure. And believe me, we're not being ridiculous. Ormand is power crazy. Since Heymish gave him the rule out here, nothing has been denied him. Embur, the queen, died because she questioned his ruthlessness. He's been on the hunt for a new queen, and I have *no* doubt he's just chosen you."

As if in reply, they heard a door open inside the house, and voices leaked out through the window near where they stood. Lance and Ormand.

"Forgive me for keeping you waiting, Sire," Lance's voice said. "I wasn't expecting you back this soon. What may I do for you?"

"I've just now found your niece wandering alone in the market. She's quite the lady."

"Alone, you say? Hmm. Well what about it?"

"That isn't acceptable for the king's intended."

Aaro and Rowan looked at one another.

"I'll kill him," she hissed.

Aaro made a shushing motion and pulled her around the side of the house away from the window, his chest nearly bursting now with panic. They had to get moving, to get away from there. He pulled her into a corner where the gardener's tool shed hid them from the courtyard out front, and the shrubbery hid them from the garden and stables.

"I have a better idea," he said. Somehow he'd gotten hold of both of her hands, and held them. She was only a few inches shorter than he, but they stood so close that she had to tilt her face upward to meet his gaze, her fiery eyes questioning. He thought he'd have to force the words out, but no. He was more confident in this than he'd been about anything in his life.

"Marry me."

* * * * *

"What?" Rowan stared at him, her mind grasping to make sense of those words.

"Tonight."

"*What?!*" She couldn't think of a thing. Not just something to say, but anything at all. She must have looked as shocked as she felt, for Aaro hurried on, almost desperate.

"I love you, Red." He reached up and snatched his hat off, probably just remembering, then hurried on. "Love is a lot of different things. It's a feeling, and I've got that. It's also a decision—one I've already made. It's a commitment. I've already stated my intention to marry you, and my word is as good as an oath. If there's anything more you need, name it."

"Some time might be nice!" She rubbed her forehead. Her brain seemed to be working again. Her thoughts flew around so fast now that she couldn't follow them. The worst part of it was that she could see Aaro's point. If she married him, they could tell the king they'd eloped before they heard of his intentions. Her uncle knew nothing about their plans. They were just two young people madly in love and ready to get married on a whim. Then there would be nothing he could do.

Except kill them

Did Aaro have a plan for that? Did she trust him? Did she love him? Or perhaps a better question would be: *could* she love him? But she already knew the answer to that.

His blue eyes pleaded with her, so intense she could feel his impatience. And he was right to be impatient. They needed to move immediately. But get married? The very thing she'd left home to avoid?

Although, if she were honest, the boy her aunt had picked out for her was just that. A boy. Aaro was definitely a man. And if she was even more honest, it wasn't him that scared her—it was herself. The fact that she would even consider marriage to him would normally send her running. But she didn't have time to run, or to play games with herself.

She glanced up at him. He was still watching her, his eyes even brighter than before, while he gripped her hands more tightly than he probably realized. She certainly couldn't ask for a better-looking man.

But she'd known him for all of a day.

But he was Aaro.

Which somehow made sense—putting him in a category all his own. It seemed natural.

She met his gaze fully, and drew a breath, her heart stuttering around the words. "Aaro D'Araines, I accept our proposal."

A grin spread across his face, changing it entirely. He looked boyish, his eyes dancing, as though he might whoop and throw his hat in the air. For the first time, she saw him as a prospective—nay—a soon-to-be—husband. Her heart flapped like a pigeon trapped in her ribcage.

Instead of tossing his hat in the air, Aaro settled it back on his head, though the grin never left. He raised one of her hands and kissed it before letting them both go. "I promise you, I will never give you reason to regret this day."

"I seriously doubt that," she said. "Though the sentiment is a good one."

A twig snapped on the other side of the hedge, and they both tensed.

"There you are!" Dustan peered at them through the shrubbery.

They both shushed him. Rowan beckoned him into their corner. "What's happening?"

"Exactly what we were afraid of." Dustan

looked grim. His eyes flickered between her and Aaro. "Ormand has declared you are to be his next queen."

"And what did Uncle tell him?"

"He hinted that you would soon be returning east, under King Heymish's rule. Ormand got angry and forbade it. He said he'd have you brought back, and my father executed for treason. Though he made it sound much more gracious than that."

"He's a pig," Aaro broke in. His eyes snapped with hate.

"What's your plan?" Dustan asked. "I find you back here whispering together, so I assume you must have a plan."

Rowan exchanged a look with her new intended. "We're getting married."

Dustan gaped. "What?"

"It will save Rowan from my cousin," Aaro said. "At least for the moment. Once we're married he can't do anything about it, except try to kill me again, which I'm sure he will, but I already planned on going to Heymish to tell him the situation out here. It's time someone did. And he'll believe me, if anyone."

"I see," Dustan answered slowly. He looked back and forth between the two of them. "We all saw the possibility of this, but I don't think any of us actually thought it would come to this. I'm sorry, Red. This might actually be your best option. Maybe." He eyed Aaro.

"Don't be sorry. None of this is your fault. It seems my fate is to be wed to *someone*, and of all my options, I like this one the best." She winked at Aaro. "But we'll need your help."

"Name it."

"I'll need a few things from my room. It would be best if we not go back into the house now. Your father can claim his ignorance. Get my things for me and meet us at the chapel in Old Town." She glanced at Aaro to confirm, and he nodded. "We'll need you to witness the ceremony."

Aaro added, "Once it's done, make sure some of the town gossips hear of it right away. We don't need Ormand claiming it never happened."

Dustan nodded. "What do you need from your things?"

There wasn't much. It wasn't as if she was going off to live in the woods. Her belongings could be sent for when it was convenient. What she really needed at the moment was a gown to get married in.

Dustan took off to pack her saddlebags. Out in front they could hear the clatter of the king's horses leaving. Still, they took care not to be seen as they stole around to the stable.

Rowan mentally apologized to Dyllan for running off with one of his horses as she saddled the mare she usually rode. They took their time, giving Ormand and his men the chance to get well out of sight before they snuck back onto the road, leading the horses. Aaro reached for her hand as they began passing more houses.

"We're supposed to be lovers eloping," he said. "We should look the part."

"Well, we are eloping. I don't see where 'looking the part' comes in."

He leaned over and kissed her cheek. "True. But we're not lovers. Yet."

She raised her hand to cover the burning kiss and shot him a look. "So much for honorable intentions."

"Marriage is honorable. And I'm a patient man—most of the time."

Old Town had been built centuries ago, with stone quarried from the hills, and oak hauled in from the wilderness to the north. It had a ponderous feeling of history about it. Rowan had not spent much time there in the months since she'd come to live with her uncle and cousins. Most of the upper classes lived there, and she and Aaro led the horses past their estates with courtyards and manicured lawns. The main avenue brought them to the central square, where a fountain bubbled. A few shops lined the square, but New Town, with its marketplace, held more interest for her.

Instead of going to the chapel, Aaro took them down a side street crowded with row houses. He handed her his reins, ducked into a narrow stone passage between two of the buildings, and knocked on a door.

"The priest," he explained.

An older gentleman with wild white hair and dirt stained trousers came to the door. "D'Araines!" he said, bushy white eyebrows going up. He looked past him to Rowan. "And... a young lady."

She nodded, unable to curtsy while holding the horses.

"What can I do for you? Forgive my appearance. I was just working in my spot of garden out behind the church."

"Never mind," Aaro said. "We don't have much time. We'd like you to marry us."

Those white eyebrows travelled even farther up the man's face. "Well!" He turned from Aaro to Rowan. "And you're agreeable to this? Are you of consenting age?"

"Yes and yes."

"Well then... I suppose." He still looked flustered. "I should...Well. We should go to the chapel then I suppose?"

Aaro nodded, holding his hat against his chest. "We surely appreciate it."

"Well then. If you'd like to run along, I should change into something appropriate."

When they got to the chapel, Dustan was already waiting for them, standing at the shadowed corner of the building, shifting his weight back and forth nervously. He had a pack slung over his shoulder, which he handed to

Rowan as they came up.

"The king plans to call on you tomorrow," he said, wiping his sleeve across his forehead. Late afternoon heat pummeled them. "He wanted to see you again before he left, but apparently you had slipped away as soon as he brought you back. No one saw where you went."

"Thank you, cousin."

Rowan slipped into the coolness of the stone building with her bundle of clothes. Past long rows of carved wooden benches she strode, her footfalls echoing back to her from the high, vaulted ceiling. She reached the altar and paused to send up a prayer. Then she found the priest's little office at the back, and locked herself in. She unfolded the gown Dustan had brought.

Yards of white lace bounced to life as she shook out the garment. White lace over top of white silk. Green ribbons laced the bodice in front and trimmed the waist and wide neckline. She'd brought the dress from the East and never worn it.

"Well, I suppose you'll do," she said as she struggled with the row of tiny buttons down her back. It took a long time before she was able to get herself free of the old dress and slip into the new one. At least this one she could ride in. And get into and out of by herself without half an hour's struggle. Her hair, on the other hand...She put a hand to the coil at the back of her head, and found most of it slipping loose. She'd never be able to put it up again by herself without a mirror, so she pulled the pins out and let it fall around her shoulders and down below the middle of her back. Not exactly high fashion for a wedding. In fact, it was more what she'd imagine for the wedding *night*.

She let her back thump against the door, leaning on it for a moment. They would be waiting for her.

Marriage. Not quite the adventure she was expecting when she came to the frontier. Not, at least, without a long and exciting courtship in front of it. But still an adventure. *Life is only as bad as you make it*, mama used to tell her. *No matter what happens to you in life, you will only become a victim if you allow yourself to.*

"Right." She put her hand on the door, squared her shoulders, and stepped out.

Three pairs of eyes turned to stare at her. Aaro audibly sucked in his breath. Dustan strode over and took her hand, escorting her to the altar. The priest looked from one to the other of them.

"Your witness today is..."

"Dustan Keir."

"And you have no objection to this man and this woman being wed?"

Dustan paused. "I don't."

The priest cleared his throat. "Aaro D'Araines, do you vow to treat this woman, in word and in action, with love, care, and respect, to honor her and provide for her, in the best and in the worst, as the Almighty is your witness, until death parts you?"

"I do." Aaro seemed never to have stopped grinning since the moment she'd told him yes.

"Rowan Keir, do you vow to treat this man, in word and in action, with love, honor, and care, to respect him and provide for him in the best and in the worst, as the Almighty is your witness, until death parts you?"

"I do." She heard herself say it, but felt like it had come from someone else.

"Then by the authority of the Almighty and of the king, I proclaim you husband and wife."

Chapter 5

They stood there looking at one another. Rowan's world seemed to have shrunk down to the space of those two ice-blue eyes. Her mind felt disconnected from the rest of her. Surreal.

"It's customary to seal the marriage vows with a kiss," the priest said. "If you wish, of course."

Aaro searched her face, silently asking permission.

She quirked half a smile at him, and that was all he needed. He closed the gap between them and owned her lips with his burning kiss. She closed her eyes and was suddenly, ridiculously, glad that she was standing in front of an altar with this man.

Dustan cleared his throat, raising eyebrows at them as they parted. "You two better be on your way, before someone comes looking for us."

Rowan backed away from Aaro and wrapped her arms around her cousin. "Thank you," she whispered in his ear. "I'll see you again soon."

"Yes, you will. Now get going." Despite his rushing them off, Dustan followed them back to the horses. Aaro turned to him.

"My foreman is in town getting supplies.

You know Jake."

Dustan nodded.

"Tell him we've gone ahead home, and to catch up with us once he's done."

Again Dustan nodded, his eyes going to Rowan, his frown deepening. "You're sure you're alright with this?"

"It's a little late now. I'll be fine." She hugged him again, reluctant to let go.

"You know where home is," he whispered. "If you ever need to, you come running." He pulled away and looked her in the eyes. "Promise?"

"Of course."

They left him standing by the chapel and headed toward the open prairie, riding in awkward silence. Their shadows stretched further across the long grass as the evening deepened. The horses' hooves clumped dully in the packed dirt of the wagon track. Saddle leather creaked. Aaro looked over at her.

"I'm sorry it wasn't the wedding you probably hoped for."

She waved him off. "Nonsense. We'll have a marvelous story to tell our children."

"Are we having those?"

Rowan shot him a sideways glance. "It's assumed, I suppose. At some point. Honestly, I hadn't given it much thought until this moment, so I don't know." She shifted in the saddle, her thoughts suddenly heavy with all the unknown things. The simple fact that she didn't even know what her new home looked like.

Aaro didn't say anything for a long moment. "I guess there's a lot of things neither of us had a chance to think about."

She snorted. "Well, we'll have all the time we need to figure them out now."

"Yes..."

She glanced over at him, his figure straight in the saddle, looking ahead as he rode. His brows puckered together into a frown, and he lifted his hat and ran his fingers through his hair before settling it back on his head.

"Before we got married—this morning—I planned to ride east and see if Heymish wouldn't do something about his brother. I hoped I could get your promise to wait for me before I went away. Now I wonder... we may both need to leave for a while. I can't guarantee either of us won't be in danger once Ormand learns our good news. I don't expect he'd move against me outright. But he will certainly try to stage an 'accident' for us. I wish I had had time to explain everything more fully before."

"I knew well enough what the situation was. And now what you want to know is if I will go with you." She laughed softly and looked over at him again, finding him watching her. "It's not what most people do on their honeymoon, but I've never been like most people."

Aaro continued to watch her in the

softening light. He drew a breath to speak, but let it out in a quiet sigh instead. The dusk deepened. He gestured to the trail ahead. "Home is just beyond that line of trees. We'll be there in under an hour."

In the distance, she heard the low of cattle. Night insects were out and singing.

"I said I was sorry, before, about the wedding," Aaro said. His eyes were shadowed, almost invisible beneath his hat in the dusk. "But I'm not. It was perfect. Mostly you. You were—are—perfect."

Most of the sunlight had gone out of the sky, and the moon come up by the time they rode through the line of trees. A sprawling ranch complex, almost a small village unto itself, hunkered in the wide basin of land beyond. The trail led them through the middle of the cluster of buildings, past bunkhouses, cabins, and stables, and Rowan heard the murmur of conversation and laughter from behind lighted windows. An aging cowpoke sat on the bunkhouse porch and lifted his hand in a lazy wave. Aaro spoke a greeting as they passed. Somewhere beyond all the buildings, but close this time, another cow lowed.

Aaro's horse drifted to a stop of its own accord in front of a stable and corral, and Rowan's mare followed suit. He jumped down, then turned and reached up to lift her down. It was the same gesture as King Ormand's hours ago, when they'd arrived in her uncle's courtyard. Except that having Aaro's hands linger on her waist seemed sweet, like awkward budding attraction, rather than Ormand's disregard of her dignity.

Aaro's eyes shone silvery in the moonlight as she looked up at him, and for a moment she though he would kiss her again. But there came a rustle of movement from the stable, and a man stepped out.

"Boss," he said, tipping his hat in greeting as he reached for the horses. "Who's the lady?"

"My wife. Rowan."

The cowboy's eyebrows shot up. He started to whistle and caught himself, tipping his hat again toward Rowan. "Ma'am." He squinted at them. "Were you planning on getting hitched today?"

"I wasn't, actually." Aaro grinned and slapped him on the shoulder. "Just turned out the Almighty was smiling on me today." He untied Rowan's pack from her saddle before the horses were led away, then offered her his arm.

The main house, even though it had been built with logs instead of stone, had a tower that loomed against the moon as they crossed the wide front lawn. Rowan had a hard time getting an idea of its size in the dark, but as they drew closer, it felt massive. She looked up at the tower just before they passed under the shade of the front porch, and saw a glimmer of lantern light.

"My watchman," Aaro explained. "You can see out of the valley to the open prairie from up there." He led her across the wide front porch, and gave the door a thump. "Miz Emrella is persnickety about bolting the door after dark." He shrugged.

"Miz Emrella?"

"My household manager. And cook. Here she comes."

They heard the bolt being lifted away, and the door opened to reveal a tall, thick woman with a red face scowling at them. As tall as Rowan was, she didn't have to look down at the other woman, who barked out as soon as the door was open, "And where have you been?"

"Miz Emrella, meet my wife, Rowan."

Emrella looked from him to Rowan and harrumphed, sounding a little hurt. "You didn't tell me you were getting married. Poor excuse for a wedding supper, is that pot roast that's all dried out now because you didn't come home. For the second day in a row, I might add." She sized Rowan up. "Nice to meet you dear. Welcome home, and all that. You'll please excuse our lack of preparedness, since we didn't know the young boss was going courting."

"Thank you. And any sort of dinner sounds good right now."

Emrella went back to giving Aaro the stink eye. "Tell me you didn't get your new bride any dinner."

When they finally made it past the cook, Aaro led her though the enormous front room toward the back, taking a lantern with them. They passed the kitchen, brightly lit and loud with laughter, down a hallway and around a corner. He opened a door into a long, spacious bedroom, and set her pack down next to the door.

"This is it."

Rowan stepped into the room, her boots smooshing into a braided calico rug that covered the open section of the floor. Moonlight shone through a window, gleaming on the polished wooden bedframe. She crossed slowly to the window and looked out into a moonlit garden courtyard, realizing that the house was shaped like an L. The courtyard butted up against the house on two sides, one side had a stockade style wall, and the other ended in a flash of moonlit water and shadow of trees.

Aaro followed her into the room and set the lantern on top of the unlit fireplace, illuminating a door leading out to the courtyard, and another to a darkened side room. Probably a closet or sitting area. The house was luxurious in a rustic, frontier way, without the imported elegance of the nobles' houses in town.

She wanted to ask: *Is this my room—or our room*? But she wasn't ready to face the answer. Not yet. Probably not by the time bedtime rolled around either. Again, it wasn't him she feared, rather the part of herself that she struggled to squelch. That she was unreasonably already in love with her husband, and part of her would be disappointed to have her own room. On the other hand...

"Do you want to eat?"

"Yes!" She spun back from the window, grateful to escape her thoughts. "I'm starving!" Which had to be why her stomach felt like it was trying to crawl up her throat.

Emrella and several others joined them at the small kitchen table, easing some of the awkwardness as they plied Aaro with questions. Had he been planning on getting married today? Why didn't he tell them? Why such a hurry? What news from town? Had Ormand done anything else horrible? And where was Jake?

"As it turns out," Aaro explained, "Ormand was planning on forcing this lovely lady to be his queen. Fortunately, I sent her uncle my proposal a full half day in advance of him."

"Fortunate is not a word I would have chosen in regard to anything that's happened this day. Though for you, perhaps, Providence was smiling." She gave him her best saucy look. "There were a dozen other less arrogant young men bidding for my attention, any one of whom I could have been with on this most unfortunate day."

Emrella gaped at her.

Aaro's eyes twinkled. "Indeed. Fortunate

for me. Unless I am mistaken though—which I never am—none of your other young men submitted a marriage proposal which your uncle could show the lesser king in evidence that your hand had already been claimed. However, I would dearly love to know why you did choose me over the others. You aren't the girl who would pick a man based solely on his looks." He grinned at her. "Unless your uncle made the decision for you."

Rowan could feel her face growing hotter by the second. "*No* man makes my decisions. Of all the people in this insufferable, suffocating place, you were the only one who made any indication that it was *I* who must be convinced, and not my *guardian*. I'd take an arrogant man any day over one who thought he could own me. That was why I chose you. Though whether I was right remains to be seen. I *have* made mistakes before—unlike you, apparently." She set her fork down and pushed her plate away, suddenly remembering that she had started the day tired and out of sorts, and realizing that she was still tired. Plotting against a king, getting married, the possibility of still having her life in danger very soon... it was a lot to process, even for her.

She stood from the table. "Thank you for supper. It was wonderful. And my apologies for my outburst. It has been a long day. If you'll excuse me."

Back in the bedroom, she dropped the bolt

across the door. Whether it was *her* room or *their* room, she was claiming it for the night.

The lamp still burned above the unlit fireplace, adding its warm yellow light to the cold, white light of the moon. She sat down on the edge of the bed and flopped backward, her red curls splayed out around her, and covered her face with her hands. She groaned and shook her head. "What have I done?" She sat up again slowly, and went to retrieve her pack from where Aaro had left it beside the door, emptying it onto the bed.

Dustan had packed her a set of his clothes, of all things, along with a day's worth of dried travel rations, her boots, and her little jeweled dagger, which she'd been too flustered to put back on when she changed that morning. She found her extra set of throwing knives as well. But no nightgown.

Apparently, her cousin was more worried about if she decided to run away than if she decided to stay. She snickered. At least he'd packed her hairbrush. Granted, her hair was not something easily forgotten about, since it was just as outspoken and unmanageable as she.

She slipped out of her gown and stood in front of the mirror in her light summer shift, taking a swipe at her hair with the brush. Coppery-brown eyes stared back at her.

"Don't look at me like that," she told her reflection. "You're a married woman now, so you might as well own it. It's not as though you were repulsed by him." She aimed the brush at her mirror image, accusing. "Admit it. You wanted him."

Her reflection rolled its eyes at her.

"Well of course you had a choice. You could have run away and become a fugitive. You just chose the lazy option. For all your preaching about being smothered by men, you went and chose a man."

She set the brush down and leaned her palms on the dresser, bringing her nose-to-nose with her reflection. "And now you're talking to yourself."

She picked the brush back up, but by that time her hair had become a cloud, puffing out like flaming dandelion fuzz. She sighed.

The door leading out into the courtyard rattled suddenly, and Rowan froze, staring at it in the mirror. Who would be coming in from the outside? When the latch moved again, she spun from the mirror, made it back to the bed in one leap, and swooped up both throwing knives and her dagger, spinning back to the door as it creaked open.

The first blade left her hand and embedded itself in the doorframe next to Aaro's head at the same second that she recognized him. He jerked sideways, blinking at it.

"What in the..." He turned back to her, and his blue eyes widened.

That was about when she remembered she was wearing nothing but her shift, whose translucent white silk didn't leave much to the imagination. Face flaming, she tossed her other throwing knife back onto the bed, though she held onto the dagger.

"Don't scare me like that."

"Where you aiming for me?"

"Of course not. I didn't know who would be sneaking in from outside, and a knife beside the face tends to give people pause."

"Yes it does." He tugged the knife free and tossed it onto the bed. "Do I have to knock from now on when I come into our bedroom?"

Rowan tilted her chin up a fraction. "You never specified that it was ours, and not mine."

His eyes traveled the length of her figure before coming to rest on her halo of wild red curls. "I thought the marriage ceremony made that obvious."

"And I thought the fact that we've known one another for all of a day made it ambiguous." She caressed her dagger's tip with her fingers. "Why did you come in through the courtyard?"

He cocked an eyebrow at her as he stepped fully into the room and closed the door behind him. "Because you had the other door locked."

"Of all the... So instead of knocking, you thought you'd just sneak up on me from outside? How does that make sense?"

"My thought was that I didn't want to wake you." His eyes twinkled as he rounded the bed toward her. He reached for the dagger. "May I?"

She stepped back out of his reach. "Not until I finish deciding whether to stab you for scaring me like that."

"I could think of better things to do."

"You're insufferable." She turned her back on him to hide her grin, but he stepped up behind her, his hands going around her waist as he rested his chin on her shoulder. His breath brushed her cheek as he stepped closer, and goosebumps raced over every inch of her. His work-roughened hands snagged at her silk shift and warmed her skin. Her heart stopped for a moment, then she whirled on him, bringing them nose-to-nose, and stabbed a finger into his chest.

"What happened to being patient?" She drove him backward with her finger until his back thumped against the wall. "You think you can barge in here and scare the starch out of me, and then do *that*, whatever that was, and expect me to fall into your arms?"

He put his hands up in surrender. "Fine! I can be patient. But if that's what you really want, then find something else to wear." He winked.

Rowan's lips parted. For a moment she had nothing to say. A phenomenon that only ever happened when she was with *him*.

Scream, laugh, stab him or kiss him. Land

sakes! Figure out what you're going to do, and do it.

She raised the dagger she still held and used the point to draw small circles in the air over his heart. He wore a shirt that laced together at the neck, but the laces were undone, dangling down his chest, baring a generous amount of skin below his neck.

"Very well." She set the dagger point at the base of the V where his collar hung open, angled the blade, and sliced downward. The shirt fell open as Aaro sucked a startled breath. The view was not disappointing. "If you can catch me, you can have me."

She leapt away from him, vaulted the bed, and was out into the courtyard and running in under two seconds, stabbing the dagger into the log wall outside so she couldn't kill herself with it as she ran.

The door slammed open behind her.

He caught up with her in a moment. Her bare feet skidded sideways in wet grass as he grappled her from behind. She twisted in his arms, bringing them face to face, hooked her foot behind his leg, grinned, and gave him a shove. She sprang away again as he flailed backward, heading for the stream that crossed the back side of the courtyard. This time when he caught up, Aaro dove for her legs, toppling her, shrieking, into the water. The shock of cold went over her head, and then she was up, spluttering, while he knelt on the grass, hands on his knees, laughing so hard he sobbed.

She lunged out of the water, wrapped her arms around his neck, and shoved backward.

* * * * *

It was well past dawn when Rowan drifted into a disoriented half wakefulness. She lay there with her eyes closed, sensing that she wasn't home, and wondering where she was. Flickers of memories tickled the edge of her consciousness. Something had happened yesterday. Something big. Something that...

She felt someone stir in the bed beside her, and shrieked, trying to jump away. But she was tangled in blankets and ended up on the floor, taking most of them with her. Blue eyes blinked down at her blearily as she struggled.

"Good morning, my love."

She stopped struggling.

Aaro. Her husband. She pulled the blankets over her head and groaned. "Ohh. What have I done?"

"Got married," Aaro said from above her.

"I thought I dreamed that." She uncovered her face and looked up at him. He lay on his stomach, his chin propped on his forearms, looking over the edge of the bed at her. He gave her a sleepy grin. She groaned and rolled further into her blanket cocoon.

Aaro yawned. The straw mattress shifted, and his fingers brushed her hair. "Come back to bed with me?"

Rowan sat up in her cocoon and crawled back onto the bed, where he tried to pull her back into a cuddle, but with all the blankets wrapped around her, it didn't work. He started unrolling them, and by the time they found each other again they were both giggling. She tucked her head into his chest.

"I thought all of this was a dream when I woke, and it made me so sad. I can't believe it's real."

He kissed her forehead. "And you've ruined me. How can that happen in just one day? You're my world, Red."

The swift thud of boots in the hallway intruded itself, followed by pounding on the door.

"D'Araines!"

He rolled over and sat up, groaning. "What?!"

"Better come out here. We're getting visitors."

"What time is it?" Rowan asked as he rose and pulled on trousers and boots.

"Near noon, I'd say."

She slid out of bed and lifted her shift off the floor. It hung from her fingers, wet, muddy, and torn. She dropped it back onto the floor with a snort. Thankfully her gown was layered enough that no one would notice the loss.

Aaro finished buttoning a fresh shirt, then

came over and put his arms around her as she was lacing her dress.

"That isn't helpful."

"Kiss me then, so I'll go away."

"I have doubts as to whether that would help."

He tilted her chin up and kissed her, blue eyes sparkling with a new kind of danger. "Come join me when you're done."

He slipped out the door, leaving her to finish cinching her gown and trying to tame her hair. Without help and without anything to smooth it after her dunking last night, the best she could do was put it in a braid.

She checked the mirror, hoping she looked more put-together than she felt, then stepped into the hall. The strangeness of it all pressed on her. That everything outside the bedroom felt so unfamiliar, that she could hardly remember how to get back out into the front room, and that this was her home.

Voices helped to guide her, and she paused in the hall next to the kitchen and listened.

"What can I do for you, Cousin?" Aaro's voice.

Another voice, similar yet very different, replied, "I believe you stole something of mine."

Rowan's joy popped like a soap bubble in a hurricane. She felt her face flame, and her breath hissed out between her teeth. *Ormand*. If he had heard about the wedding already, it could only mean that he had come to her uncle's house to collect her either last night or just after dawn this morning. The pig. But there was nothing he could do about their marriage now. And no forced annulments, since it had been consummated. She was suddenly fiercely glad for that. Whatever Ormand did now, he couldn't take away what they shared in each other. She lifted her chin, becoming every inch the proud and gracious new wife, and opened the door.

Chapter 6

"Stole something?" Aaro feigned innocence while rage stabbed through him. "I don't believe I've stolen anything of yours."

A soft footfall sounded behind him, and he half turned as Rowan slipped her hand around his arm, giving it a squeeze. Even with Ormand there, she made his pulse spike. She looked like a queen, straight and regal, with her hair braided and pinned into a crown around her head. She kept her arm linked with his as she dropped a half curtsy.

"Ormand, I believe you've met my wife, Rowan."

Ormand's eyes snapped. "I see it's too late for an annulment. You've already ruined her. Very clever."

"King of the West you might be," Aaro said softly. "But you shall not speak about my *wife* as if she were your dog. Not to my face, not in my house, and certainly not in her presence."

Aaro was treading on thin ice, and he knew it. A part of him demanded caution, that he bide his time and follow through with the plan to go to Heymish. Another part of him was done with patience and caution. Ormand's arrogance had gone on too long, and spread too far, and he wished to end these little games, confront his cousin, and be done with it. He had the backing of the entire county, and probably the entire West Talva.

Ormand studied him for a moment through slitted eyes. Silent. Calculating. "You pose an interesting problem," he said finally. "You defy me at every turn. You're untamable. You withhold the respect due me..." he paused.

"My respect goes to those who've earned it."

Ormand held up a hand. "Please. I already know how you feel about me and my methods of keeping the peace. No need to rehash."

Manipulation and intimidation. And murder, Aaro wanted to say, but he held his tongue. He looked past the king and the half dozen guards who'd come in with him, out the front window. It looked like half an army out there, waiting. No matter what happened, the outcome of this meeting wouldn't be a good one. Not for him, or for Rowan.

"I have not dared to kill you outright," Ormand went on. "Somehow you attract loyalty—whether you seek it or it seeks you I have not discovered, but that's irrelevant. Most of the West would put you on the throne, if given reason. If I were to make a single bold move, such as a king should be able and willing to make, and the people didn't like it, they would revolt and rally around you. So I can't let you live. On the other hand, killing you could upset my position too much to mend. What would my brother do if I killed you outright, unprovoked? You see the tenuous situation I'm in? I can't kill you, and I can't let you live."

He lifted the silver circlet from his head and ran his fingers through his hair before replacing it. His gaze shifted from Aaro to Rowan and back again before he continued. "Now you defy me openly, marrying the woman I intended to make queen. Indeed, I called on her last evening, intending to make my intentions known, and even informed my friends of my decision. That changes a few things. Defiance. An open strike against me." He smiled.

"I made my intentions clear when I sent Lance Keir my proposal," Aaro said. "You had made no claim to her." Beside him he felt his wife stiffen, though she remained outwardly calm. He squeezed her hand, trusting her to know he spoke at Ormand's level, and not that he considered her a property to be claimed. "We met, loved each other, and wished to be married."

Ormand smiled a tight-lipped smile. "Still, I can hardly let the matter go. I can't let you win. Perhaps you fail to understand the situation completely. The moment I let you win, I am no longer king."

Aaro's gaze flicked from Ormand to the soldiers awaiting his command outside. "Let my wife go then. She can return to her home back east. Western politics don't concern her. She's innocent in all of this."

"It's always the innocent who shoulder responsibility for the rest of us. She should have thought of that before she came here and married you."

"But if she hadn't married me by choice, she would have married you because she was forced. That's hardly her fault. Let her go, and we can figure this out as we should have done months ago." He glanced at Rowan. Her lips had thinned out. She still held herself like a queen, and she was wisely biting her tongue, but if a person could spontaneously turn to sculpted ice, then she was in danger of doing it. Her hands on his arm felt warm, though, as she squeezed it.

Ormand ran his hands down his embroidered vest, tugging it straight. "Perhaps. Still, I can't dismiss the matter. The fact that you're begging for her safety only confirms that you know I'm right." He snapped his fingers at the guards. "Bring them both."

Mitchell, the hired hand that had come to get Aaro earlier, still lingered at the doorway. He stepped forward at the same time the guards did. Out of the corner of his eye Aaro saw him slug the guard. Another guard drew a gun, and a third a sword. Aaro ignored them and stepped toward Ormand, moving fast enough to grab his cousin by the collar of his fancy vest before the other guards could step in. He punched him.

Ormand rocked back on his heels, but

Aaro's grip on his shirt kept him upright. Two guards grabbed hold of him, and he heard Rowan's cry of anger. He half turned, and a gun butt slammed into his head. Explosions went off behind his eyes, and he felt himself fall. Then nothing.

* * * * *

Aaro woke with a spasm of coughing, which turned into retching.

"Take it easy. Almost there," someone said.

Something crashed nearby, and he became aware of intense heat and smoke, and the roar of flames. He coughed violently again, and tried to roll over, but someone had him by the arms, dragging him. His boot heels scraped over wood.

Everything hurt. Bad.

The man dragging him started coughing too, and swearing, and he realized it was Jake. He pried his eyes open to a wall of smoke, tinged orange with flame. Then they were out of it, onto the porch, and he started coughing again. Jake helped him get onto his knees, and together they stumbled down the stairs to the front path, and out onto the rutted road leading in from the prairie. The buildings around them were all burning. The grass was starting to burn. Jake hauled him around behind the main house to the stream. The same stream that he and Rowan had played in the night before.

"Reckon we'll be ok," Jake said, splashing

through to the other side, still hauling Aaro along with him. "It's starting to rain now."

He let go, and Aaro landed on his knees. Jake sat down and waited while he coughed and retched, involuntary tears stinging his eyes. When the spasm passed, Aaro remained kneeling, his eyes squeezed shut, waiting for the pain and dizziness to pass. His chest ached and his head throbbed, as well as his ribs and several other places. His arm burned, the pain intense enough to drown out most of the others.

"Rowan?" He asked. His voice sounded ruined, and the single word sent him into another coughing fit.

His coughing quieted, and he looked up, but his foreman still didn't respond, staring off across the prairie. Aaro would have demanded he speak, if he'd been able to talk. Or he would've strangled answers out of the other man if he had the strength. But breathing and not collapsing were all he could handle at the moment. He was at Jake's mercy for finding out what had happened to his wife.

"Guess they beat you after they knocked you out," Jake said finally. "Thought you were dead. Probably the only thing that saved you was that you were on the floor where the smoke wasn't so bad."

Aaro felt the truth of those words. He felt mostly dead. He hurt like he'd never hurt before. Even getting shot once hadn't been this bad. But all he wanted was to know that Rowan was still alive. That she was waiting for him somewhere. Even if he had to find her and rescue her. She had become his entire world in a single day. He silently begged Jake to speak.

When he did finally open his mouth, his voice came out low, the same as he'd use for calming spooked horses. "I stayed in town last night. Had a few things I couldn't take care of till the bank opened up this morning, then got delayed..." His voice drifted off. He coughed once and cleared his throat before continuing. "I met Ormand and half his army on their way back to the palace. He told me to get out. If I left West Talva, he said he'd let me go. Or, if I was a fool, I could come and bury you. Said you attacked him. So I rode like the wind back here. Guess Ormand thought he'd killed you. Or that the fire had."

"Rowan?" Aaro croaked again.

Jake shook his head. "Ormand told me. She's dead. She wasn't in the house with you and Mitchel, but there's a lot of bodies..." He let his voice trail off.

At that moment a crash and roar came from the house. Both of them looked up in time to see the whole thing collapse, the lookout tower toppling over. Flames shot upward with the billowing smoke.

The first sob took Aaro by surprise, and nearly broke him in half. He turned from the fire, still on his knees, and bowed almost to the ground as his body shuddered and rocked. His throat burned and he started coughing again, gasping and sobbing all at once till he thought he'd choke to death.

"Take it easy," Jake said. "Breathe now, cry later." When Aaro finally regained control, he handed him a canteen. "We need to get out of here. Ormand thinks you're dead. He'd try to finish the job if he knew otherwise. We'll find someplace to hole up till you can travel, then go to Heymish together."

Aaro shook his head. "No." He took another sip from the canteen. The rain was coming down harder now, washing the smoke and soot from his face, soaking through his shirt and cooling the burn on his arm. The fire had spread through the grass nearly to the creek on the other side. Now it smoked and started to die down.

Jake sat down in the wet grass and tilted his hat back on his head, creating a miniature waterfall off the brim. "No?"

"He killed my wife," Aaro whispered, making Jake lean forward to hear him over the rain and the roar of the fire. He waved a hand around at the destroyed ranch. "What happened to our people?"

Jake didn't respond, but his face did.

"Mitchell? Emrella?"

Jake shook his head.

"Heymish's got nothing to do with this,"

Aaro said, still at a whisper. After another sip of water, he went on. "This is between me and Ormand now. I'm going to destroy him."

"Revenge is a fool's mission."

"You don't have to help me."

Jake sighed. He mopped water off his face with a wet handkerchief, smearing the soot and dust into streaks. "What you going to need?"

"A mask."

Chapter 7

Rowan rode in silence, sandwiched between two guards in Ormand's carriage. She hadn't bothered to struggle against the ropes around her wrists and ankles. Nor had she bothered to speak, cry, or beg. Ormand had tried baiting her into a conversation. "I didn't think you were the kind of woman to pout," he'd said of her continued silence. She merely looked at him.

When they had met Aaro's foreman riding out from town, and Ormand told him she was dead, one of the soldiers held a knife to her ribs. She didn't speak then, either.

She watched the king, matching his stare, studying the faint lines around his eyes, the day's stubble on his face. She compared him to his twin brother Heymish, and found him better looking, though nowhere near as gorgeous as Aaro.

Aaro again. Again, she ruthlessly forced her thoughts away. If she thought of him, she would see him curled on the floor, unconscious, his body jerking as Ormand's guard kicked him. The same guard who now sat to her right in the carriage. Then she would think about the others. Emrella, and the young cowboy who'd tried to defend them, with bullets through their heads.

If she thought about Aaro, she would hear the gunfire and the clash of swords as the guards dragged her to the carriage, and Ormand's quiet command to fire the buildings. Then would come the worst part. The imagining. Imagining the bodies charring in the flames. And Aaro. It would come back around to Aaro, and she would picture him with fire roaring around him, limp, as the house collapsed, and the lookout tower fell and buried him there.

Then she would remember him from before. How perfect he had been in every way. How completely she'd fallen for him. How...

She ripped her thoughts away as her eyes stung and her head pounded with the effort of holding everything back.

She returned her stare to the king, forcing the calm and the ice to return.

Ormand leaned back in his seat facing her and the guards, watching, as he'd been through their journey. "I admire you, Lady D'Araines," he said finally.

Rowan started a little at the use of her married name. In truth, she hadn't even tried the name on. *Rowan D'Araines*. She rolled it around silently. She could have grown to like it.

"You would have made a fine queen," Ormand went on. "Even now you won't acknowledge that I've won. You refuse to give me any kind of satisfaction, I suppose." He leaned against the door, looking out the window at the prairie passing by. "It would have been satisfying, perhaps, to watch you weep. But not necessary."

He turned away from the window and met her eyes. His gaze traveled down to her neck, where the copper wolf pendant still rested in the hollow of her throat. "The truth is, I have won. Whether you acknowledge it or not." He leaned forward and fingered the pendant, bringing his face close.

Rowan didn't flinch, though her skin crawled as his fingers brushed her throat. One finger strayed from the copper, stroking her skin, soft as a breath.

"So beautiful," he whispered. "I can only imagine what last night must have been like for my cousin."

"How are you going to kill me?" Rowan said, breaking her silence. She didn't have a bullet through her head yet, so she imagined he must plan on making her punishment more public.

Ormand sat back abruptly, and the skin at her throat tingled.

"I'm not. I have something much more interesting in mind for you. You'll wish yourself dead. And death won't be far off. But it won't be by my hand."

Rowan held his stare.

He chuckled. "It must be killing you. All of this." He waved a hand around the interior of the carriage, encompassing the memories and images that rode invisibly with them. He shook his head. "Yet you remain regal. How I wish you could have been my queen."

An hour or more later the carriage creaked to a stop, and Rowan raised her head and opened her eyes. She'd wearied of Ormand. His face, his voice, his words. So she had closed her eyes and shut him out. She wouldn't allow the thoughts of Aaro either though. Not yet. She thought of Dustan, and Annalie, and wondered what they were doing. She wondered if Annalie had heard of her marriage, or if Dustan and the others were worried about her.

The carriage door opened, and Ormand stepped out, pausing to smooth his vest, then strode away. One of the guards got out. He leaned back into the carriage and dragged Rowan across the seat, putting her over his shoulder like a sack of potatoes.

"Please!" Ormand called, turning from the doors of the palace to glance back at them. "Untie her feet and let her walk. Such indignity is embarrassing. I just rode in a carriage with that woman."

The guard set her down and kept an iron grip on her arm while his partner cut the rope around her ankles, then grabbed her other arm. She walked between them, head held high.

Ormand disappeared through the massive, ornate oak doors, but the guards led Rowan a different way, along the ancient stone building and around the corner, where a shoulder height wall formed an alleyway between the palace wall and the drive leading back to the carriage house.

A locked iron gate let them into the alley, and another led them down a narrow stone stairwell that seemed never to end. Their feet slapping against the stone echoed back at them in the tight space, until it dumped them out into the dungeon proper.

An involuntary shudder ran through her. For the first time since they'd taken her, she jerked against the guards. They both tightened their grips. The door behind her was locked. Her hands were tied. And she didn't have any of her knives. She stopped struggling. If she got out of this, it wouldn't be by kicking and screaming. So she kept her mouth shut and marched with the guards, even though waves of panic kept crashing through her till she thought she might drop dead from her heart giving out.

They passed a row of cells and a room with a heavy door standing ajar, where she glimpsed instruments of torture. She expected to turn aside, either into one of the cells, or even the torture chamber, but they kept walking. Silent. Only their footsteps echoed through the stone hallways, making her think the dungeon must be empty. Apparently Ormand didn't keep his prisoners around long.

They left the dungeons behind, following a narrow corridor lit by candles mounted intermittently on the wall. After a time, Rowan realized it must be a tunnel, not a corridor, for they had walked far beyond the width of the palace, their feet smacking on damp flagstones. The walls were a haphazard mix of brick and stone, and they, too, glistened with moisture in the dim light. No doors or passages branched off, and the floor remained level.

It must have been a mile that they walked before the tunnel ended against a single barred door. One of the guards lifted the bar and leaned it against the wall. The other escorted her inside, where he let go her arm, taking up position in front of the door.

"Well this is something new," someone said behind her. She turned, her gaze skipping over the bookshelves, desk, and panels of mirrors that lined the walls till it reached the room's occupant, a wiry little man with dark bronze skin and short white hair. He peered at her over top of wire-rimmed spectacles, reminding her instantly and achingly of Uncle Lance.

"I can't say Ormand has ever sent me a young lady before." His face creased into a thousand wrinkles as he smiled. This time he reminded her of the merchant woman she and Aaro had met at the market in New Town. The Shonnowan woman.

She hadn't steeled herself, and the unbidden thought of Aaro choked her, blotting out her panic for a moment. She gasped, hunching over with the force of the tears demanding to be let loose. Her face twisted, and she drew deep, shuddering breaths. She mustn't cry. Not yet. It wouldn't be put off much longer, but for now, she had to keep herself together.

A muffled sob escaped, and she covered her mouth with her hands, still bound together with cord. She struggled for a moment, finally forcing herself upright, clearing the escaped tears from her face with her bound hands. Her throat still ached, but she pushed the thoughts of Aaro away relentlessly, raising her head and blinking at the little Shonnowan man, whose eyes were level with her chin. He peered up at her, his thousand wrinkles slanting into a frown.

"Fallen amuck of Ormand have you? If he has a weakness for anything, it's usually for a beautiful woman. He doted on Embur, until she found fault with him in front of his advisors. What can you have done that he would bring you to me?" He pushed his glasses up again and scratched the tip of his nose, his frown deepening. "Worse, what is he going to demand I do to you?"

The little man sighed and glanced at the guard. He took Rowan's elbow and led her gently toward the other side of the room, beneath a domed ceiling with a pyramid shaped skylight at its apex that let in weak daylight. Raindrops spattered the glass.

"Don't talk much, do you? Hmm. You can't bottle it up forever. But I do hope you hold out till... I just hope you don't give him the satisfaction of breaking down."

Rowan smiled faintly. "I've made it this far."

He nodded, pulling her over to a bookcase at the far side of the room. Mirrors separated the bookcases, angled so they augmented the natural light. The little man reached up to put his hands on her shoulders, whispering, "Before the king comes, you should know that magic is never permanent. There's always a way to undo it. I don't know what your curse will be yet, so I can't tell you how to break it, but there is *always* a way."

"Curse?" A chill swept through her, beginning in the pit of her stomach, and so much worse now than the shiver she'd gotten from Dustan's mention of magic two days ago.

The Shonnowan man pushed his glasses up and glanced at the guard. "Usually the breaking is directly opposed to the purpose of the curse. Whatever way in which it disables you, if you can overcome it, you can break the curse. I wish I had time to explain more. It's a vastly complex system, with infinite variables, but whatever happens, don't give up hope."

Rowan reared her head back, staring at him, her lips parted.

"Oh, and another thing about curses. They're never complete. You'll see what I mean. The best craftsman in the world can't render a curse without flaws, and I am nothing like the best."

"What...?"

"Oh, be assured. If Ormand has you here, he's got something unpleasant planned for you. I hope for your sake it's not *too* unpleasant. But...I doubt it."

She felt like the world was dropping out from under her. Magic? Curses? She'd only ever heard stories and gossip about such things before today. How could she deal with that?

The door opened, and the little Shonnowan man looked sheepish as Ormand strode in. His eyes went from one to the other of them, and the corner of his mouth lifted in a smile. "Rigall, at what point will you give up trying to help these people? You can't win any more than they can."

Rigall, the Shonnowan magician, peered at the king over his glasses, then pushed them up and looked through them. "I've stomped on every belief I ever held for you, King. If I cannot keep my faith, I must keep my humanity."

Ormand flicked a hand in dismissal. "You realize, of course, that your efforts accomplish nothing but to ease your own, weak conscience. And that your folly doesn't worry me in the least."

Rigall glared at him, retreating behind his desk. "And my son?"

"Still ambling about the countryside wearing the body of a bear, so far as I know. You'll be free to seek him and his cure the moment our project is complete, as promised. I am a man true to my word. I also have many things to attend to today, and petting your needy emotions is not one of them." He grabbed Rowan's arm and pulled her into the center of the room, beneath the skylight, glaring at the guard. "Do I have to do everything?"

The guard hustled from his post and dragged a stool over to Rowan, pushing her down onto it. He glanced at Ormand questioningly before he returned to his spot by the door.

Rowan felt goosebumps prickle along her arms. She had been working at trying to free her arms, but her wrists had been bound with strong cord, wrapped several times around and between, and tied much more securely than a thicker rope could have. She could barely even move her arms, let alone wiggle them free.

"And in the meantime, as ever, I am at your disposal," Rigall said to the king, sitting down with a huff and flipping open a giant book. He perused its pages. "What is it going to be today? A tongue binding? Blindness? I hope not the foul odor curse. It took me a week to get the stench out of here when you demanded that one."

"I should have taken your head for that one," Ormand replied. "The results were disappointing, at best. And the other crippling curses never work out well either. People tend to find ways around them. The viper you made me the other day was also a disappointment."

"Serves you right. The Shonnowa well know the danger of abusing the Gift. Only a fool would do what you're doing. And just because you give a garden snake a viper's skin, doesn't mean it will act like a viper."

"You're a liar," Ormand answered, ignoring Rigall's retort about the viper. He strolled over and leaned against one of the bookshelves. "Your people have been using the Nawassa to their own ends for generations."

"The Shonno-mara? They are fools as well."

Ormand waived a hand in Rowan's direction. "Shall we get on with it?"

Rigall sighed. "What do you want done to her?"

"Have you seen the pendant she wears? A gift from my late cousin, if I'm correct, and perfectly fitting. Turn her into a wolf.

Rowan squeaked involuntarily. A wolf! Was that even possible? She looked at the magician to see his response. He just looked weary, and sad. A new round of panic exploded through her chest, making her vision dance, and tingling through her numb fingers. She jerked against the ropes again, and only managed to wrench her arms. Thankfully Ormand wasn't watching her. Somehow, it was important not to let him see fear. Defiance was all she had left. After a final look at the guard and the bolted door, then at the skylight a full story above her head, she sagged on the stool.

"I don't want her going back to her old life," Ormand was saying. "I offered her power, and love, and she defied me."

Defiance. She could have laughed to herself, if her heart wasn't beating loud enough to drown her own voice. She drew a long breath, and met Ormand's eyes, and suddenly her fear broke. Her panic washed away like a candle in a flood. Whatever was coming, she couldn't stop it. So she let her fear and her hope slip away together. *My life is in Your hands, Almighty One, as it always has been.*

"What you offered was neither power nor love," she said, holding Ormand's gaze and feeling only a fierce joy now in speaking the truth. "You bend the truth. You manipulate and you intimidate. Rigall is right. You are a fool, and someday you will know it."

Ormand merely regarded her with one eyebrow raised. "Trying to comfort yourself?"

"No. I have no illusions right now. But you, for all your arrogance and condescension, you are the one falling for your own lies. You've become absorbed in creating your own reality, and you believe it's true, and force everyone to play along. That's why you hated Aaro. He wouldn't play. You keep saying you've won, and you have. For now. But there will always be someone else—another Aaro—who won't live in your false world. You'll always have someone you have to destroy, and eventually the cost will be too great. You will have to face the truth for what it is, not what you make it. Then all that you've built, and all that you are, will be undone."

"Well said," Rigall muttered.

"Truly, it was spoken like a dying prophecy." Ormand smirked. But the smirk slowly melted as they stared at one another for a long moment. He snapped his fingers at his magician. "Get to it."

The little man shuffled out from behind his desk carrying a vial of green liquid which he shook before he uncorked it. He put his finger over the opening and upended the vial quickly, then dabbed his wet finger over Rowan's pendant. He repeated the process and touched her forehead.

"My own blend," he explained. "It helps to focus the energy I draw out of the air. It would be better if it wasn't raining today. The more sunshine the better. Or moonlight. Depending on what you want the end result to be." He glanced at Ormand. "It could make for a stronger outcome, but our dear king is always in a rush, and doesn't seem to care when a job only gets three-quarters of the way done. For that matter, with this type of curse, moonlight *would* be better suited. But who am I to argue?"

He returned to his desk to consult his big book, glancing up at her. "This next part involves drawing the Gift out of the air, and sound is one of the things I'll be using. You may think it's a good idea to make some noise of your own to disrupt things... I beg of you, though, for your own sake, don't do it. Being turned into a wolf is bad enough. Who knows what distortions would manifest if the process is interrupted. You wouldn't want to be a wolf with seaweed for fur."

"Enough!" Ormand cried. "Would that *I* could use magic, so I could silence your babble."

Rigall glared at him. "Enough yourself. You be quiet too, if you don't want the Gift to latch onto you and turn *you* into a wolf instead. I can't say I'd be sorry."

Ormand growled, but said nothing more. Rowan almost could have laughed.

Rigall pushed his desk back against one of the bookcases and took down a small gong that Rowan hadn't noticed before. Then, from other shelves, he brought out a number of bells, and a pan flute that he hung around his neck.

"Nawassa—the Gift, my people call it—is a mystery even the best of us haven't entirely figured out," he said as he touched one of the mirrors to adjust it, focusing the light on Rowan in the center of the room. "It lives in the atmosphere around us, like air, yet not like. It can be summoned, harnessed, and commanded, yet it seems to have a will of its own sometimes. Perhaps that was a balance put in place by the One who created it for our use, so that we could not abuse it fully." He broke off and shot Ormand another glare as he swiped a little folding fan, similar to the one Rowan carried, off his desk. Except this one was made of some kind of exotic metal.

"At any rate," he continued, and Rowan wondered if he was simply flaunting his opportunity to talk without Ormand's interruption, "Our relationship with it is tenuous. Any disturbance could disrupt the whole process. A strong gust of wind, or a very loud and out-of-place noise. Of course it would depend on the spell being worked, and how far along it was, how bad the results would be. You might end up with a disaster, or it might just dispel the Nawassa altogether." He shrugged. "Now. Silence." He looked at each of them pointedly, then took a deep breath, and of all things, began to dance.

Rowan watched, and a tinge of fear crept back over her. Yet she was fascinated. The little magician moved, he and his fan, high-stepping and twirling around the room. The metallic fan flashed in the light, sometimes fluttering, sometimes beckoning or waving, and then Rigall began to hum. At intervals he would strike the gong, ring one of the bells, or blow a note on his flute.

Nothing happened.

But then it did. It began so subtly she didn't notice at first. The air began to change. It felt thicker, warmer, yet cool and tingling like oil of peppermint rubbed against her skin. Always the reverberations of the gong or the flute lingered, and as the air thickened, the vibrations seemed to remain longer. The light and the vibrations coalesced around her like a second skin, soothing but slightly itchy.

Rigall moved closer, his movements like liquid. He snapped the fan closed and touched the tip of it to her forehead, speaking a single word that she didn't understand. Instantly though, the image of a huge, coppery wolf flooded her mind. Then he said, "Sleep."

The colors of the wolf image leaked out. The room faded to black. She felt like she was floating. Then nothing.

* * * * *

She woke to the sound of birds and insects, and the overpowering aroma of wet earth and grass. She was lying on her side, and long stalks of grass and tangles of weeds waved in front of her eyes and dripped water on her. She blinked. Something didn't seem right. The colors looked different. The smells were stronger, more varied. Her body felt... She shifted and tried to sit up. And screamed.

But the scream came out as an agonized, wailing howl from a throat that was no longer human. The cry of a wolf.

They'd actually turned her into a wolf.

She managed to get her haunches under her and sat up, raising one giant coppery red paw to stare at it. She tried to turn it as she would have turned her hand to look at her palm, but found the movement awkward.

She tried to stand up, but that too felt off-kilter and strange, so she sank down to all four paws, swinging her head back and forth. Movement caught the corner of her eye, and she spun. Whatever it the thing was remained just beyond comfortable sight, so she spun some more. Then the other direction. A flash of white and red. She could almost see it. Almost reach it...

Rowan sat back down suddenly in horror. Cautiously, slowly, she stood back up and ducked her head down to see between her arms, now acting as front legs, along the length of her shaggy belly, and beyond. She had a tail.

And she'd just been chasing it.

"Of all the..." she tried to say, but it came out garbled, more of a throaty whine than words. She tried again. Her tongue felt too big and floppy, but she slowed down and labored over each sound. Nothing would work right. Not her tongue, not her lips. All she got was something that sounded like "O waaarr eh..."

She snapped her mouth shut. *Of all the...* and her last spoken words had been to Ormand. The slime. He should be the one wearing an animal hide and trying to walk on four legs. But thinking of Ormand, where was he? Where was she? The last she remembered had been Rigall's underground study. The magician's command to sleep. She had been fighting tears for hours, her head pounding. They'd killed Aaro, and she hadn't been able to cry over him.

Now, looking around, she saw that she was alone on the prairie. Not a building or a person in sight. The only animals she could see were birds. They had just left her here? How far was she from town? But what was she thinking? She couldn't run back to town like this. She'd be shot on sight. Maybe that's what Ormand had meant when he said she might not live long anyway.

She lay back down on her belly and covered her face with her hands.

Paws, she corrected herself.

Well. She would stay alive, if only to spite Ormand. And she'd find a way to break this curse. The magician had said it was possible, and if it was possible, she'd find a way. What else did she have to lose? Ormand had taken everything from her. Her home, her family, her love, even her identity. Going back was dangerous and delusional. She could only go forward.

But first, she would cry for Aaro. If she must be a wolf, then she would mourn as only a wolf could. So she raised her snout to the red, overcast sky and howled. She couldn't cry, but the sky wept for her.

Chapter 8

Aaro rested, his back against a tree, feet stretched out toward the stream. His throat still felt raw, and the rest of his body throbbed. Rain fell again, soaking his clothes and plastering his hair to his neck, cooling his hands and face, and his throbbing arm. He had dozed a little, though he knew he shouldn't, while he waited for Jake to get back from town. It felt like all his energy had been washed away, drained into the wet ground under him. If any of Ormand's troops came back and found him now, he'd never be able to fight them. He could barely move his head without fighting not to throw up, and was sure several of his ribs were cracked.

But he didn't think Ormand would send anyone back. Not right away. Tomorrow maybe, to scout for survivors. Or when one of the nobles with enough influence demanded it.

Flames still licked through the collapsed buildings despite the afternoon's on and off rain showers, and black, reeking smoke hung in the shallow valley with no wind to blow it away.

Aaro felt another coughing fit coming on, and braced himself for the assault of pain that would come with it. He wrapped his arms around his ribs and coughed until tears streamed down his face. When the fit had passed, it left him breathing in ragged gulps while more tears leaked from his eyes, their warmth mingling with the cold rainwater. If he could have laid down and died on command he would've done it. Except for one thing. Ormand. Ormand was the ember that blazed hot against the cold inside him. He would stay alive long enough to kill Ormand, and anyone who supported him. Then he would find some way to die.

The sky had turned red with the coming night, while the rain continued. Over the rain, he heard pounding hooves approaching. That would be Jake, riding hard to get back to him before nightfall. In another moment two horses and a single rider appeared, slowing down as they made their way through the destruction. Jake walked the horses across the stream and dismounted, his face as bleak as the day.

"You able to ride?" he asked.

Aaro twitched a shoulder by way of a shrug.

Jake nodded toward the other horse, which Aaro saw was one of their own. "Found him wandering the prairie. Haven't seen any of the others. One of us'll have to ride bareback, 'cause I couldn't buy another set of tack without raising suspicion."

"The mask?" Aaro rasped.

"It's here. And you're right. It ain't an ordinary mask. Got everything else, too." He offered a hand, pulling Aaro to his feet and then steadying him when he swayed. "I'm thinking we ride to the cabin and stay put till it quits raining."

The cabin, a shanty some of the hands stayed in occasionally when they were working the eastern section of range, was a good two hours' ride away. But it would likely be safe.

Aaro limped to Jake's horse and winced his way into the saddle, leaving his friend to ride bareback. He tossed Jake the reins and hunched over, one arm wrapped around his ribs and the other hand gripping the horse's mane. "Go," he whispered.

"There's already rumors going around," Jake said as they turned east and left the burned-out buildings behind them. "Some of 'em are even true. But the official word is that you defied the king, then attacked him, and the soldiers killed you to protect him. Ormand's calling it a tragedy that should never have happened. That you forced his hand. I didn't hear anything about Rowan."

Aaro didn't react to the news. Mostly he just felt numb.

Soon the prairie hid all but the smoke still pouring into the sky. For a few minutes the rain slacked off. The overcast sky glowed red. In the distance, they heard a wolf howl, the cry sounding eerie and out of place. It went on and on, rising and falling, dying off finally to be renewed a second later. Jake muttered under his breath and urged the horses on, but Aaro felt no fear. He listened to the wolf's cry and thought it sounded like how he felt.

The rain started up again, but the howl continued, and Aaro let the sound and the cold wrap around him and lull him into a stupor as they rode on into the deepening night.

* * * * *

The smoke led Rowan back to the ranch, after she had howled her throat raw. It reeked, spreading for miles like a beacon in the night. One good thing she'd discovered about being a wolf was that she could travel fast, once she got used to using four legs instead of two. She topped the final knoll, slowing down as her ridiculously heightened sense of smell went crazy. *That*, she had already decided, was not a good thing. She could smell everything. And so far, it hadn't done her any good. She couldn't sort out or make sense of the smells. She only knew that they were there, and there was no escaping them.

In the bowl of land below her, what remained of the ranch sat in blackened heaps against the dark gray of the prairie. She could see better in the dark than she used to, but the sight wasn't comforting. Fires still glowed here and there among fallen timber and charred sections of walls that remained standing. The building that had fared the best looked to be the stable, but even of that only half remained standing. Nothing stirred except the smoke and the rain. She turned away.

She couldn't go back to town. She'd be killed before anyone knew any better, and the ranch was no more. What to do?

A slight breeze picked up from the north, clearing the smoke away and bringing a distant smell of pine. She'd heard that where the prairie ended, a wilderness began. The place from which the ancients had hauled stone and timber for the town, the place where you could go and vanish. When she lived back east she had heard rumors that the Shonnowa lived there now, scattered among canyons and mountains and forests. There were towns up there as well, though they were wild and unsafe.

But who was she to worry about safe? She bared her fangs in a bitter grin. North it would be. If she could find the Shonnowa, maybe they could help her break the curse, if they didn't kill her first.

Her stomach rumbled, and she looked longingly toward the burned-out ranch. No help there. She could only hope her taste buds had undergone a significant change as well. The thought of catching field mice or rabbits and eating them raw... not appealing.

* * * * *

Two days later the wilderness began, with forested foothills, rivers, and lakes. Another three days, and the foothills had become steeper, broken by gullies and waterfalls, caves and canyons. Hunger and sorrow traveled with

Rowan, but also wonder.

A few times she'd caught whiffs of what she learned to identify as human scent, though she only saw them from a distance, cutting and hauling lumber, or traveling in small groups. She sat and watched them several times, debating whether to approach. But they were all armed and rough looking. Of course, anyone out here would likely look rough. The problem was, how would she ever show herself without getting killed? Even if she did find the Shonnowa. They must not have any better feelings toward wolves than her own people. She didn't have any great love for wolves herself, and she *was* a wolf.

Her constant hunger was what tempted her the most toward approaching the men she came across. She'd managed to catch a couple of rabbits and a mouse, and didn't like to dwell on the memory. The raw meat didn't taste like she had expected—it also didn't taste good. And a couple of rabbits in five days was hardly satisfying.

On the sixth day she wandered into an ancient forest of towering pine, the forest floor broken by intermitted rocks stabbing up through the carpet of needles and moss. The hillside sloped steeply down toward a churning river.

She lay down on her belly, front paws stretched out, panting and watching the river below and wondering if raw fish would taste any better than raw rabbit meat, or be any easier to catch. The breeze kicked up, wafting a distant smell of smoke and cooking food. The smells of a campsite or small village. Her stomach rumbled.

Twilight was coming on, and a big, round moon hung over the horizon, not quite at its full, but nearly. She had a clear view, and her skin tingled as she looked up at it, her fur standing on end. The air around her felt congealed. She knew the breaking of the curse could not be as simple as staring at the moon, yet for an instant her heart leaped, and she rose, still panting, yearning toward the light and her human form, and she cried. The lonesome, hungry, heartbroken cry of a wolf.

A yelp of surprise from just beyond the rocky ridge startled her, and she fell silent, ears perked toward the sound. She heard the snap of a twig, then nothing.

She looked from the ridge back to the moon, knowing that if someone was here, she should hide herself, yet reluctant to wander from the patch of moonlight, which was growing stronger as the twilight deepened. She could still feel the prickles of magic along her skin, and remembering what the magician had said about the curse being incomplete, half expected *something* to happen, though she didn't know what.

Several minutes passed, and she thought perhaps she had imagined the sound of someone's voice, or that her longing ears had changed the sound of a fallen branch or another animal to that of a human. She lowered her head to the ground, covering her face with her paws, and shuddered. That single sound, or imagined sound, had wrenched her heart. She missed them so much. Dustan, Annalie, Uncle Lance. Aaro. Most of all Aaro, though she'd known him for the shortest time. A strangled sob escaped her, though this time it sounded less wolfish and more human.

She jerked her head up. Red curls, their color dim in the fading light, fell around her face. Long, human fingers splayed on the ground in front of her. She picked up her hands and looked at them, bewildered, then at the rest of her. Fully human, bathed in moonlight. The white dress she'd been wearing when Ormand took her was rumpled and smudged, but still intact.

"Oh..." she breathed. "Am I...?" The words felt strange in her mouth, and she dare not finish the thought. She could still feel the tingles of magic, tickling the skin on her bare arms, raising goosebumps. She rose unsteadily to her feet, taking a moment to get her balance, and stepped out of the moonlight, into the dark shadows of the trees. For several minutes, nothing happened. Her heart pounded, and her eyes stung. It felt like a burlap sack full of moths had been let loose in her stomach as she held her breath.

Then, as she watched, her hands grew stubby and furry, her slender arms turning into the forelegs of a wolf.

"No!" she cried, jumping back into the moonlight. "Please...no." In another moment, her human form returned. She dropped to her knees in the pine needles and sobbed.

"*Ellowaha*?" said a voice.

Rowan startled, sitting up and choking back a cry as a human—a man—stepped through a gap in the ridge, spotted her, and hurried over. He spoke as though he were in a panic, looking about wildly and beckoning for her to come, but she couldn't understand a word he said.

"Who—" she croaked. She cleared her throat and tried again as he rushed to her side and pulled at her arm, still looking alarmed. "What's wrong? And who are you?"

The man paused for a moment in concentration, then switched to her own language. "Please, woman, you must hurry. Did you not hear the wolf here a moment ago?"

She stared at him for a second, his earnest expression and dark Shonnowan features, and then she laughed. She must truly have gone mad over the last several days, to laugh now. But still she laughed, and a tiny bit of the burden lifted from her heart. So she had found one of the Shonnowa. And he hadn't tried to kill her. Yet.

She let him pull her to her feet, aware that he was watching her warily now. Probably thinking her a raving lunatic. She tried to drop a curtsy and nearly fell over.

The man still looked worried, glancing around at the rocks and forest for the wolf he thought to be hiding nearby. But he also looked confused, and guarded.

"Forgive me," Rowan said. "There is no wolf. Well, there is, in fact, but that wolf is me. Lady Rowan D'Araines. So very pleased to meet you."

"D'Araines," the young man said, butchering the name as he mulled it over. "This is familiar. But you are not a wolf."

"I am cursed," she said, and hoped that taking a direct approach would be safe, for she hadn't the time to hedge. The man wasn't reaching for weapons yet, so she took that for a good sign. "My people's king, Ormand D'Araines, killed my husband, his cousin, and made his magician curse me into the form of a wolf." She glanced up at the moon. "Apparently the moonlight turns me back."

The young man was shaking his head. "King D'Araines, his name I know. And you are his...cousin? But of this thing called a magician..." he spread his hands and said something unintelligible. "This *magician,* this is a person?" He eyed her curiously.

"Yes. One of your people."

He shook his head again. "Not one of us, if he is making curses. Perhaps one of *Them.* My people do not fashion the Gift into curses." He looked at her again, really looking now, and reached a hand to touch her wild hair. "Why are you so far from your own people?"

Why did men find her hair so fascinating? Rowan withdrew a fraction of an inch, not wanting to offend, but after Ormand's slimy fingers caressing her throat, she had no desire to be touched.

The stranger caught himself and withdrew his hand, looking sheepish.

"My people would have seen only a wolf and killed me."

"Ah, of course. But why are you here then?"

"I was looking for you!" Rowan felt impatience gnawing at her. "I have to break the curse! But I don't know how. The magician said it was possible. That no magic is ever permanent. And I thought if anyone could help, it would be the Shonnowa."

"Magic, magician." The stranger shook his head again, his eyes wandering back to her halo of red curls as he spoke. "If you are speaking of the Gift, Nawassa, then he was right. It can be bound to people or things, but that bond is...what is the word? Unsteady?" He shrugged. "I am not a craftsman, so I know little about it. But there are others who might be able to help. You will come with me to see them?"

"Please!"

"Good!" His eyes danced. "In the morning, we will go."

"Oh." Rowan felt herself droop. Her stomach rumbled, and the Shonnowan man looked at her. "I'm not very good at being a wolf yet," she said.

He burst out laughing, like it was the funniest thing he'd heard in his life, then beckoned her toward the rocks at the ridge crest. "Come. I have food."

She followed, leaving the moonlight behind with a reluctant glance, plodding up the hill. By the time they reached the rocks she had resumed her wolf shape. The man led her to a cleft, sheltered by a tree, and turned to speak. He started when he saw her in wolf form, but then he smiled.

"Ah! I see!" he said. "But you are a very beautiful wolf, as you are a very beautiful woman."

If Rowan had known him better, she would have growled.

"Can you speak?" he asked.

She shook her head.

"I am unhappy for this. But you can understand, so it is..." he shrugged. "Enough. It is enough. My name is Sorrell. Be welcome. Perhaps tonight you can help me keep watch for real wolves." He sat down and dug through a leather satchel, offering her dried fish and flatbread that was reasonably fresh.

She went to sleep that night with her belly full for the first time in a week, and didn't stir till morning. But she dreamt of dancing with Aaro, kissing him under a full moon.

* * * * *

The next day they walked down toward the river, with Sorrell keeping up a steady, one-sided conversation the whole way. Sometimes he asked her questions, then apologized. For some reason, Rowan had always pictured the Shonnowa people as being silent and mysterious, perhaps having magical abilities. But the more time she spent in Sorrell's company, the more he reminded her of a masculine version of Annalie. Bursting full of life and energy and words, though sometimes he couldn't think of the one he wanted, so he would fill in with a Shonnowan word instead, then try to explain it.

They crossed the river, walking along a fallen log overtop of the water, then continued on for the rest of the morning. Rowan could smell the Shonnowan village drawing nearer, distinguishing the aromas of meat and baking bread, leather, herbs, wood smoke, and people. She kept expecting to see it over every rise, but it was another hour before they came in view.

Sorrell paused at the top of a ridge, and when Rowan sat down panting beside him, she saw the clearing below with its dozen or so little cabins, a corral, and children playing around the buildings. Fires burned in front of most of the houses.

"Our people have become nomads," Sorrell

said. "Since *They* drove us out of our cities, and then your people came and rebuilt the abandoned ones. Now we live in houses that we can leave when we need to. This is a good place. Perhaps we will make our own town here, in the next years. Some of our people have begun to build again, some of the other clans. And our women are always eager to plant and to be welcome in one place."

Rowan sensed a wistfulness in him as he spoke, and glanced up. His gaze had gone from the tiny village below them, to the valleys southward. She wished she could ask. But even if she could talk, these were not her people, nor was this her heritage. She wouldn't know the first thing to ask without sounding like a jackass. For the first time, it pressed on her and annoyed her how little she knew beyond her own life. Longing she understood. Longing to be home, to be free, to have Aaro back. But what things did a Shonnowan man long for?

He shook himself from his reverie and grinned down at her. "Come. And be welcome." He started down the hill, and she followed.

The first person he saw, he called out to them in his own language, waving toward Rowan. The other man stopped and stared, then grinned. He ducked into one of the houses and came out with a woman, pointing to Rowan again. If Rowan could have blushed, she would have been red as a tomato again as people gathered around them, with Sorrell speaking in Shonnowan. She sat down beside his feet, her head coming level with his waist, and curled her tail around herself.

Children joined the crowd, pressing close to see. They were cautious at first, then bolder, reaching out to touch her coppery fur, squealing with delight, then chasing each other in and out through the crowd.

The conversation seemed to focus more between Sorrell and an older man, until they were joined by a young woman. She spoke, and they listened, and then she knelt down in front of Rowan, looking her in the eyes.

"My brother says you understand the speech of the king people."

Rowan dipped her head in a nod.

The young woman, not much older that Rowan, if she had to guess, giggled. She reached out a hand, then paused. "May I?"

Rowan returned her gaze, unable to respond with words, and slightly taken aback. The woman must have taken her lack of response as consent, for she reached out and ran her fingers through the thick mane of fur around Rowan's neck, cooing to herself in her own tongue. "Beautiful," she said. "Yes. Sorrell says you are even more beautiful as a woman though."

Rowan heaved a sigh. All the cleverest wit in the world was of no use to her now, when she needed it.

The woman laughed, seeming to understand. "Have no fear. Be welcome. We will speak tonight when the moon is shining, yes? My name is Willow. It is one of your words, I believe. Our father spent many years with the king people. He was a merchant." She stood up and beckoned Rowan to follow. "Come with me. We will get away from the noise."

Willow led Rowan to one of the little houses, built of slender, supple branches woven together, layered with woven grass, and covered on the outside with animal skins. Inside, tools and supplies hung from the walls, and a stone fire pit with a chimney sat cold in one corner.

"This is our home, my husband and I, and one more, soon," Willow said, rubbing the slight bulge of her belly that Rowan hadn't noticed before. "Be welcome here, for as long as you need. Rest if you are able. It is a long journey from the king city to our mountains. I am the clan's healer, so we are accustomed to having guests stay with us."

Rowan's gazed flicked from Willow's pretty, round face to the bump of her growing baby, to the tidy little shanty she called home. Her chest ached, and her head filled with a roar. *Aaro. This should have been us.*

She turned and fled back out the door, past the startled crowd, back into the forest. Behind her she could hear Willow and Sorrel calling, the thud of footsteps following, but she kept running. Her big copper-red paws flashed in and out of dappled sunlight, and the trees blurred around her.

Why?

Why couldn't it have been them?

Her paws slid in the thick layer of pine needles as she charged down the valley, and she slipped and rolled, crashing through underbrush before she came to rest, belly up, in a shallow stream. Ice cold water soaked through her fur, tingling along her back. Rocks dug into her. She rolled over and slogged back to shore, shook herself, and lay down.

Why?

And she couldn't even cry. Not as she should be able to. Her cries came out as whining, guttural noises that scared even her.

In rage, she screamed—a long, deranged wail that sent birds scattering out of the trees and echoed back at her from the hills. Truly the sound of a beast.

If the Shonnowa were still following her, that should have turned them back. But no. From the top of the hill a rustle of brush announced company. Rowan didn't want company. She wanted to be left alone. She wanted to cry. A real, human cry. But if she couldn't do that, then to scream out her frustrations in whatever voice she had.

She covered her face with her paws and lay still, hoping they wouldn't see her. But the footsteps shuffled closer, and someone sat beside her, the soft rustle of linen and doeskin sounding next to her ear. A hand touched her head, stroking it.

"I am sorrowing to cause you this," Willow said. "I did not think. What must have happened to you these past days? Sorrel says your husband was killed. I cannot imagine that. Even if I try...no, I cannot try. It hurts too much." She stroked Rowan's ears, her head, her back. If Rowan kept her eyes closed she could almost imagine it was her mother, long ago, rubbing her back, petting her hair, telling her all would be well when her childish troubles got the better of her.

"Don't go," Willow said. "Come back with us, and we will find a way to break your curse. Or we will do everything we can to try. Tonight you will tell us your story. With more learning, we can have more ideas what could...eh, remove? This curse."

Rowan heaved a shaky sigh. That *was* what she'd come here for.

That night the moon rose full as the sun set, a huge red orb hanging in the cleft of the eastern mountain peak. Rowan sat and watched it from the wide clearing in the valley northwest of the village, where a fire ring and trampled grass evidenced other gatherings.

Willow sat nearby with a stack of slender green twigs and a pile of linen strips which she worked at weaving together. Rowan could only guess she must be making some kind of soft basket to carry the baby around on her back when it arrived. She watched her for a moment, acid rising in her throat, then turned back to the moon.

She could already feel the curse tingling along her skin, the air congealing around her. She lifted a paw to look at. Not yet.

Willow started to sing softly as she wove, a lilting, longing murmur of music, and words that Rowan couldn't understand. Her eyes stung, and she felt tears running down her face. She lifted her hands to wipe them away, and saw that they were human. Willow looked up at her soft gasp, and her eyes widened. Her hand stilled, resting the basket in her lap.

"*Darsaw!* I believed you, but to see you a woman...!" she said. She put her work to the side and shuffled over on her knees, reaching out to touch Rowan's hair and face, wearing an unreadable expression.

Sorrell strode over and sat down on Rowan's other side, flashing a white smile at her in the twilight. Soon the circle around the fire had filled in, and two of the men worked on getting the fire started. Rowan felt all of their eyes on her. She touched her hair, running her fingertips through the silky curls. It felt strange, after just a week. What if they never found a way to break the curse? What if moonlit nights were all she ever had to be...real?

She ducked her head, but too slowly to hide the terror in her eyes as Willow looked at her. She felt the other woman's arm go around her shoulders.

"It may take months...or years. But we will find your cure."

Chapter 9

Three years later.

The buzz of voices, the roaring fire, the constant thump of beer mugs slammed down on tables, and the plink of the cheap piano in the corner blended together into a drone that Aaro had ceased to hear almost from the moment he stepped through the door. As usual, the noises faltered when they saw his mask. He heard the whispers, but when he made no move other than to sit down at the counter and order coffee, things resumed, just as they always did.

"More coffee?" The bar maid stood in front of him again, holding the tin pot with a towel wrapped around the handle.

He let go the mug and gave it a push with his fingers, sending it sliding to her. She filled it and set it back in front of him.

"You ever take that mask off?" she asked, cocking her hips as she leaned an elbow on the counter. She blinked at him slowly, making sure he got a good look at her long, black eyelashes.

"Wouldn't be much point in wearing a mask if I took it off, would there?" he growled.

"We get men in here who are on the run from time to time," she said, not to be put off so easily. "They'll take their masks off eventually.

With help from the right person." She gave him a lazy wink. "Haven't seen one like yours before though. It looks foreign."

Aaro took another sip of his coffee and didn't answer. If the wind wasn't whipping into a blizzard out there he might have considered riding on. Then again, his horse needed rest. It was too cold to push on relentlessly, and he had nowhere to go for the moment.

"Will you be staying a while?" the girl asked.

"Maybe."

"Don't talk much, do you? I figure most men, if they're wearing a mask, want to brag about why. Who they killed, or how big of a reward they've got on their heads. Or what kind of a job they're on their way to do."

Aaro looked up at the girl finally, his mask shifting slightly with the movement. He'd been wearing it for so long now he didn't even feel it most of the time, like a second skin covering his cheeks and the upper half of his face. The only time he took it off any more was to shave.

"Well! Look at those eyes!" she cooed. "Eyes like those don't deserve to be hidden. You're quite the looker, I do believe. Play your game right and you might be able to get some free company for the night."

Aaro stood with a growl and threw a coin down on the bar. "Get me a room. *Alone.*"

She pocketed the coin and shrugged.

"Can't blame a girl for trying. We don't exactly have the top pick of men around here. You on the other hand," she said, coming out from behind the bar, "something tells me you're at the top of the top."

Aaro remained silent as she prattled on, shouldering his bedroll and saddlebags and following her up a narrow flight of stairs to an equally narrow hallway. The girl opened a door and waved him in.

"Here you go. Will you be coming down for supper?"

"Yes."

Still she lingered, leaning on the door, watching him drop his things onto the bed and shed his overcoat. "You must at least have a name. Or a nickname."

"No."

She sighed. "Alright then. We're serving food in half an hour. Don't be late, if you don't want leftovers." She turned and disappeared down the hallway, leaving him alone finally.

He set his hat down on the bed and pulled the leather thong out of his hair, retying it into a short tail. The mask stayed in place, held by the Shonnowa magic infused into it, rather than by any physical ties. No one but he could remove it. So it stayed. His face hadn't been seen by another soul other than Jake since the day Rowan died. And Emrella. And Mitchell. And Hank.

Now even Jake had left him.

Justice I understand, Jake had said before he rode away, now almost a year ago. *But this is bloody revenge, and it's eaten you alive. I don't know you anymore, and all my helping is just helping you turn into worse of a monster. Killing for money? No. I'm done.*

He was one of Ormand's bootlickers, Aaro had retorted. *We can't go forever without income, and I'm not stopping for a couple years to raise beef.*

You're a damned murderer, Raines. You decide to go to Heymish, like you always planned, and I'm with you every step. But I'm not killing people for money. I don't care what they done.

Aaro wondered fleetingly where Jake was now. If he'd found someplace to settle down again. Maybe got himself a girl. He'd be better off. He was right, after all. Revenge had turned Aaro into a monster. A man with no face, no name, and no life. And for all of that, he still hadn't killed Ormand. But what Jake didn't understand was that if he gave up now, it would all be for nothing. Blood on his hands, with no way to redeem it.

* * * * *

Back down in the common room, more of a crowd had filtered in, and it was impossible to get a table to himself, so Aaro settled for a seat in the corner, facing the room, at a table between two old-timers who looked at his mask suspiciously but said nothing. It was not entirely uncommon, wearing a mask. Ormand's list of wanted men was ever growing, and if you were wanted and no one saw your face, then no one would have to lie. Or tell the truth.

The meal of meat pies and thick slabs of bread was served, and the flirty bar maid came back around and filled his coffee mug, giving him another hopeful wink. Aaro hadn't realized he'd been chilled to the core until the hot food and coffee started to thaw him out.

The door slapped open, bringing a small blizzard of ice and gusting wind with it. Half a dozen men filed in, tipping the room from comfortably full to over-crowded. They were soldiers.

The innkeeper, busy filling mugs and talking to patrons, looked alarmed, hurrying over to greet them.

"Good evening! Hello! Ah, please, find whatever seats you can. Will you be supping tonight?"

The captain nodded, scanning the room. "We're also looking for someone." He fumbled with his icy overcoat and pulled out a roll of paper. Every eye in the room was on him as he unrolled it and held it out, revealing a detailed sketch of the Shonnowan mask Aaro wore. "Has anyone seen this man?" Every eye in the room went from the sketch to Aaro. The captain followed their collective gaze.

Aaro rose slowly, his hands spread,

hovering over his weapons belt. "Looks like you found me."

The captain looked relieved as he rolled the paper up and strode over. He touched the brim of his hat. "Captain Alonso Fernand." He glanced at the two old men Aaro had been sharing the table with. They grabbed their plates and hustled away. Alonso sat down, while his men found places here and there throughout the room. He studied Aaro's mask. "Shonnowan work, isn't it?" He asked.

Aaro dipped his head in a nod, returning to his meal cautiously while keeping one hand on his gun under the table.

"What can I call you?"

"Nothing."

The captain studied him for another moment. He was a tall man with sharp brown eyes, which were about the only thing Aaro could see of him beneath layers of wool and ice. He took off his hat and set it on the table, unwound his scarf, and tugged at the fingers of his gloves.

"Well then, Nameless Sir, King Ormand D'Araines demands an audience with you, as soon as we can make it back to the castle."

"Ormand does nothing without demanding."

Alonso nodded. "That's true enough."

"What does he want with me? And what has he ordered you to do if I don't come?"

The corners of Alonso's mouth twitched.

"I'm to kill you, of course. But I believe the king has somewhat more benign plans, at least for the moment. You've gained yourself a reputation, Nameless One. Shall I call you Mask? For that is all anyone knows of you, is your mask." He smiled as the bar maid brought him a plate of food. Unfortunately for him, her eyes stayed on Aaro, and he had to endure another round of attempted flirting before she left.

"And what are Ormand's plans?

The captain stabbed his fork into the meat pie and took a bite. "This is fabulous," he said with his mouth full. "I'm cold through and through, and the pepper is almost as good as liquor for warming you up. Well, perhaps not. But being on duty, pepper will have to do." He brushed his napkin across his moustache. "I believe Ormand has a job for you."

"Why?" Aaro asked. "He's got plenty of men to do his killing."

The captain shrugged, saying between bites, "I don't know if it's killing he has in mind. Then again, who *does* know what goes on in the king's mind?" He shrugged again. "He's got plans of some kind. I believe he'd take over the world, if he had the resources."

"No doubt."

Aaro sat in silence, watching the other man eat. The reason he hadn't killed Ormand yet was simply that he hadn't had an opportunity. After the destruction of Aaro's ranch, Ormand had become more careful, almost paranoid, no doubt fearing some of Aaro's more outspoken supporters. Someone who had had enough and was willing to do something about it. And there had been a few incidents, though only one of the would-be assassins had been caught. He'd been hanged in the market square. The other attempts had been unsuccessful, but the men involved had been able to vanish. And Ormand had upped his guards. He never walked the market any more. He rarely stepped outside the walls around the castle grounds, and from there it was impossible to get close enough.

But if Ormand had sought him out for an audience... That might be the chance Aaro needed.

"So, will you be coming with us tomorrow, or shall I kill you?" Alonso asked.

Aaro grinned, bringing his hand holding the gun out from under the table and setting it on top, the gun pointed at Alonso's chest. "You could try," he said. "But I have my own reasons for wanting to see the king."

Alonso nodded, polishing off the last of his supper and washing it down with a gulp of coffee. "Good. We leave at dawn. Provided this blizzard doesn't pick up."

* * * * *

It was two days' ride east through a foot of snow before they saw the dark blot of Skybreak against the white horizon. Aaro hadn't been truly warm since they left the inn, though it had warmed up considerably. Winter hadn't even fully set in yet, though winter solstice celebrations were only a few weeks away. His mask kept the brunt of the cold off the upper part of his face, while his hood and scarf protected the rest. His wide-brimmed hat was pulled down over top of the hood, snugging it closer to his head and keeping the wind from blowing it off. But the rest of him felt chilled through by the time they rode through the gates and into Ormand's stables, where they handed the horses over to be cared for. He decided it was high time to find someplace to hole up for the winter, once his business with Ormand was over.

"Come to the barracks and get warm before you see the king," Alonso said. "A man half warm is a man with half his wits."

"Thanks."

He followed the captain past the soldier's barracks, long buildings newly constructed of rough pine, and into the officers' quarters, which they had to themselves. The castle had had a garrison before, of course, but the three buildings they passed had been put up within the past year.

The two of them crowded around a pot-bellied stove, dripping melted snow onto the floor planks. A boy brought them coffee, which they couldn't drink until they'd shed scarves and gloves and several layers of coats.

"The king wants to see you within the

hour," the boy said, bouncing from foot to foot as they struggled out of their wraps. "Captain, sir, he said to make sure you and the...the..." he faltered as he looked at Aaro's mask, and his voice dropped. "The mercenary, both of you are to come to him in the throne room."

Alonso waited for the boy to leave before grumbling unintelligibly under his breath.

"Ormand is building his army," Aaro said, flicking his fingers by way of gesture back toward the new buildings they'd passed. "Where's he getting his men?"

Alonso shrugged. "Here and there. Criminals, mercenaries, some that don't speak the language too well, and some that would rather not be here. Some of 'em are too young. In my opinion. And he's got his regular troops that Heymish commissioned to come out here years ago."

"Who is he going to war against?"

The captain just shrugged. "Who can say."

"How many?"

"I wouldn't be any kind of a captain if I told you that. But you've got eyes. Those three barracks are full, plus another three over on the other side. We put up a stockade around everything over the summer."

Aaro made a quick estimate. Ormand must have close to two thousand men on the premises. He turned his attention back to the captain, studying him. The other man didn't appear to have any great love for the king, and even his loyalty seemed questionable. That could be useful. Unless it was simply his manner to be flippant and off-hand, or unless he was putting on an act. Though, after two days in the snow together, he didn't think the latter option likely. A man tended to show his true nature when he was cold and uncomfortable for extended periods of time.

Alonso left the stove long enough to get a fresh uniform, and a clean shirt for Aaro. He set his empty coffee cup on the stove and peeled off the oversized wool socks he wore over top of his boots, then stripped down to his trousers, which were also wool.

"Trust Ormand not to leave time for a decent bath, then likely give the stink-eye for showing up smelling like wet sheep."

When they'd changed into clean shirts they set out for the castle, a short walk from the barracks, but far enough to chill Aaro all over again now that he wore lighter clothes. He'd strapped his weapons belt back on, waiting for Alonso to forbid it, but the captain said nothing.

A shoulder-height wall separated the officer's quarters and new barracks from the castle proper, and once they stepped through a wrought iron gate, they had to cross a cobbled carriage way and flagstone paved courtyard before they entered a heavily guarded vestibule. A fireplace at each end warmed the long room, ensuring no winter drafts entered the castle.

"You'll have to leave your weapons here," one of the guards said, coming forward to take Aaro's belt with the twin daggers and guns. Aaro unbuckled it and handed it over, but the man paused with it in his hands. He looked up and met Aaro's eyes through the mask.

"Problem?" Aaro said. Inside he'd gone icy. He had recognized the guard the second he walked in as one of the ones who'd been there the day they burned the ranch. He was on Aaro's kill list.

"No..." the man still hesitated. "Seems like I've seen this gettup before. You got anything else on you?"

Aaro gave a noncommittal shrug and pulled another knife from his boot, adding it to the pile.

"Search him."

Two more guards came forward and patted down Aaro's trousers and shirt.

"Take off your boots."

Aaro complied, tipping them upside down to show that they were empty. The guard inspected them anyway before he tossed them back.

"Now the mask."

"No."

The guard stepped up to Aaro, grabbed the edge of his mask, and tried to rip it off. Aaro's head jerked sideways as if he'd been struck, and he felt the magic tingle against his face. The guard backed off and stared at him.

"I'm here at Ormand's request," he said. "I'm happy to go back to minding my own business, if he can't take me the way I am."

The guard growled, but at a warning look from Alonso, and he waved them on.

They entered a ballroom, huge and echoingly empty, with a grand staircase ascending to a balcony at the far end. Alonso led him through a side door and several smaller rooms before they entered the throne room, situated, Aaro guessed, at the heart of the palace, and also heavily guarded, and where he was searched a second time.

Aaro didn't know what he expected to feel, coming into Ormand's presence after three and a half years. Burning rage, perhaps. But all he felt as he looked at his cousin was bitter cold. Colder than the blizzard and the coming winter. Colder than the wind across the frozen prairie. Numb, aching, cold. He stood before the man who had killed his wife, and imagined what he would do if he had his weapons. Every move played out in his head in detail. He'd make sure there was lots of blood. But not so much that death could come too soon.

Ormand returned his scrutiny with the same intensity. He still wore his usual fine embroidered vest, with a decorative sword and dagger strapped to his waist on a fancy, silver buckled belt. "I had begun to wonder if you existed," he said when the silence started to become burdensome. "Our phantom assassin." He drummed his fingers on the armrest of his throne. "Do you have a name?"

"No." Aaro lowered his voice to a gravelly pitch. Ormand cocked his head, listening, but no hint of recognition touched his expression.

"Have it your way. But you've been killing an alarming number of my supporters over the past several years. Who is paying you?"

Aaro remained silent.

"Alright then, I am willing to buy the answer. What is your price?"

Aaro allowed a hint of a smile to reach his lips, but still ignored the question. "For what purpose did you bring me here? My secrets are my own to keep."

"Excellent." Ormand sat back. "There were several reasons why I hunted you down. I cannot afford you working for my enemy, whoever he may be. So you will work for me now. Your secrets can't be bought, which is good, however I still desire to know who is trying to cut off my support. They won't succeed, of course. But it is always wise to know one's enemies. Perhaps we can come to an understanding.

"And I admire your work. It's clean. Surgical. As I said, I doubted your existence. A good quality for an assassin. Yet here you are, in the flesh. And just in time for the mission I have for you."

Aaro raised his eyebrows. No one could see his expression beneath his mask, thankfully, for he was showing his surprise. He stifled the sudden urge to laugh. A bitter, ironic laugh it would have been.

"Name your price, Mask," Ormand demanded, leaning forward, searching his face again as though he could see beyond the leather and silver.

"First, name your mission."

Ormand nodded slowly and sat back. "Fair enough." He snapped his fingers and a servant stepped forward with a small, flat wooden box, about the size of a man's hand. Ormand took the box, then the key which the servant drew from a string around his neck. He unlocked it and flipped the lid back, holding it out for Aaro to see a silver medallion resting inside, with three smaller, separate pieces to one side.

"This is a piece I had commissioned from a Shonnowan magician in my employment. I believe you are familiar with the work of the Shonnowa. If I'm not mistaken, your mask is another example of it, which is probably why I have not been able to gather any rumors as to your identity."

He snapped the box closed and locked it, but did not return it to the servant. "This particular set has been over four years in the making." He ran his hands over the smooth wood, reinforced with iron bands. "I need a man to deliver it to the Shonnowan king without letting it fall into anyone else's possession. No one must touch it except for him."

"The Shonnowa have no king."

"Ah, but they do." Ormand smiled.

Beside Aaro, the captain shifted, and he shot him a quick glance. The man's lips were pressed together, and he had a slight pucker between his eyes. Again, Aaro had the impression that his loyalty to the king was being stretched. He was uncomfortable with something about the situation—perhaps he had an idea what Ormand's plans were and disapproved. Yet the king didn't question him coming into his presence fully armed, so he must not suspect. That could be *very* useful.

"We know the Shonnowa as reclusive folk, nomads who hide in the hills save for the merchants and traders," Ormand went on, his eyes roving across the high, vaulted ceiling. "But those are the outcasts. The people so kind as to build this town and then leave it vacant for us to settle in. The real Shonnowa nation is much stronger, but even more elusive. And more treacherous." His eyes glinted, his gaze returning to Aaro. "I desire to negotiate with their king. To at last form an alliance with our neighbors to the north. And you will be my emissary."

Aaro was taken aback. Was this a trick? "And how do you plan to form an alliance with a nation you deem as treacherous?" he asked.

Ormand lifted the box with the medallion from his lap. "With the help of this. But it must be done this winter. Before the snow melts. And no one can hear of it. You don't sell your secrets. That is well. If you do, you will die. Now what is your price?"

"Where is this Shonnowan king?" Aaro asked. "How far?"

Ormand heaved an irritated sigh. "No one knows. My information only tells me that their place is to the north, beyond the mining settlement of Silver Rock. Once there, hopefully you will be able to hear more rumors. Any other questions, please direct to my captain." He waived at Alonso. "Now. What is your price?"

"A thousand in silver coin."

"Preposterous."

Aaro tilted his head. "You are buying nearly two weeks' journey both ways, and probably much longer, in the start of winter. And also my silence, never forget."

"Fine then. Done. You'll be paid fifty now and the rest on your successful return. It would never do to go wandering the wilderness overloaded with payment. A man could get his throat slit that way."

"True." Aaro bowed stiffly from the waist.

Ormand held out the box to him. "Remember, do not touch the medallion. Do not let anyone touch it, save the king."

"And if I must give a reason?" Aaro said. "What does it do?"

"Do not give them reason to ask. Only tell the king that it is a powerful gift. It is the highest magic, wrought by a master. No such device has ever been successful before."

Aaro took the box, feeling like he held a viper.

"Do come back alive," Ormand said. "I have other work for you to do."

Aaro turned away, the captain at his side, and moved toward the door.

"One more thing," Ormand called. When they turned back, he said, "I keep hearing rumors from my garrison at Silver Rock. There is a wolf that has been spotted in the area. A great red beast that has no fear of men, that they say the Shonnowa—the outcasts—have tamed. I have an interest in this creature. If you see it, and if it's as tame as they say, it may be possible to snare it. An extra hundred coin if you bring her back to me alive."

Chapter 10

Aaro raised his brows, wondering what this new piece in Ormand's mad game could be. What use could he have for a wolf? He nodded to the king, then followed Alonso back through the palace, retrieving his weapons from the guards, and returned to the officers' quarters. The pot of coffee on the wood stove had been refilled, and they had the place to themselves.

The captain pulled a couple of chairs from the table strewn with charts, books, and coffee mugs, over to the stove. He sat down and started tugging his boots off.

"'Bout time," he muttered, peeling off layers of socks and stretching his bare feet in front of the fire. "I don't envy you this job."

"I don't envy me either," Aaro grumbled, following the captain's example and stretching his feet toward the warmth.

"Why did you take it?"

Aaro didn't answer. He'd taken the job as another chance to get close to Ormand, to kill him or to learn his plans, whichever came first. The more opportunities he had for being in his cousin's presence, the sooner he'd get the chance to kill him. But he could hardly tell the captain that.

"I might be able to guess," Alonso said

after a moment. He glanced around quickly, double-checking that they were alone. "I've seen my share of mercenaries. I know what kind of men they are. You're not that kind."

Aaro looked at him, waiting, holding his gaze through the eyeholes of the mask.

"You disguised your voice when you spoke to the king," Alonso said. "I have to ask myself why? If you were a stranger, it would hardly matter what you sounded like. So you must be someone the king knows. You aren't like any assassin I've ever met, so you've got something driving you other than money." He shifted, turning his eyes away as though suddenly nervous, but went on. "Back at the tavern I saw how the girl threw herself at you. You never so much as flirted. So you're a man of honor, who probably has, or had, a girl of your own.

"Now, if I put all that together, I might be able to guess at a few things. I might be wrong, of course. But I might not. I don't think anyone hired you to kill Ormand's people. I don't think you're keeping anyone's secrets—except your own. You're the kind that would kill for honor, not money. So you've got some grievance against the king. Something, possibly, to do with a woman."

Aaro watched him, creeping his hand toward one of the daggers in his belt. Alonso didn't move. Only his eyes, wandering around the room, occasionally flickered back to Aaro.

"There was an incident, a few years back." Alonso spoke haltingly now, openly nervous. "Rumors, mostly. That Ormand was all set to name his new queen. Then his cousin jumped in and eloped with the girl the very same day. Now I don't know, but maybe you've got a similar story. Maybe you've just been waiting for a chance to get close to the king."

"That's an awful lot of maybe's," Aaro said.

Alonso nodded. "That's so. That girl that got killed though, the one the king was going to marry. I used to be a good friend of her cousin. Worked on his ranch before I came here. I had an eye on that girl myself. She was something. Red hair brighter than sunset, most as tall as some men, and just as sharp as they come..." His voice trailed off.

Aaro felt like someone had twisted a dagger in his heart. Unconsciously his hand moved from the dagger on his belt to rub a spot on his chest. He could see Rowan as though she stood before him now, picturing her as she'd been that night, all curves under a silk garment as thin and translucent as frost. He could feel her kisses, and hear her heartbeat.

"I see my guesses weren't too far off," Alonso said quietly.

Aaro jerked back to the present, his hand returning to his dagger. "And what do you want with so many guesses?" he growled. "Too many could be bad for a man's health."

"A better question, Aaro D'Araines, is whether you really want to throw your life away on revenge, or if you could do more good by fighting for us. Ormand is building an army. He plans on going to war."

After a silence that stretched into minutes Aaro said, "The best thing for West Talva would be for Ormand to die."

"But not murdered at the hand of the man they would flock to as a hero and a martyr—if they knew he was alive."

"I have no desire to be a hero. All I wish is to avenge my wife and my people."

"Perhaps you will change your mind. If you do, remember that you have allies. Both here and throughout the country.

Aaro eyed him, scrutinizing his expression, his voice, his words. He'd had suspicions about Aaro's identity, yet did not accuse him to the king. Slowly he nodded. "I will remember."

* * * * *

The weather warmed back up, thankfully, as Aaro travelled north toward Silver Rock. A reprieve before the full force of winter hit. But by the time he reached the town, ten days later, his bedding and spare clothes had all succumbed to the damp from melting snow and dripping trees. He and his horse were both caked with mud that never seemed to dry, and neither of them had been in a good mood since they left the palace.

During that last day, the weather had grown cold again, and snow flurries swirled.

They plodded down the muddy street, past a bank, a mercantile, an office building for the mining company, several weathered-looking cabins, and finally a tavern advertising rooms. At the end of the street he glimpsed the stockade surrounding Ormand's garrison.

Aaro dismounted and led the horse through the gate into the tavern's muddy, trampled yard. He flipped the gawking stable boy a coin to take care of his horse, grabbed his gear, and headed inside. After a week and a half of travel in the cold, walking into the common room felt like stepping into an oven. It was late afternoon, and the place was mostly empty. The innkeeper came out of the back, took one look at Aaro's mask, and shook his head.

"You'll take that off if you know what's good for you," he said. "This town isn't fond of strangers to begin with. Especially not when they wear masks. We'll have some of King Ormand's men in here tonight, and they're like as not to rough you up."

"Thanks for the warning. I need a room."

"Sure. But just you mind what I say. I don't want my place destroyed when you get into it with someone." He led Aaro past the door leading to the kitchen, through another open doorway, and into a hall running the length of the building. Half a dozen doors led off to the right. The innkeeper, who introduced himself as Kinnly, opened the first door and waved Aaro in. "It's late in the year to be getting travelers. You going to be wintering in the area?"

"I truly hope not."

Kinnly laughed. "Don't blame you. I'd move to more civilized regions myself, but business is good here. At least for the tavern."

"I'm looking for information," Aaro said. "What do you know of the Shonnowa?"

The man's face fell. "Well now...what might you be looking to find out?"

"Their whereabouts. And anything else useful. I have business with them."

"What sort of business?" Kinnly asked, still looking doubtful. "Mostly they're folk I'd rather not have dealings with. I reckon they aren't all bad. There's a few that come from the village once in a while, and they seemed decent enough, until they started bringing that wolf with them. Beast is huge—most the size of a full-grown man. Like to make my skin crawl every time I see it."

Aaro kept his mouth flat, the rest of his face hidden by the mask. Kinnly likely didn't realize just how much information he'd given. "This village—have you ever been there?"

Kinnly shook his head. "Not me. Two or three of the soldiers have been down there. It's small. No more than a couple dozen people, they say."

Aaro settled his saddlebags and bedroll on

the floor inside the doorway. "I hear there's more than one kind of Shonnowa. The nation is divided."

"That's true enough." The innkeeper nodded, leaning against the wall, and picking at a splinter in the rough wood of the doorframe. He seemed happy to talk, and more useful than Aaro had hoped, though innkeepers were bound to hear more gossip than most. "The nation divided generations ago, so I've heard," he went on. "And each side thinks they were in the right, so they still both refer to themselves as Shonnowa— 'People of the Gift.' It's blasted confusing, if you ask me. But there's a marked difference. We get some of each in here, and you never know whether they're the decent kind, or the more feral variety, until your purse is gone, or your dog is cursed, or your neighbor's daughter is missing. Get my meaning? If you have dealings with them, be wary."

"Again, thank you," Aaro said. "Do know where the place is for these other Shonnowa—the 'feral' ones?"

Kinnly shook his head. "No, and I don't want to. Talk to Robbel, the captain of the garrison out here. Maybe he could tell you. But for mercy's sake, take the mask off!"

Once Kinnly had left, Aaro shook out his blankets and draped them over the bed posts and bathing screen to dry out. His spare clothes got hung over the chair and dresser. There was a basin of water, which he used to wash up and then shave, checking the lock on the door and the window first, before he took the mask off.

His face tingled with magic and the rush of cool air against his skin. In the warped and scratched mirror, the upper half of his face looked unnaturally white, while the lower part maintained a decent tan underneath the stubble. His eyes were empty. They might as well belong to a stranger.

When he'd finished shaving he re-tied his hair back out of the way and replaced his mask and hat. This was a view of himself he'd become much more used to, and the eye-holes of the mask shadowed the deadness of his eyes. He left the room.

Already a crowd began to gather in the common room. He found a table in the corner and sat down with his back to the wall, ignoring the suspicious, angry glances. Kinnly spotted him and shook his head, scowling.

Aaro didn't have long to wait before several soldiers came in, off-duty and ready for a wild night. They headed to the bar, their voices the loudest in the room. They didn't spot Aaro right away, which was fine by him as he sat and watched, biding his time. He hadn't expected as many people from such a tiny town, but then, what else was there to do on a winter's night besides drink their money away.

Kinnly came around to his table. "Don't

say I didn't warn you," he said. "Are you going to want something stronger than coffee?"

"Not tonight."

Another group of soldiers came in while Kinnly was refilling his mug. The innkeeper glanced at them and said, "There's your man Robbel."

This new group were officers, and more observant than their underlings. They spotted Aaro right away, their expressions going sour. Aaro allowed a small smile as he lifted a hand and beckoned them over. They looked surprised.

Aaro pulled the letter signed by Ormand out of his pocket and handed it to the captain when they stopped at the table. Robbel looked even more surprised as he read it. He folded it slowly and handed it back to Aaro.

"It's Shonnowa you're looking for, huh? Well, I wish you good hunting, but I don't envy you. My advice is, grow a pair of eyes in the back of your head. Don't let them touch you. If one starts dancing or singing, or talking funny, get out of there." He shook his head, sizing Aaro up. His lip curled. "Good to know our king is hiring mercenaries now. But better your kind tromping through the wilderness than one of us."

"Can't imagine what King Ormand wants with the Shonnowa," said one of Robbel's men.

Robbel shrugged. "I'd say he's a fool, if it wasn't a hanging offence. Sure, they'd be useful, if you could control them. He's playing with forces he doesn't know a thing about... unless he's managed to learn something, sitting down there in his comfy palace, that we don't know."

The other man snorted.

"Where can I find them?" Aaro asked.

"Who knows?" Robbel turned to look as the door opened, and waved a dismissive hand toward the man who came in. "Why don't you follow one and find out."

The newcomer had dark, wary eyes, and a face that managed to look tan and peaked at the same time. He sat down, stiff as a scarecrow, at an empty table. Already Aaro was considering doing exactly what Robbel suggested. Following the Shonnowan man. But he wasn't done asking questions, either.

"There's a village here, somewhere," he said. "How can I find it?"

Robbel waved the question off. "Those aren't the ones you're looking for. They're outcasts." He nodded toward the Shonnowan man sitting at the table sipping a drink while watching the room warily. "But he's not." He turned back, headed to the bar, calling over his shoulder, "Good hunting."

Aaro watched him walk away, feeling frustration boiling inside. Now what? He had more questions, and not all of them were directly related to carrying out Ormand's orders. The beginning of a plan had begun to form, but he needed more answers.

Before the meal was done he slipped back to his room and packed his things, taking only what he could carry on his back. A few days' rations, his bedroll, his weapons. He left them packed and ready at the door, then returned to the common room, pulling Kinnly aside. He pressed a few coins into his hand.

"I'm leaving tonight. Keep my horse, and the rest of my things, till I get back."

Kinnly raised his eyebrows. "And when you don't come back?"

"Then put them to use," Aaro growled. "But give me three weeks."

"Alright," Kinnly said, still with his eyebrows up, sounding unconvinced.

Aaro slipped back into his place in the corner and waited. When the Shonnowa man at last got up to leave, Aaro slipped back into his room, quickly putting his coat, scarf, and gloves back on, and grabbed his things. The box with the medallion he slid inside his coat before he went out. He detested having the thing on his person. Whenever he touched it he could feel the tingles of magic from inside.

On the street, he caught sight of the Shonnowan man a moment before he disappeared between two of the building, and followed, keeping well back and going quietly. The man had had a few drinks, and he swayed as he walked, muttering under his breath. He never bothered to look around him.

Aaro hoped the man would lead him back to the rest of the Shonnowa. But he hadn't decided what to do when he got there. He wished there was some way to know what Ormand's medallion was capable of, and what kind of people these other Shonnowa truly were. If he could, he would see where their town was, then try and find the smaller village. The people Kinnly had thought were decent. Perchance they might be able to give him some answers. If not, there was still the matter of the wolf.

They walked for hours. The moon had risen a couple of hours past sunset, and now rode high in the sky, blotted out occasionally by the clouds, or hidden as they walked beneath the trees. They were headed west, more or less, through a gap in the hills, following the northern bank of a stream. The man never turned around once, but still Aaro remained cautious, keeping well back. He neither saw nor heard any sign of trouble until a blow to his shoulder and sudden pain sent him stumbling forward.

He had just enough time to register that he'd been shot with an arrow, before the Shonnowan man in front of him cried out and fell, the moonlight shining along the arrow shaft embedded in his neck.

Aaro dropped to the ground, gun already in hand, searching the trees and hills that rose on either side of the stream. No sign of anyone. But he could hear voices now, speaking a language he didn't know, what sounded like arguing. He scooted on his belly over to a group of boulders, dropped his pack, then slowly got his feet under him, crouching between the rocks. He could feel hot blood trickling down his shoulder blade, sticking to his shirt. Reaching over his shoulder, he snapped the arrow shaft, flinging it aside.

The voices drew closer. He dared a peek over the boulder, and saw half a dozen men standing around the fallen Shonnowan. Two of them argued, while the other four spread out, looking for Aaro.

He drew the hammer back on his revolver, pausing. Once he fired, they would know where he was. He steadied the gun against the rock, waited a beat, then fired. The man closest to him went down, missing half his brain. He pulled the hammer back again, but they were running now, scattering into the trees and circling back toward him. All he had were flying shadows to aim at. He fired again, heard a cry, and was ready for the next shot, only now he didn't have a target at all.

The next arrow came out of nowhere, striking his gun, sending it flying out of his hand, and slicing the flesh between his thumb and index finger. He grabbed his wrist out of reflex, and when he looked up again, a Shonnowan man stood before him, holding a sword in front of his face.

The sword point described little circles in the air in front of Aaro's nose. Its wielder tapped it against Aaro's mask, then used it to try and pry it off. When that didn't work, he drew nearer, reaching a hand to grasp its edge. Meanwhile, Aaro had found his left-hand dagger and drew it suddenly, swiping the sword aside. He lunged forward and slammed his mask into his enemy's face.

The man stumbled backward, holding on to a gushing nose, and Aaro followed him with the dagger, sliding it into his stomach and upward.

A third arrow took him above the knee as he turned. His world shattered as the point drove into the bone, and he staggered to his knees with a scream, blinded for a moment by agony.

"If I wanted to kill you, I could," someone said from above him.

It was all Aaro could do to raise his head and open his eyes. This man didn't make the mistake of coming too close. He stood a couple yards away, an arrow nocked to the bowstring, ready to pull back and shoot in the fraction of a second.

"Why were you following one of my people?" he asked.

"Why did you kill one of your people?" Aaro ground out through clenched teeth.

"Because he was a drunken fool and allowed himself to be followed," the Shonnowan replied coolly. His remaining three companions stepped out of the trees, drawing closer, one of them cradling an arm black with blood in the moonlight. "Why were you following him?" the leader asked again.

"Was sent..." He gasped for a breath past the pain. "King Ormand seeks to... negotiate with your king. Sent a token." With his good hand he touched his coat where the box with the medallion and its accompanying disks waited in an inside pocket.

"Our people stand alone. Our king does not barter favors." He nodded to one of his men, who stepped forward and ripped Aaro's coat open, pulling out the box. He showed it to the leader, who asked, "What are these?"

Aaro blinked, trying to work his way through an answer. "I don't know. Some kind of magic. Made by one of your own people."

The man scoffed. "What do we want with it then?"

Aaro's thoughts kept scattering like leaves in the wind, while blood pumped around the slender cedar shaft in his thigh. He muttered under his breath.

"What?" The leader took a step closer.

He blinked again, and managed to gather his thoughts. "High magic, wrought by a master. Only your king shall touch what's inside."

The man holding the box said something in his own language, at which the leader glanced at it curiously. "Where is the key?" he asked.

Aaro reached up, his hand shaking, and

drew it from around his neck. He held it for a moment, his mind clearing momentarily. If he had any chance to live at all, it was in satisfying the Shonnowan leader. Yet what was he doing here? Dying to fulfil a last mission for Ormand? The irony nearly choked him.

The man holding the box snatched the key out of his hand. He opened it and presented it to the leader, who peered inside, his eyes alight with greed.

"Don't touch it," Aaro warned.

"Why? Is it poisoned?"

"I don't know." He wilted further toward the ground.

"Our mages will determine if it is," the leader gave a nod, and the other man snapped the box closed and locked it. He turned his attention back to Aaro, watching him coldly. "Your mission is accomplished. However, you won't be retuning with a message for you king." He turned to one of the others, still speaking in Aaro's language. "Kill him."

Blood dripped from Aaro's right hand. His left leg wouldn't even move. The Shonnowan man stepped forward, raising his sword. Aaro drew his left-hand gun and fired, point blank. The sword thrust went wild, slicing down across his chest, through his coat. His enemy stared at him with round eyes, dropping the sword and grabbing at his heart. He toppled sideways.

In the distance, the mournful wail of a

wolf call shivered through the night.

One of the remaining men stepped forward, but the leader waved him off, looking around at the trees, suddenly nervous. He said something in his own tongue, glanced back once at Aaro, and walked away. His people followed.

The wolf cried again. The moon still shone, though clouds were gathering in the east, blotting out the stars.

Aaro collapsed back against the boulder, cradling his hand in his lap while he tried to pull his coat closed over the gash in his side and chest. One-handed, with numb, clumsy fingers, he dug for his ammo and replaced what he'd fired. He searched along the ground with his good hand, but couldn't find the other gun that he'd dropped. Then he leaned back against the rock, shivering, and swore softly.

He'd known all along that Jake and Alonso were right, but he'd never expected to die like this. If anything, he was supposed to die taking Ormand's life, not completing a mission for him.

"Forgive me," he slurred. Whether he addressed the Almighty or his dead wife, he didn't know or care. He knew he wasn't ready to die.

Across the creek the brush rattled, and a big furry head emerged into the moonlight. For a moment he couldn't decide whether it was a wolf or a bear. As the rest of the animal came into view, he saw it was a wolf, but a big one.

He raised his gun, but his hand shook, and weakness dragged at his arm. His breaths huffed shallowly, and he forced himself to squeeze the trigger before he passed out.

The echo of the gunshot was the last thing he heard.

Chapter 11

Rowan had been trying to avoid Sorrell every moonlit night since the beginning of fall, and it hadn't been easy. Normally, she'd want to spend every moment she could as a human, even if it meant being up with the moon at all hours of the night, but he had almost cornered her a dozen times. So she avoided both moonlight and Sorrell, and the prolonged, self-imposed social fast was making her grouchy.

Tonight was different though. Tonight everyone was out, bundled in coats and furs, their breath puffing white in the light of the bonfire and the paper-thin bark lanterns that the children hung from the bare branches of trees and bushes around the edge of the clearing. The moon shone bright, keeping Rowan in her human form, clothed in Shonnowan fur-lined trousers, boots, and coat. She sat on a log bench and handed strips of prepared bark to her friend Willow, who nimbly wove them into the little luminaries that were beginning to light the clearing like fallen stars.

"You must dance in the celebration this year, if there is moonlight," Willow said, stopping for a moment to blow on her cold fingers.

"Please, no." Rowan said, handing over the last strip of bark as her gaze strayed across the clearing to Sorrell, who was trying to catch her eye. She pretended she hadn't seen.

"But you talk of dancing so fondly. It would do you good."

"Yes, ballroom dancing, or barn dancing," Rowan replied dryly. "I feel like a stork when I attempt your Shonnowan dances."

Willow laughed as she finished the last bark lantern and handed it off to a waiting child. "You're just trying to avoid my brother still."

"There's that, as well." Rowan sighed.

"You will have to speak with him eventually."

"I was hoping the problem would go away if I ignored it long enough."

Willow gave her a look, though one cheek dimpled as she fought a smile. She finally gave up trying to be serious and jumped to her feet, laughing as she extended a hand to Rowan. "Come, I'll show you the dance again. You have a full week to practice it, before the solstice." When Rowan pouted, she wiggled her fingers, insistent. "For my sake? I must enjoy my freedom while Jannen has the children, and if I dance by myself I will look silly."

Rowan took her friend's hand and reluctantly allowed herself to be pulled into the clear space around the bonfire. Several of the children clapped in delight, and soon there were half a dozen others standing with her and Willow in a line, with their backs to the fire, facing the outer circle of benches. Someone hauled a drum out into the clearing, while several pan flutes and a weathered guitar made an appearance as well. The dance and the music both began with a clap from the dancers, and then the line started to move.

In truth, Rowan knew the dance by heart from her three previous years with the Shonnowa. She just felt awkward performing it. The movements were raw and sensual, in an earthy, lithe manner, though it was a group dance and not performed with partners. Plus, her tall, lean frame didn't lend itself well to jumping or spinning. It made her feel conspicuous, and really, wasn't having red hair and fair skin outlandish enough when one was surrounded by dark beauties? Even now, she could almost feel Sorrell's gaze following her, though she and the other dancers moved too fast to see more than a blur beyond their circle.

They moved around the perimeter of the bonfire, coiling, circling, spinning, catching hands, ducking beneath each other's arms or jumping over them when they were lowered, weaving a pattern that Rowan had difficulty keeping track of. She finally ducked out of the rotating bunch of dancers, huffing mist into the air and smiling as she watched the others continue. Several more dancers joined in, more than making up for Rowan's absence.

While she didn't enjoy participating in the

dance, she could happily watch it all day. She backed up and sat down on one of the benches. With the intense focus she'd been forced to give the dance, she had forgotten about Sorrell, and as soon as she sat down, he was at her elbow, his face and his voice all full of admiration.

"Your beauty has frozen the moon in the sky," he said, giving her a wide grin.

Rowan sighed, letting out a cloud of white, frosty breath.

"You don't believe that I am sincere?"

"Sorrell—" she started, her insides twisting in frustration.

"My dear Red," he said, more serious this time. "I know you've been avoiding me. Have I hurt you in some way?"

"No," she sighed again, resigned to facing the conversation she'd been trying to avoid for so long, though she slid down the bench to put a few inches of space between them.

"I have not tried to hide how I feel about you, but I know our people are very different. Have I unknowingly been offensive?"

"No, Sorrell, you're a good friend, but..."

"I love you, Red. You know I will wait for your curse to be broken. That is why I have sought so diligently for a way to undo it. Please, I just want to know there is hope for us."

"There's not!" Rowan's heart wrenched at the hurt that showed in her friend's eyes before he masked it. "I don't think about you like that.

You and Willow and the rest of your people have been the best of friends to me, but..."

"I know you can't think about such things as a wolf, but you must know I think about you the most as a woman."

"No, it's not that..."

Sorrell paused a moment after she trailed off, pressing his lips together, his hands clenching his knees. When he spoke again it was with hesitation. "You are still thinking about your husband."

She nodded, looking away. She could try to tell him, and the words could flow until they both froze to death sitting there, but how could she ever make him understand? Even Willow sometimes seemed incredulous that she hadn't moved on yet. But her dreams were haunted. Not so much by his voice or his face, but by his presence. And in the half-wakeful moments before she fully remembered that he was gone, she would still pray the Almighty for His care over Aaro. It was always worse around the full moon, for then she would dream of standing in the moonlight, kissing him. Then she would wake, and her pain would drive her into the hills to howl her lament at the sky.

How could she ever explain that to Sorrell?

"It has been three years," he said gently. "I am in admiration of your loyalty, but my heart aches that I must still watch you mourn." His dark eyes, far too close for comfort, pleaded. She had run out of bench to put more distance between them.

"I'm sorry," she blurted. "Truly, I'm sorry that both of our hearts must break. But I've never sought anything but friendship, and I haven't anything else to offer." She stood and rushed away, aware that Sorrell also leapt to his feet, though he didn't try to follow her as she ran back to her little cabin at the edge of the village. Frustration and tears twisted her face, and she ducked through the door before anyone could see her. Several unladylike words slipped out before she got ahold of herself, and squelched the tears. Then, blocked from the moonlight, her curse took hold again and she felt the tingling buzz of magic as her form shifted. She stood once again on four feet in the middle of the one-room shanty, and smacked the sandy floor with a paw, which did nothing to vent her feelings. *Curses on you, Ormand. I hope someone slits your throat.*

* * * * *

Rowan could smell more snow coming the next morning, and she sought out Dinarrel, the town elder, to tell him, scratching the Shonnowan word for snow in the semi-frozen mud outside his house.

He smiled, though his eyebrows puckered together. "Each winter seems harder than the one before," he said. "I dread each one coming. But I suppose that's because I'm getting old. Never fear, Red. We shall send out hunters today, before the storm comes. You shall go as well, if you'd like."

She did like. The tracking and chasing part, anyway. After more than three years of being a wolf, she still was not fond of sinking her teeth into a living animal. Having the quivering muscles in her mouth gave her the crawlies, and it always took forever to get the loose fur off her tongue, since she couldn't spit properly.

She trotted back to her own cabin after seeing the village leader, and found Willow there, with little Minnoa toddling around the room, and baby Sol in the basket on her back. She sat cross-legged on the pile of blankets and fur in the corner that Rowan used for a bed, and when Rowan came in, set a steaming bowl of food on the floor.

Minnoa waddled over and stuck her fingers in the bowl a second before Willow could pull her out of the way. "No, no, child! We already broke fast. Remember? Papa cooked fish."

Fish was what was in the bowl they'd brought for Rowan as well. She had smelled it even before she went inside.

"You were over to see Dinarrel this morning," Willow said as Rowan nibbled at the food.

She nodded.

"Is all well?"

Rowan nodded again. Sorrell and the

others who had built her house for her had hauled buckets of sand from the stream for the floor, making it possible to scratch a few words when she wanted to be understood. She wrote SNOW again for her friend.

Minnoa thought the whole thing hilarious, and toddled over, swiping her chubby palms through the word, erasing it. Next, she attacked Rowan's fur. Rowan didn't mind usually. Unless she found that one spot that... Drat. She felt her paw start to twitch as the little hands scratched her neck.

Willow corralled her daughter again, saving Rowan the embarrassment of involuntary scratching. "We'll be sending out hunters today then," she said. "Are you going with them?"

Rowan nodded. She finished eating and gave the bottom of the bowl a swipe with her tongue to pick up the crumbs, then scratched out THANK YOU on the floor.

"You're welcome. Always." She hesitated and pinned Rowan with a keen look. "You spoke with my brother last night," she said.

Rowan nodded reluctantly.

"And he confessed his love?"

She tilted her snout skyward and heaved a sigh.

"I'm sorry, my friend," Willow said. "I tried to dissuade him."

Rowan nodded.

After another moment's silence Willow

went on, hesitating, and obviously picking her words with care. "Perhaps...perhaps it is difficult for us to understand. It is not we who live with your curse. You have done well here, and our people love you. But you cannot often share your heart, and choose to withhold it even more often. So perhaps we sometimes fail to see the depth of hurt you still carry. It cannot be an easy thing to shake off, when you are caught forever in this wolf's body. What I mean to say is—you cannot move on and pretend to have any kind of normal life, like you might if you were still human. You have died, in a way, even though you still live."

Rowan watched her friend, who stared at the wall as she spoke, as if she were watching something at a great distance.

"So perhaps," Willow went on, brushing dark strands of hair from the squirming Minnoa's face, "we assume too much." Her gaze snapped back into focus, and she smiled at Rowan, her round cheeks dimpling. "I am just happy you have found a portion of happiness here, even if it is incomplete. And please be patient with my brother." She laughed. "Of course, he cannot marry you while you're a wolf anyway, and perhaps by the time we break your curse, things will change."

Rowan nodded, though her heart gave a twinge at the mention of breaking her curse. She didn't hold out much hope for that.

Within an hour most of the men in the

village had headed out. Instead of joining one of the groups who would eventually split up and try to drive game out to each other, Rowan set out alone. Unlike the humans, she had no aversion to being out after dark, and that was usually the best time to hunt anyway, so if she found nothing during the day, she would stay out until she did.

At least she planned on going by herself, until she heard Sorrell hail her, running to catch up. "Red!" he shouted again, far louder than was necessary, as he reached her a moment later. "I hoped to join you today."

And she had been hoping to avoid him again. His smile was as brilliant as ever when he caught up to her and gave a wave toward the hillside in front of them, as though she hadn't broken his heart the night before. "Lead on."

She started off again through the ankle deep snow, glad to be a wolf now, and not expected to say anything as he trudged after her.

For the past three and a half years Sorrell had been the one who sought relentlessly for a way to break her curse. He'd gone to other Shonnowan villages asking questions, he'd sought out and read as many of the ancient texts as he could find, which was no easy feat. But in all of that, they hadn't learned anything more than what Rigall had already told her. That the breaking of her curse would be something that directly opposed its purpose. So they had tried to figure out its true purpose. That never went anywhere either. But even though their search had been useless, he only became more intense. It made her uncomfortable.

"You were hoping to avoid me again," Sorrell said as they walked.

She twitched an ear, feeling a little guilty that her intentions were so obvious.

He sighed, his bright smile slipping. "I keep thinking about our conversation last night. I am sorry to make you uneasy. But I feel there might have been more to say."

Her ears sank slowly toward her skull. *Wonderful.*

"Forgive me. I just need to know. It isn't because I'm Shonnowan, is it?"

She shook her head.

"Is it our way of life? Because, if you desired it, I would follow you to your own home, and your own people."

Her ears went the rest of the way back, pinning themselves to her head. That. That right there was why she had wanted to come out here alone. So he wouldn't be able to make her feel guilty. Again. Because he was utterly devoted to her, and she couldn't return any of it. Even with Willow's pretty speech that morning, the truth of Sorrell's arguments gnawed at her. It had been three years. She was free to move on. She should move on. She liked Sorrell immensely.

She just couldn't love him.

"I see," he said. "But forgive me if I am not

yet content to give up on you."

The sun shone bright and cold as they walked, though the sky had a grayish caste to it. By the time they stopped for lunch the little bit of early snow still clinging to the ground had turned soggy. They hadn't seen anything larger than squirrels, though their trail zigzagged across the hills, covering an enormous amount of ground. The other animals must sense the storm coming as well, and not only her.

"I have been thinking some more," Sorrell said as they shared a snack of jerky and slightly smooshed flatbread, breaking a long silence. "There is one place we haven't looked for a cure for you."

She cocked her head to the side, which was the easiest way of telling him to continue.

"The Shonno-mara. They hold most of our sacred texts, and they know much more about curses than we do."

Rowan's ears plastered themselves back again in response to her fear. She shook her head and gave him the best scowl she could contrive.

"It may be the only way to find out," he said.

NO, she wrote in the mushy snow.

He shrugged. "I know it would be dangerous. But if it means we could have a future together someday..."

She erased the word 'no' with a vehement swipe and wrote it bigger. NO! NO NO NO.

He looked taken aback. "But why? You want to be human again, don't you?"

She sat and fumed for a moment before she wrote again. TOO DANGEROUS. Swipe. YOU WILL NOT RISK IT FOR... she stopped, swiped the words out again, and stared at the ground for another moment. Oh, that words could be had for the speaking! When she wrote again it was more carefully. YOU WILL NOT RISK YOUR LIFE FOR MY LOVE. I FORBID IT.

He threw his hands up. "What do you want to do then? To stay a wolf forever? If I don't do it, who will? And if not for love, then for what?"

She couldn't spell it out for him in the muddy snow. You can't break someone's heart and dash your own hopes with crooked letters written on the ground. So she got up and ran. Again.

"Red!" he shouted after her, rising to his feet with a strip of jerky still in hand.

But she kept on running. Both of them knew he'd never catch up with her. Not when she really ran, with the cold air stinging her eyes and her paws barely touching the earth.

* * * * *

When she had put a safe distance between herself and her would-be suitor, she slowed, returning to her zigzagging hunt, sniffing the wind, watching for game trails. She didn't know what else to do. She couldn't go back to the village yet, she wasn't ready to explain to Willow why she'd come home early without any meat, and she couldn't face Sorrell. She was careful, though, to remain within howling distance of the village. If she did bring down a deer, she would have to call for help. She'd never be able to drag it home by herself. As it was, even with her wandering, when night fell she had gone as far as she dared, so she changed directions and headed back, taking a different course and covering different ground.

The moon came up, and the bitter, damp smell of the impending storm increased. She kept to the shadows, not wanting to turn human on a night like this. It would be two or three hours' walk back to the village from here in human form. As a wolf she could make it in less than half that, if she had to. But she kept to her zigzagging course through the hills, still hoping to spot something to show for her hours of wandering, though now with the storm closer it was doubtful. In truth, she just didn't want to go back before everyone had gone to bed. Then she wouldn't have to face Sorrell and his lovesick pleading.

A gunshot shattered the night.

Rowan's head snapped up, and she perked her ears toward the sound.

It wasn't the Shonnowa shooting. Most of them either couldn't afford Talvan guns, or scoffed at the amount of noise they made. Which would mean it was one of her own countrymen.

Boom, again.

She jumped as though propelled by the sound itself, running toward it, down a shallow gully and up the far side. As soon as she topped the hill she could smell blood. A lot of it. And all human.

A final *boom* cracked through the air. And then the howling started, off in the distance.

Whatever was happening was down in the valley below. She slowed her pace, then stopped, letting out her own spine-tingling howl that dipped and rose again into the sky in a pattern that would bring riders out from the village, though it would take them a while to get there. Then she trotted silently down the slope, slowing again when she heard voices.

"Leave him," a man said in accented Shonnowan. "He's a dead man anyway. The wolves come." He and his companions moved off upstream. Three of them, Rowan saw, peeking through the brush. She scanned the stream banks. Five bodies. Except, she reminded herself, one of them must still be alive.

She stepped into the open, feeling the moonlight tingle along her skin. Sure enough, the man slouched against the rocks across the stream looked up at her. He raised his gun, struggling to hold it steady, and squeezed off a shot that went wild. His arm dropped, and his head fell back against the rock, knocking his hat off and exposing his mask to the moonlight.

Rowan stopped in her tracks as shock bolted through her. That mask! Even after more than three years the sight of it took her back to the blistering hot marketplace in Skybreak, where Aaro had bought her the wolf pendant and hung it around her neck.

She forced herself to take a step forward, then another, sniffing the air. The scent of blood was so powerful it covered everything else. His pant leg was soaked with it, while a dark pool of it gathered in his palm from a slice at the base of his thumb. His coat and shirt hung open, revealing a long, ugly gash.

Rowan stood over him, her heart twisting at the familiarity the mask had ignited. There was something else about him that felt familiar as well, but with her focus on the mask, she couldn't tell what. He looked to have a lean, muscular build under his winter layers, and neck-length hair frizzed out of its binding, curling darkly at the edges of the mask.

She looked up at the moon, feeling the tingling magic congealing across her skin, and waited for the transformation. She wouldn't have much time, with the storm rolling in. The moonlight would be gone soon. But that was just as well, with real wolves howling after the scent of blood. In the meantime, she had to get him into some kind of shelter.

The rocky hills were overgrown with

brush and trees, and it was hard to see, but she thought there might be a rocky place near the top of the slope. Possibly someplace that could conceal a cave. If it didn't, then it would still be better to have stone at their backs than to be sitting in the middle of the bloodbath when the wolves came.

The second she felt her form shift she stood up and went to work.

Willow had provided her with a couple changes of clothes for when she was in human form. Whatever she wore at the time became a part of her when the curse turned her back to a wolf, but still, it was good not to be stuck with the same white dress she'd been married in. That dress had too many memories. Now she wore soft doeskin trousers and light boots with a simple linen tunic.

She found a dagger laying near the masked man, and used it to cut strips from the dead men's clothing to use for bandages. With nothing to help remove the arrow in the man's leg, and fearing to rip it out backward, she wrapped the makeshift bandages around it, tightening them as much as she dared. It was when she went to lay the man down that she realized he had another arrow in his shoulder, broken off a few inches out. This must have been the first wound. They must have shot him from behind and further away, for the arrow hadn't gone all the way through. She hastily wrapped that too, winding the bandage around either side of the arrow shaft, under his armpit, and around.

The man groaned in his sleep as she wrapped his hand.

"Good. You're still alive," she muttered. Her fingers ached with the damp cold as she tied off the strip of cloth. She regretted not having anything cleaner than a dead man's shirt to use. Willow would have a fit when she saw it.

Now she just had to get him up the hill to those rocks. Hooking her hands under his arms, she leaned backward against his weight, huffing as his body scraped over the rocky stream bank. "Come on, friend. Help me out here. You're a whole lot heavier than you look." She heaved backward another couple of feet. "Too much..." another heave, "...muscle. On you. Not on me, sadly."

How was she ever going to get him up the hill? And the wolves were howling closer. Soon they would go silent, and then she'd be worried. A glance at the moon showed her it was still holding its own, even as the first few snow flurries fell.

After a few more feet she gave up and went back to the bodies. Two of them were wearing belts. Good. She buckled them together in a big circle and looped it across the man's chest and under his arms. It gave her some leverage, which helped. She got him into the trees, and from there was able to brace herself against them and haul him further. One tree, then on to the next. Up and up. By the time she reached the rocks she was soaked in sweat. The man stirred and muttered.

"Of course. Wake up *now*."

It was hard to tell, in the dappled moonlight and with the mask shadowing his eyes, but she thought they flickered open for a minute, resting on her. The man gave a sob, which turned into a moan in the back of his throat, and he lay still again.

"You, sir, are worthless."

Rowan left him and went looking for a cave. This area had many of them, and the place she'd dragged him to looked even more promising up close, with ledges rising out of the hill, cracked and broken, with many shadowy gaps.

The wind gusted, driving a fine flurry of snow into her face, and she glanced at the moon, broken by the bare branches of trees. Still a little while yet before the storm blotted it out. She returned to the man and fumbled through his pockets until she found his flint fire starter. Feeling suddenly frustrated and overwhelmed, she ran back down the hill and took off what clothes remained on the bodies that were dry and would burn, and bundled them together. A bulky object laying near the rocks caught her eye. A pack with a bedroll. She snatched that up as well and raced back up the hill.

The wolves had stopped howling.

There was a hollow in the rock that had caught her eye. Not quite a cave, but if she used her imagination it could be. It curved inward enough to provide shelter from the wind on three sides, and the rock overhang above would keep some of the snow out, though it let the moon shine in. There would be plenty of room for both of them in there, so she dragged him over to it.

She gathered a few armloads of wood, frantically snatching branches, twigs, leaves, anything she stumbled across, and tossing or carrying them back until she had a small pile collected next to the bundle of clothes. It only took her a moment to stack the driest cloth and wood together, then struck flint and prayed that it would light. It did. She almost laughed in relief. She coaxed the flame along, blowing gently on it, adding more twigs, silently begging it to burn.

She cast glances toward the stream, which she could just see between trees, as she worked, watching the flashes of movement down there. Gray fur under a white moon. Hopefully they would stay busy with the bodies for a while. She added more fuel to the fire, making it bigger, longer. A wall between them and the wolves. She gathered as many fallen branches and sticks as she could without going far, and stacked them nearby. Then she turned back to the man.

Her first chore was opening his bedroll and pulling and tugging him onto it, then covering him with a blanket. She slid him as close to the fire as she dared. He shivered and mumbled something, mostly unconscious. If Willow were here... but she wasn't. And Rowan didn't have a way to get her here any time soon. Men from the village should be on their way, but even when they got there, they would have to go back and get Willow. It would be three hours at the least before she arrived, and in the meantime Rowan had to stop him from losing more blood. Nor did she have much time left to do it.

She found a flask of alcohol and a needle and thread among the man's things, and put them to use cleaning and stitching up the gash across his chest. Willow would be horrified when she saw the sloppy stitches, but Rowan had never been any good with a needle, and tugging it through human skin threatened to make her queasy.

Finished with that, she checked his leg again. She guessed the arrowhead had struck into the bone, and she had no way of getting it out without causing more damage. *What do I do, Willow?* She touched Aaro's wolf pendant that still hung around her neck, visible when she was a human, smearing blood across it. The day she'd faced Ormand and been cursed, she had put her life in the hands of the Almighty, giving up on all her hopes and fears. Was this stranger's fate in her hands any more than her own life had been then? Was it not the Almighty who still held her, and him as well?

Ah! Forgive me. Your will be done.

She broke off the arrow shaft and bound up his leg again. That one would wait for Willow.

The moon, sinking toward the west and staying just ahead of the storm, shone into their little shelter, faithfully keeping her human as she worked. But the storm kept following it, drawing inexorably nearer. "No you don't," she muttered. "Give me a little more time."

His shoulder wasn't as bad. Kneeling beside him, she rolled him slightly, propping him against her knees, where she could cut his shirt and coat away. The arrow had gone almost all the way through the muscle on top, missing the bone. Running her fingers along his shoulder, she could feel the bulge of the arrowhead beneath his skin.

"Have to cut you out," she muttered as she worked. She set his dagger blade in the fire for a moment to sterilize it, then slit along the bulge of the arrowhead. Blood coated her fingers as she guided the flint out, pushing the arrow shaft gently from the back. Breaking off the feathered back end, she pulled it the rest of the way out, then used a generous splash of alcohol to clean both sides, stitched it, and rewrapped it.

Another glance at the moon. Almost gone. Fine snow pellets swirled around, hissing in the fire.

Hurrying now, she unwrapped his hand

and cleaned it with the alcohol as well, holding it in her lap as she stitched it closed. Yes, Willow would have a fit when she saw the butcher job Rowan had made out of the stitches. Clouds swallowed the moon, leaving the fire as her only light source as she re-wrapped his hand. Her curse tingled along her skin, and she grunted in frustration as she fumbled with the knot.

She felt the buzz of energy, and the shift in form as the knot left her fingers. Then, just as suddenly as always, she was sprawled in the most awkward position possible for a wolf, on her tail with her four legs all tangled up together. The scent of blood washed over her again as she lost her balance and toppled over backwards, missing the fire by a few inches.

Righting herself, she took a second to regain her bearings, and then sent up another howl to guide her friends, who must be getting close by now. Soft growls, and an inquiring bark replied to her howl, and the soft scraping of dead leaves stirred by silent paws out beyond the fire. The wolves were headed their way.

Chapter 12

Aaro felt himself being dragged through brush and over rocks, twisting his wounds. He faded in and out, slogging through pain and weakness just to peel his eyes open, though all he could see were dark shapes of bare tree branches. He must have lost track of time, for the next thing he knew, he lay beside a fire with a woman at his side, talking to herself as she worked over him.

Rowan, his heart cried.

He must be hallucinating. Probably he was still propped against that rock next to the stream, waiting to die. But if he must die, he was glad to see her one last time.

"Red," he whispered. But she didn't hear him, intent on sterilizing his dagger. His eyes closed, and when she started tugging on the arrow in his shoulder he faded out again. Not so much unconscious as lost in a dark world where nothing existed except pain.

When a wolf howled directly over him, he knew he had nothing left to do but wait for the final wash of agony before he died.

Nothing happened.

He forced his eyes open. Shaggy, coppery-red fur filled his vision. He flinched, scrabbling backward on his elbows, gasping out a cry as the movement tore his shoulder and chest. A massive red paw came down on his chest, pressing him, squirming, back onto his bedroll. He blinked his vision clear, twisting his head. His bedroll? And a fire roared bedside him, hissing at the snowflakes falling hard and fast outside their rock shelter.

The wolf lowered its head toward his face, sniffing at this mask. Big, intelligent eyes surveyed him, gleaming like hammered metal in the firelight. When he stopped struggling, the paw moved from his chest to his face, the claws brushing gently across his cheek, hooking under his mask. His head tilted to the side as the beast tugged at his mask. When it didn't budge, it—*she* he corrected, since he could see down the length of her shaggy belly, gave up. But then she seemed to follow his line of sight. Her ears pinned down, and her paw came back, swatting him upside the head. She backed off and sat down, glaring.

Not a normal wolf.

"How?" he rasped. *How did I get here?* he wanted to ask, but his voice refused to work.

The wolf stuck her nose in the air and turned her back on him, curling her tail around herself and staring out into the night, for all the world like an offended woman. He became aware of noises beyond the fire's light. Snapping, occasional snarling and growling, but from a distance. Closer to their shelter came a short bark. The wolf sat like a statue, her ears following the sounds. She sniffed the wind, and howled again, sending an involuntary shudder through Aaro.

Outside the firelight, her howl was answered by growls and movement. Eyes gleamed, reflecting the light.

The red wolf pushed another stick into the fire, backing away as sparks flew up, outlining her in flame and shadow. She whined softly.

"How?" he asked again.

She turned her head enough to give him the stink-eye and a curled lip.

He let his head fall back and he sighed out a groan.

The wolf eyed him for another minute, then something beyond the fire caught her attention, and she turned, her ears forward. Her tail swished slowly back and forth once across the ground.

Aaro heard a yelp, and then another. A distant whinny, and then a human shout echoed up to them. The red wolf barked once, standing up now, waiting. Her tail hung motionless behind her as hoofbeats pounded up the hill. Two riders materialized in the firelight, shouting in Shonnowan. The wolf replied with a bark.

One of the men dismounted and came around the fire, talking to the wolf, though she never answered him. He knelt on Aaro's other side, lifting the blanket to survey the damage, and grimacing.

Aaro could have sworn the wolf tried to

speak then, carefully manipulating her velvet lips into something that sounded like "Illuoh."

The man nodded. "Willow," he said. He turned back to Aaro. "We will bring our healer, but it will be some time before we get back. Red will keep you safe."

Aaro let his eyes close, again retreating to a place that was not sleep and not waking, just drifting in pain and the sensation of floating. At some point he must have slept though, because he woke up shivering, with cold air rushing across his chest, biting at the gash. The cold clawed its way deeper, becoming an ache all its own, and he felt sick with his shivering. He forced his eyes open to see a young Shonnowan woman kneeling beside him. When she saw that he was awake she smiled and replaced his blanket.

"Hello, stranger. You found trouble tonight in a portion and a half, I would say. Do you have a name?"

"No," he whispered, his gaze seeking the wolf, wondering if he'd dreamt her, like he'd dreamt Rowan. But she sat off to the side, watching. Dawn streaked the sky beyond the fire, and snow coated the trees and ground.

"Hmm. I hope you will live, but I do not know. It is too cold to lose so much blood, and you will lose more, for I must get the last arrow out. Do you understand?"

He nodded.

She raised his head, pressing a cup to his lips. He tried to turn away.

"It will help stop the bleeding," she said.

He swallowed, tasting earthy, bitter herbs. He kept his eyes squeezed shut until he'd drained the cup, and she laid his head back down on the blankets.

The wolf padded over, and the blankets shifted as she laid down at his side, radiating warmth, while the woman threw more blankets over top of them both, trapping the heat. Snow continued to fall outside the cave, deadening the world.

Another of the Shonnowa, a man, appeared around the corner, dragging a bundle of branches to the fire and building it up before disappearing again.

Finally, when the fire was roaring, warming one half of him while the wolf warmed the other, the woman pressed a strip of leather between his teeth. "Forgive me, for causing more pain," she murmured.

Aaro sank back into the darkness, the leather still clamped in his teeth.

* * * * *

Rowan rested her chin on her paws, drifting off to sleep in the excessive warmth of the blankets and the fire. Willow sang softly while she worked, and the man slept. Even to her wolf senses the snow had a cleansing effect on the world, lulling her, after a long day and longer night, to rest.

She dreamed again of kissing her husband under the full moon, but this time, instead of ending, the dream went on. In it he ran his hands through her hair, covering her face with kisses, laughing with her. They snuggled in a blanket together beside a roaring fire.

The dream lingered when she woke, disorienting, so that for just a moment she thought she was still lying next to Aaro, waiting for him to wake up and kiss her again. Another moment, and she remembered it wasn't Aaro asleep next to her, but a stranger wearing a mask that she couldn't remove, struggling to stay alive.

Her heart broke.

"Good that one of you is finally awake," Willow said. She sat cross-legged next to the fire, measuring out dried herbs from her collection, and crumbling them into a kettle of water. "Our friend still lives, but you have both been sleeping for hours now. I have hope for him, provided we can keep him from getting infected."

Rowan stretched and yawned, then lay there panting, watching her friend. She wanted to get up and go out, beyond the fire, where the snow still fell, already over a foot deep. But the stranger needed the warmth for the moment more than she needed the cold. She turned her head, studying him. Even in his sleep his lips pressed into a flat line, his jaw clenched in pain. He still seemed achingly familiar. Even his scent, though mingled with blood, whispered to her. She couldn't resist trying the mask one more time, nudging it with her nose.

The man groaned in his sleep, soft as a sigh.

"I tried that as well," Willow said. "It's one of ours, infused with the Gift. Only he can take it off."

Rowan cocked her head, looking at her friend.

Willow laughed. "No, not even Dinarrel can undo the spell. If he could break a binding like that, he would have been able to break your curse as well. I'm sorry, Red. I want to know who he is as badly as you do."

Rowan seriously doubted that. She didn't just want to see his face. She *needed* him to live. She needed to know who he was, and why he made her heart break. Why he reminded her so much—she allowed herself to think it for just a moment—of Aaro.

* * * * *

The snow stopped that afternoon, and Willow's husband came shortly afterward to bring her home, saying that the baby would not stop fussing, and Minnoa kept crying, after hearing the wolves howling in the night, thinking they had taken her mother away.

"It seems I'm needed," Willow said, laughing. "But our friend should be well for now. You and Sorrell can watch over him, and I will return in the morning. When the tea simmers, try to get him to drink again. It will help ward off infection and bring healing."

"I would like to know what happened," Sorrell said, looking over top of the fire at the sleeping stranger, "that he was ambushed by our people."

"But not our people," Willow reminded him. "They have become the people of the Curse, rather than the People of the Gift."

"Yes—but still. Even *they* do not attack strangers without cause. Was he known to them? Or did he have something of value that they would want? Who knows whether one unusual incident might be the harbinger of something more? That is why I desire to know."

Willow shook her head, her ever-present smile playing at her lips. "Then I will leave you and Red to find out. I must go care for my children." She leapt lightly onto the horse behind her husband, and they picked their way downhill through the snow and the trees, headed back to the village.

Rowan watched them out of sight, then lay back down next to the stranger, nudging her way into the blankets. She glanced at Sorrell, feeling the awkwardness that they had put aside in the excitement descend around them again now that they were alone.

He returned her look with a rueful smile. "I am a little envious of our stranger. Though as you know, I prefer your human form."

She shook her head.

"Forgive me," he said. "But I can only long for the day when you are fully human, and I can win your love properly. I still cannot understand why you refuse help."

She rested her chin on her paws and heaved a sigh. If she could speak, how could she explain, further than she had already tried to, that she could never give him the love he hoped to gain at such a great risk.

And how long would it be before the stranger woke up and took off his mask?

Sorrell went to gather one more load of wood before night fell, and built up the fire again, then set about preparing a meal. After he and Rowan had eaten, he poured a cup of Willow's strong herbal concoction and added a scoop of snow to cool it off before coaxing some of it down the stranger's throat. The man roused enough to swallow, but his eyes never opened. Sorrell set the cup aside and leaned back against the rock, his brows drawn together as he watched the stranger sleep.

Rowan followed his gaze to the mask, fierce and unmoving, and wondered what micro-expressions moved the face beneath while the man slept. She realized she'd given him Aaro's features in her mind. Since the moment she'd seen the mask, she had imagined Aaro's face beneath it. Dead for three years, and he still haunted her.

She looked away, her heart feeling like it'd been shredded. She needed to return, to keep the stranger warm, but revulsion took her. She'd felt so drawn to him. Had, without realizing it, projected her deepest longing onto this man whom she knew nothing about, simply because he wore a mask. She'd lain beside him to keep him warm, and dreamed he was her man. But he wasn't. Aaro was dead. And who knew, when this man woke, whether he would prove that he'd have been better left to die as well.

Her hide twitched as if a fly had landed there, and her ears swiveled backward, flattening again her head.

"What is it?" Sorrell asked, watching her.

She shook her head. This was another thing she could never make him understand, even if she could speak. Not Sorrell, who was in love with her and had high hopes that one day she would return the feeling.

"If you think you know him, please tell me," Sorrell said.

She shook her head. She knew what she had been imagining, the subconscious thought that her longing had driven her to. But she didn't know this man.

She turned and slipped out past the fire into the cold evening. The sun had set already, turning the world blue with dusk. Walking back down the hill toward the stream, she sniffed the air. Sorrell had dragged the bodies of the wolves they had killed the night before a distance away, but she could still smell blood both from them and from the stranger's battle by the creek. Snow had covered the stains, leaving white mounds over the bodies of the Shonno-mara that had fallen, but the smell of death remained.

The boulders where the man had made his last stand were nothing but blue mounds under the blue of the evening sky. She sniffed around them, digging her nose into the snow, moving it aside with her paws until she'd unearthed a revolver, its wooden grip scored deeply, and drenched in blood. They must have shot it out of his hand. Its twin lay next to his hat where he'd dropped it after he tried to shoot her. Not that she held it against him. She was a wolf, after all.

Scouting around two of the other bodies produced nothing new. They had been mauled and partly eaten by the wolves, but enough remained to get a hint of what had happened. Three of them had been killed by the stranger. One shot through the heart, one ripped open by his dagger, and one shot in the head. The next body had an arrow through the neck. He'd been killed by the Shonno-mara then. But he was either Shonnowa or Shonno-mara himself. Why would they kill one of their own?

She returned to the rocks and took the man's hat in her teeth, shaking the snow from it, then, sighing, dropped the guns inside the flat crown and carried the whole thing back up the hill. How she longed not to have to carry things with her teeth!

Sorrell examined the things by the light of the fire, but he came up with no more clues that she had. Willow had removed the man's weapon belt earlier, and now Sorrell returned the guns to their holsters, and the dagger to its sheath. He set the belt off to the side, out of the stranger's reach.

Rowan dug down in the leaves and pine needles near the campfire until she'd cleared a patch of dirt, smoothing it with her paw. Sorrell moved to kneel beside her as she scratched into the dirt, ONE MAN KILLED BY SHONNO-MARA.

"They killed one of their own?" Sorrell asked.

She nodded.

"My opinion of our brothers grows lower at each encounter," he said. "But still I wish I knew the reason behind it all."

Rowan silently agreed.

When Sorrell wrapped himself in his fur cloak and stretched out by the fire, she reluctantly returned to the stranger's side to keep him warm through the night and the dropping temperature. Within minutes Sorrell had fallen into a light snore, which, she thought, was another excellent reason not to commit to a relationship with him. Tonight's gentle rumbles were quiet compared to what she'd heard at times coming out of his cabin at night.

The blue of evening deepened into night, and still Rowan lay wakeful, listening to the sounds of winter and the distant howls of wolves.

* * * * *

Aaro woke up so gradually he didn't realize he was awake until he'd been laying there staring at the fire and feeling the gentle whoosh of breath on his neck for several minutes. He turned his head, not sure what he was expecting to see, but the big, coppery wolf laying at his side was not it.

He startled a bit, and the big metallic eyes opened, regarding him coolly, the ears perked toward him. The black nose quivered, only inches from his shoulder, and the jaws parted as the beast panted. She lay underneath the blankets with him, warming the side of him that the fire couldn't reach. The fingers of his uninjured hand brushed against her fur.

"What are you?" he whispered, his voice cracked and rough.

She shook her head.

"You can understand me?"

She nodded.

"But you can't speak."

Again, the big copper head shook a negative. He wanted to ask more, but his weariness held him prisoner. The idea of asking yes or no questions until he had the answers he sought was too daunting. He sighed, letting the tension go back out of him. His whole body ached with weakness.

"You saved my life?"

She nodded.

"Thank you."

The big eyes continued to watch him, almost hungrily, and she shuffled one paw forward and nudged his mask, her intention clear. This time it was he who shook his head.

"No, friend. I have no identity any more. None that matters."

Her eyes pleaded, almost desperate, if a wolf could look desperate. He turned his face away. Within moments he slept.

When he woke again, morning had come, and the smell of herbs and meat drifted to him from the fire. A Shonnowan man sat with his back to him, hunched next to the flames. The wolf, on his other side, breathed steadily, a continuous stream of warm air puffing against his chin and neck. Her breath didn't smell like rancid dog breath, thankfully.

The man turned around, and his expression lifted when he saw that Aaro was awake. He took a cup from where it sat near the fire and brought it over.

"Be welcome," he said, sitting down cross-legged by Aaro's shoulder, opposite from the wolf. "It's good you are awake." He put a hand behind Aaro's back, helping him sit up, and placed the cup in his hands. "Another of my sister's remedies. I don't envy you."

Weakness dragged at Aaro, begging him to lay back down, and cold air swirled past the displaced blankets, making him shiver. He lifted the cup and drank, hating the weariness that threatened to smother him. The healer's brew didn't taste good, but it was warm, and it soothed the tremble inside him. When he'd finished, the Shonnowan man laid him back down gently, but even still Aaro bit the inside of his cheek as the movement twisted the gash across his chest. Sweat beaded under his mask, and he panted.

"My name is Sorrell," the Shonnowan said, sitting back and looking at him with a mix of compassion and curiosity. He nodded toward the wolf. "You've already met Red."

Aaro closed his eyes as his breathing steadied and his heartbeat returned to normal. "Who is she?"

"A friend. She can tell you her own story someday—if she chooses. I'm anxious to hear your story though, stranger, if you feel up to tell it. Or at least give me your name."

Aaro shook his head. "I have no name."

"Surely at one time you did."

For a long time he didn't reply. Then, "That man died."

"I see. You've given up your self. But to what end?"

"Vengeance."

Sorrell nodded, his expression tightening.

"Vengeance is a treacherous master to give yourself to. Perhaps you have learned that, though."

"Aye," Aaro whispered. "But I serve her, nonetheless."

Chapter 13

Rowan spent most of the rest of the day dozing in the warmth of the cave and the blankets and furs piled on top of the sleeping stranger. Sorrell kept the fire going, and that afternoon, Willow came back to check on them. Her face and her low laugh showed her relief when she undid the bandages and found no signs of infection. But he wasn't out of danger yet.

"Tomorrow," she said to him, "we will bring you back to the village. I have my man working on a, hmm—*torenna*—a bed? That he can pull behind the horse."

"Thank you," the man who refused to give a name said. His voice was still husky and lacked strength.

"Be welcome, *Omen*," she said.

"Omen?" his tone whispered of surprise as he looked to Willow to explain. Rowan looked at her curiously as well.

"In our tongue it means 'wanderer,'" Willow said. "But perhaps it is used with different meaning for you?"

"Omen. It's a portent. A sign, or a warning, of something to come," the man answered softly.

"Ah! Perhaps that is true as well. I hope not. But we shall see. Perhaps when you tell your story before the chieftain, more will become clear. In the meantime, rest, *Omen*. Red will guard you for one more night, and my brother will not let the fire die."

When she had gone, Sorrell resumed his seat across from Rowan, meeting her gaze for a moment before he turned his attention to the stranger. "My sister calls you *Wanderer*, but I wonder if *Omen* is not more accurate. What happened two nights past? Why did our brothers attack you?"

"Because I was following one of them," the stranger replied, his mask giving away none of his thoughts.

"And why did they kill one of their own?"

"Because he was drunk and allowed himself to be followed." The man shifted, his lips pressed flat in a grimace until he settled again. He tentatively flexed the fingers of his right hand, swathed in bandages, and sighed, either in relief or pain, when they all answered his command. He let the hand rest across his chest, turning his head to meet Rowan's gaze.

For the first time, she saw that his eyes were blue. Shadowed by the mask, they still gleamed like sky reflected in snow. Her heart hammered as it had not done in three years, and her jaws parted. If she had speech she would have said the name that swallowed her thoughts. But all she could do was stare. And then, slowly, painfully, like driving a dagger through her chest, remember the day that Aaro had died. The soldiers' boots kicking his limp form, the flames and the smoke as she watched from between Ormand's guards, waiting for him to stagger out the door, and realizing he never would.

The man had started to speak again, but some intensity of her feeling must have translated into her gaze, for his voice faltered, and they stared at each other for a long moment.

"Who are you?" Sorrell asked again, oblivious.

When the man turned back to him, cursing either in irritation or pain, the spell snapped. "I'm a man seeking revenge, and I will do whatever I have to, to get it," he growled. And with that, her image of Aaro was gone, and in his place lay a stranger. A killer. A man wounded inside and out. "If you have to call me something, I'll answer to Mask. But tell me. Do your people often shoot each other in the back? Because not even I have ever stooped that low."

"They are not our people," Sorrell replied without acknowledging the stranger's insult. "Those who use the Gift for their own ends, or wield it against others, we call them Shonno-mara. People of the Curse. Though they are our brothers. And they call us the *Omen*. Yes, it is the same name my sister called you. Wanderer. But it has also come to mean *outcast*."

The stranger huffed a wry laugh, but didn't explain what he found amusing.

After a moment, when he still didn't

speak, Sorrell continued. "For generations they have lived in our ancient cities, while we have wandered the mountains and plains without a permanent home, because we refused to corrupt the Gift, and with it ourselves. They have no walls any more, to separate their hearts from what things should be done, and what things should not." He fell silent, his eyes drifted away from the wounded man to the fire and then beyond, wistful as he always was when speaking of the Shonnowan cities, his ancestral home. "So, Mask, to answer your question, my people do not shoot others from behind. But the Shonno-mara will do whatever they wish, if it aligns with their plans. What I fear is the day when they turn their plans toward us."

* * * * *

Sorrell's words lingered with Aaro through the day, when he wasn't sleeping. The weight of Ormand's unknown plans, and his magic pendant, now in the hands of the Shonno-mara, gnawed at him like a premonition of disaster. *Omen*, the healer had called him. He hoped it didn't prove to be true. But as soon as he had his chance, Ormand would die, and then his plans would be at an end, no matter what they were.

The next morning, Willow retuned with her husband and checked him over again, changing his bandages and re-applying salve to his wounds, nodding to herself and making her cheeks dimple as she worked. She always seemed to be either singing or laughing, and when she was silent, she smiled.

"You are feeling better?" She asked without looking up from her work.

"Some," he said.

"I would like to take you back to our village today. We have made a *torenna* to carry you. I hope the journey will not be too difficult, but it will be cold, even with the furs we brought. There isn't room for Red to ride with you and keep you warm."

"How far?"

"It will be slower than it would be walking or riding. Three hours."

He nodded. "Thank you for all of this."

"It is no great burden," she said, smiling. She finished wrapping his leg and sat back on her heels. "And Red seems to find something in you that has made her protective. For her, I would help, even if I had no other reason."

Aaro blinked, his eyebrows going up underneath his mask. He looked for the wolf, but she must have slipped out while Willow tended him. So he asked again, "What is she?"

The question met with a soft laugh. "Her story is her own to tell."

"But she doesn't speak."

"No. Most of the time not. I wish she could! She is the best of friends, but how much better, if our prayers were answered?" The young woman looked wistful for a moment, her dark features drawn together.

"Are you ready?" her husband asked, speaking in the kings' language for Aaro's benefit.

She nodded, unfolding and standing up in one smooth motion. The two men, Willow's husband, whose name Aaro hadn't caught, and Sorrel, stamped out the fire, kicking snow and dirt over it. They brought a stretcher made of saplings with blankets stretched between them, piled with more blankets and furs, and with help Aaro wiggled onto it. The whole thing tilted up at a slight angle when they hitched it to the horse, and the first few steps proved he would be in for a bumpy ride, even with the snow.

"Where's Red?" he asked as they packed up the rest of the accumulated supplies and prepared to leave.

"Do not fear. She will catch us up," Sorrell replied. "She comes and goes as she wills."

Aaro tried to doze as they travelled. His stretcher slid along the snow most of the time, but whenever he was close to falling asleep they would hit a hidden rock or a branch and jar him awake, sometimes swearing with pain, depending how hard he hit. Willow looked back at him several times, her brows puckered with concern. She spoke to her husband in Shonnowan several times, and he slowed the horse.

They'd been going for well over an hour before Red caught up with them. She came bounding through the snow, silent, with her pink tongue lolling out in a pant. She fell in beside him, sniffing him, as though checking to make sure he'd been properly cared for.

He reached out his good hand and touched her shoulder, burying his fingers in her impossibly soft fur. The color, now that he could see it fully in the sunlight, struck him as a bittersweet reminder of Rowan, and how her coppery curls had made a halo around her head. They way they'd fallen like a curtain around her face when she kissed him.

He pulled his hand back. Heat burned in his chest, and longing worse than the pain of his wounds coiled in his guts. Almighty in heaven, how he missed her! And they'd only been together for a single night.

If only Ormand's death could serve to bring her back.

When they finally arrived at the Shonnowan village, it seemed everyone had turned out to see them. Children followed the horses, some of them running after Red, gripping handfuls of fur in their chubby fingers while men and women looked on curiously. Aaro closed his eyes against the stares, feeling naked even behind his mask, and faked sleep until he felt the stretcher lower and then lift, and they carried him inside.

His eyes popped open to see the Shonnowan home. Except it was empty. A bed of blankets and furs took up one corner. That was where they put him down. On the opposite side of the tiny room a fireplace constructed from river stones and clay sheltered a blazing fire, and beside it a small stack of wood leaned against the pelt-lined wall. Other than that, there were no furnishings, or even possessions. A smooth, sandy floor stretched from wall to wall.

Red came in behind the men who'd carried him, followed by Willow, who checked his wounds again and seemed satisfied that he'd survived the trip in fair shape.

"This is Red's home," Willow said. "For now. Perhaps not for always. But it is the least crowded place for you. I am unhappy to say that I use her home at times to bring those I care for so they can rest. In the days when my people lived in our own city, there would have been a house for healing, but now this suffices. It is the most our village has ever known, and we call it the Wolf House."

Red swiped a paw across the ground, drawing Aaro's and Willow's attention. The red wolf scratched something into the sand. He couldn't read it without propping himself up on an elbow, which seemed like an enormous effort at the moment.

Willow read it, her cheeks dimpling again. "She says welcome, and to be at home."

"She can write?" Aaro couldn't quite keep his voice from climbing in surprise.

"Of course. Her mouth may not form

speech, but her mind is perhaps sharper than yours. And she was knowing the ways of your people, at one time.'

"She's not a real wolf then?"

Willow shrugged. "It is her story." She stood up and rattled off what sounded like a list of instructions to Red in Shonnowan before she left, leaving Red and Aaro alone to stare at one another.

The wolf sat down facing him, her jaws parting in a quiet pant.

"Who are you?" he asked.

One furry ear swiveled back, and one eyebrow raised. She lifted a paw and nudged his mask.

He laughed, surprising himself and setting off a throb in his shoulder and chest. He pressed his good hand over the hole in his shoulder. Almost, he was tempted to take off the mask. But for three years the only ones who had seen his face were those drawing their last breath at his hand.

"I'll keep the mask," he said. "The face I wear is a piece of the past. The mask is the present, and it serves me better."

Red dipped her head in a nod, and scratched in the dirt. He rolled enough to read, AT LEAST YOU GET TO CHOOSE.

"Aye, I've chosen. But it was the Lesser King who set me on this path. If it were up to me..." he sighed, weariness descending on him like a predator. "But my hopes for the future have passed into dreams and ashes. I might as well grasp at smoke."

The wolf's eyes gleamed, almost as if she would shed tears. He didn't know if wolves were even capable of tears. She bent her head to scratch in the sand again. HE IS A MONSTER.

"And that is why I am going to kill him," Aaro replied.

She stared at him, the emotions of her thoughts flickering behind her eyes. Finally, she wrote again. MURDER IS NOT JUSTICE.

"But only murder will serve, when murder is what he has meted out. If not death, then what? And don't talk to me of Heymish. The high king sits on his throne and does nothing. No man can be that blind unless he wants to be, or unless he is a fool."

OR HE IS DECEIVED, she wrote in reply, raising her brows. She swiped the words away and wrote again. HE NEEDS TO KNOW THE TRUTH.

"What good would that do?" Aaro spat the words. "He would never have his brother killed, even though it is the thing he deserves."

BUT IS IT THE THING HE FEARS MOST? she wrote.

Her words rocked him. He settled onto his back, fatigue gripping him as the question hammered at his mind. "I don't know," he said to the woven saplings that formed the underside of the roof. "But it is the thing in my power to serve him."

She regarded him with what looked like understanding for a moment before she ducked through the double thickness of wool and animal hide that covered the doorway, disappearing and leaving behind a whirl of cold air and loneliness. He let himself fade into sleep.

The next day he woke, and seeing Red had already gone, propped himself in a sitting position against the wall. He still felt weak, but not helpless. His stomach rumbled, and he wondered what time it was. Then he wondered how far he would have to venture to use the privy, which in turn set him to consider the state of his clothes. If he went out there he'd freeze. His one trouser leg was shredded from the thigh down, and stiff with dried blood. His coat and shirt were in ribbons. His left boot also had a fair amount of blood on it.

As if in answer to his assessment, Willow breezed in, her arms full of bundles, bringing a swirl of snow with her. Red followed at her heels, stopping to shake snowflakes from her back.

"Ah good! I though you would feel better today. I brought you clothes, if you are well enough to change. I think you will also be hungry?" The healer raised her eyebrows, smiling as she placed the clean clothes across his knees. She bent and set a pair of fur-lined boots at his feet. Then she put a steaming bowl in his hands.

Smells of venison and herbs wafted up to him, and his stomach rumbled, even as Willow placed another bundle in his lap. New smells of bread and honey joined the others, and his stomach again protested its emptiness, while his mouth watered.

"Thank you. I don't deserve all this."

She shook her head. "You must eat well, if you are to get well. The tea helps you to mend and keeps the infection away, but only food can return your strength."

As she spoke, a child pushed through the doorway, dressed in furs and boots until only her brown eyes peered from between layers of clothes. She spotted Red and squealed, waddling toward the wolf as fast as her layers of clothing allowed.

"Ack! *Minnoa, il somme du olem.*" Willow threw her hands up. "I told her to play with the others. I am sorry." She scooped the child up, tickling, scolding, and laughing all at once.

"It's fine," Aaro said. But she waved him off.

"Eat. You will have visitors soon enough." She buried her face in the child's neck, making silly nonsense-noises as she carried her outside. Red, free from her small attacker, stretched in front of the fire and yawned.

"You seem popular with the children," he said, picking up his spoon awkwardly in his left hand and going to work on the stew.

Red huffed and shook her head. She scratched in the sand, IT'S THE FUR.

He smiled into his soup bowl. "I can understand the fascination."

Her ears went back, and he laughed. He hadn't laughed in three years, and here he was, shot up and barely alive, with his plans indefinitely on hold, and he'd laughed twice in as many days. At a wolf. What was wrong with him?

When he'd finished eating, the wolf got up went out, leaving him alone to change clothes. He struggled into the wool-lined trousers, cursing as he twisted wrong. He couldn't put weight on his leg at all without agony ripping from his hip to his knee. His right hand wasn't much better. The merest brush against it had him seeing light bursts behind his eyes.

At last he stood, unsteady on one leg, wearing strange clothes and suddenly impatient with his weakness. He wanted to be away, to return to Skybreak and, he hoped, finally demand justice from Ormand, whether at the tip of his blade, from the barrel of his gun, or with his bare hands.

But justice would have to wait, at least until he could walk.

Willow came back in a few minutes with more water infused with herbs, and also a crutch. He managed a trip to the outhouse, then collapsed back onto his pile of furs and slept. He must have slept most of the day away.

He startled awake at a noise, sitting up to find four Shonnowan men, plus Willow and Red, crowded into the tiny room and staring at him. He started up, but stopped, wincing, when he twisted his shoulder and chest. Slowly he sat the rest of the way up, leaning against the wall.

"We've come to hear your story," Sorrell said.

Chapter 14

Rowan regretted not waking the stranger—he'd said to call him Mask— beforehand, when he startled awake and twisted his wounds. A hiss of pain escaped him, and his good hand balled into a fist as he eased back against the wall. He returned the Shonnowans' stare, his blue eyes shadowed by the eyeholes of his mask, but made no move to speak.

It was Dinarrel, sitting cross-legged with his back to the fire, who broke the silence. "Willow calls you *Omen*, Wanderer. Will you not give us your right name?"

Mask gave a short shake of his head.

"And you won't remove your mask?" Sorrell asked, his voice harsh in the small room. He wore an uncharacteristic scowl, his hands running up and down the worn leather of his boots, never still.

Dinarrel shot Sorrell a frown, gray eyebrows lowered over shrewd brown eyes. Rowan could feel the animosity coming from Sorrell, and wondered if the chieftain noticed, and what he made of it.

Mask shifted, looking at each of them in turn, waiting for the next question. His gaze remained a moment longer on Sorrell, his eyes behind the mask just as shrewd as the chieftain's, taking the measure of the other man. Besides Dinarrel and Sorrell, Dinarrel's son, Rorren, and Willow and her husband, Jannen, had joined them. Of all of them, only Sorrell seemed on edge. The others merely looked curious.

The small room forced them to sit elbow to elbow in a semi-circle facing the stranger. Rowan, who had been watching from behind the others, padded over and sat to the side, closest to Mask, where she could see both him and the others as they spoke.

"Please," Dinarrel invited, "Tell us your story. The actions of our brothers, the Shonno-mara, concern us."

The man shifted, his mask turning a fraction to look at her before he spoke. "I am no friend of King Ormand," he started, "but I had my own reasons for taking his mission." He went on to tell of the medallion set made by the Shonnowan magician, and his journey north to Silver Rock, then of his indecision about what to do, and how he had planned on seeking their counsel before he contacted the Shonno-mara. Then he was ambushed and left for dead, and the medallion taken.

He told his story briefly, his good hand finding the bandages across his chest as he spoke, smoothing his shirt over the sword gash, his mask turned slightly to include Rowan in the conversation. Again, she couldn't help for a moment seeing Aaro behind the mask, as the cadence of his story smoothed out the bitter, clipped edges of his voice, allowing a hint of a drawl to creep in. She shook the impression away.

Her next thought was of Rigall, the little Shonnowan magician Ormand had enslaved. She wondered if he was the medallion's creator, and if Ormand had been good to his word and released him. Somehow, she doubted it.

"And you have no idea what this thing, this medallion, is capable of?" Dinarrel asked, his brows once again drawn together in worry.

Mask lifted his good shoulder in a shrug.

The ensuing pause stretched into a thick silence, until Sorrell swore in Shonnowan. "What is it you have done, stranger? Just what have you done?"

"I don't know," Mask said, the edge in his voice unmistakable.

"What kind of power might it be that you have just given to a people with no conscience? Or to your wicked king? And only because you wanted revenge above everything else! But it is always the innocent who pay for the crimes of the guilty." Sorrell's heavy breathing sounded loud and angry in the small room. His eyes darted toward Rowan, accusing, as if her rescuing the stranger had somehow been the cause of their uncertainty.

"Sorrell," Dinarrel said softly, warning. He turned back to Mask. "You don't know at all what these things could do? Not even a—ah. I don't know the word. Not even a small amount of knowing?"

Again, Mask shook his head. He dropped his left hand from the bandage around his chest, staring down at where it rested in his lap, flexing his fingers. Slowly, he moved the fingers of his wounded right hand.

"You do not know this thing, this *medallion*, or the smaller pieces that went with it, but do you know your King Ormand?" Jannen asked. He struggled over the words, forming them with care. Of the group gathered, he had the least knowledge of the Talvan language.

Mask's head lifted a fraction. "Yes. I know the king."

Rowan's heart skipped a beat. Why? She couldn't pinpoint the reason for the heat that suddenly flooded her chest, making it feel like she might explode. Was it the voice, or the words? Who was this man?

Her paws twitched. If there had been any possibility of ripping the mask off his face, she would have done it right there, would have used teeth, claws, whatever it took. Instead, she stared at him, willing her gaze to reach beyond the magically fused leather and silver. If she had her human form, she would have screamed at him, threatened him, begged him. But all she could do was sit and stare with her ears pinned back against her skull, muscles tensed. Begging him to say something more. What if...?

Dinarrel, unaware of her struggle, picked up on the line of Jannen's question. "Yes. What can you tell us of king Ormand? If you know him, perhaps you know what he wants. This could help."

Rowan didn't even realize she'd shifted forward, almost brushing the stranger's elbow, until his mask turned toward her, and from the corner of her eye she caught the gleam of Sorrell's eyes on her as well. But Sorrell's glaring brown gaze wasn't the one that held her captive. It was Mask's blue eyes, peering at her from the shadowed eyeholes, that drew her until they seemed to take up her entire field of vision. Almost, she could read his question there. He would be wondering why she turned so intense.

He cleared his throat and turned back to Dinarrel. "Ormand does nothing that isn't motivated by power. If he gave the Shonno-mara this thing, then it is to serve his own ends."

Rowan let her ears swivel, trying to capture every nuance of every syllable. There was something familiar in his voice quality, but his tone had returned to the clipped, bitter sound of a man in pain. Not merely physical pain, but something that went much deeper. Something that had tainted his soul.

It had been three years since she'd heard Aaro's voice, and she'd known him for little more than a single day. And Aaro was dead. Even if there was some chance, she would never be able to identify him from his voice alone. Not like this. One minute she thought Mask sounded like him, the next minute she dismissed it as her emotions playing tricks on her.

"We must think, then, that whatever this thing does, it is meant to further his plans," Dinarrel said. "But what are his plans? We were not aware that he sought more than to rule your western lands. Is he now thinking of more?"

"Yes." Mask paused. "He is building his army, and now contacting the Shonno-mara. He wants more. But I don't know in which direction he will go."

Dinarrel nodded once, his weathered face unreadable, but otherwise he sat unmoving, as he had since they'd come in. "What more are your thoughts? You say your king wants power, but there are more kinds than one. Who does he mean to fight? Us? The *Whonnollo* of the south? They were once our brothers as well. Much longer ago than the Shonno-mara. Their difficult land protects them."

Mask shook his head. "Swamps, jungles and deserts. They would hold no interest for Ormand."

"What then? The People of the Gift? Would he attack us?"

The stranger paused, his thoughts protected behind the mask. "Maybe."

"What do we possess that he would want?"

"Magic," Mask replied. "But the Shonnowa are no great conquest. There aren't enough of you in one place. The Shonno-mara would be more tempting, maybe..."

"This medallion then, is perhaps something he plans for their—ah—control?" Dinarrel watched him, his dark, sharp eyes intent, though he remained expressionless.

The others watched him as well, silent. Rowan glanced at their faces. Willow had her mouth open slightly, as though holding her breath. Sorrell looked fierce, barely controlled. The others merely waited, their expressions sharp.

The stranger's lips, the only thing really visible below his mask, pulled to the side, pressed flat in thought. "That's possible. But I don't think the Shonno-mara are his end goal. It's more likely he wants to use them. To conquer his brother."

Silence fell again. Mask's gaze flickered to Rowan for a moment, perhaps sensing that she would have more interest in the affairs of the country than the others.

"Your nation would go to war against itself? Your people against each other?" Sorrell spit out the words, his voice dipping in contempt.

Mask's gaze raked over him, sharp enough it could have drawn blood. "Much like your own people," he said.

Sorrell had no reply, but his brows drew together in a glare.

Mask returned his attention to Dinarrel. "But if Talva goes to war, it will cover most of the continent. You won't be safe from it. Even the *Whonnollo*, as you call them, could be drawn in. War tends to spread out."

Dinarrel nodded. "I must think about this. We must find out first, I think, what this medallion from your king does." He rose, his son Rorren, and Jannen with him. They filed out the door, leaving Willow, Sorrell, and Rowan with the stranger.

"You seem very content for someone who just delivered a weapon into the hands of our enemies," Sorrell said.

"What do you want me to say?" Mask responded. "I told you what my intentions were. You think I planned to almost die helping the man I'm going to kill?"

Willow gave her brother a sour look as she went about preparing to change Mask's bandages for the day, now that she had room to work. She set a kettle of water in the fire, then sat down to cut strips from a length of cotton cloth. One of her last ones, if Rowan guessed right. Someone would be going into town soon. One thing Willow insisted on buying was clean cotton or linen cloth for her supplies. Many things the Shonnowa made themselves, but they didn't have access to the flax or cotton required for material, and she would only use new cloth for something as serious as Mask's wounds. Even then she took care to boil everything first, before it was cut.

"I think you are so consumed by your anger that you think of nothing else. Who will you harm before you murder this man?"

"Whoever I have to," Mask replied flatly.

A sick feeling opened up in Rowan's stomach, like the rotting of death. All the strained longing she'd felt to know his identity leaked out of her again. This man was certainly not Aaro. She didn't *want* him to be Aaro. She rose from her haunches and went out. Evening was coming on already. The hanging door rustled as Sorrell joined her, resting his hand on her head between her ears. Even knowing she was a woman, most of them had a hard time fully comprehending that when she was in wolf form, she was *still* a woman. Gestures that would have been awkward and ridiculous toward another person—like petting their ears—were enacted toward her all the time as a wolf. Most of the time she didn't mind. Especially from the children. But sometimes with Sorrell...

"Why do you favor him so?" he asked, looking down at her, still wearing his scowl, though now his expression bore hurt as well. "He is more a wolf than you are."

Then get your hand off my head, she thought. But all she could do was meet his eyes. Even if she could speak, she didn't know what to say.

Sorrell sighed. "He's dangerous. I don't

trust him."

She didn't trust him either, but that was beside the point.

The Shonnowan man squatted on his heels, bringing him a little lower than eye-level with her. "I don't have the right to do more to influence you against him. All I can do is beg you. He's a stranger, and a killer. I don't understand why you seem to care for him so much. You've known me for three years, and yet..." He paused, noting her flattened ears, and finished with a sigh. "I can't help feeling that he's won more of your loyalty simply by being mysterious and dangerous than I have by offering...everything."

Rowan put a paw on his shoulder and shook her head, cursing her wolf's tongue.

"Forgive me, please," he said. "I only have the best wishes toward you."

She watched him disappear into the gathering gloom, then turned her nose toward the sky. The moon was already up, waiting for darkness to reveal its glory. Not much of a moon, but enough to give her a chance to talk with Willow.

She turned and padded back inside.

Willow had finished with Mask's chest and shoulder, and was cleaning his hand. His mouth twisted in pain, but he said nothing. He and Willow both glanced up at her as she stretched out in front of the fire, watching. She'd stitched his chest the night of the attack, but now, cleared of blood, she had a better view, even though she scolded herself for taking advantage of it. Part of her still couldn't let go the equal parts hope and dread as she took in every detail that could remind her of Aaro.

One thing they had in common was an admirable physique. Even under a layer of bandages he was well worth looking at. If she had her human form, she'd be blushing. A faint burn scar warped the skin on his left arm. In spite of everything, disappointment crashed through her. Aaro's only scar, beyond the small white nicks that most working men carried on their hands, was from a bullet through his right thigh. Rowan's gaze traveled down below his belt level. Even if the burn was something he'd acquired in the last three years, she couldn't exactly ask him to take his pants off to confirm the other. She huffed a sigh.

"Looking for something?" Mask asked.

Rowan raised her eyes to meet his, once again thankful that she was incapable of blushing at the moment when she realized her thoughts hadn't entirely involved bullet scars.

At his words, Willow glanced from him to Rowan. Flashing dimples, she said, "Red seems quite taken with you, stranger. Something that not even my brother can boast. I hope soon to find out why." She laughed, then sobered. "Do not misuse her devotion."

Devotion? Not the word Rowan would

have used. More like a maddening hunger to know his identity. She could not go on shredding her heart, hoping that miraculously Aaro could still be alive. But perhaps, if this man knew Ormand, he would also know Uncle Lance, and her cousins, and could open up a way for her to go to them. Or could deliver a letter for her.

Willow finished his hand and stood, while he worked at getting his shirt back on. She left both fresh water and more of her herbal tea for him, with the promise of supper later, and followed Rowan out of the house, where the waning crescent moon was already high in the sky. They both looked up at it.

"I'll meet you in the clearing in a moment," Willow said, smiling down at her before she hurried to her own cabin.

Rowan wandered toward the bonfire clearing. It was deserted tonight, blanketed in snow, and waiting for the solstice celebration two nights hence. The little bark lanterns were still hidden in the trees and bushes, firewood had been stacked under a canvas tarp, off to the side, and someone had created a makeshift table by laying rough planks out between two waist-high stumps that served the same purpose every year.

She swiped a pile of snow from one of the log benches, then dusted it with her tail. It took a long time for the pale, weak moonlight to begin tingling along her skin, and longer still for it to thicken around her. In the meantime, Willow appeared, wearing her coat, with a blanket draped around her shoulders. She handed an extra blanket to Rowan as her human form finally came.

The cold air bit at Rowan as she wrapped up in the blanket, joining her friend on the cleared log. Willow had brought a lantern, and set it on a stump off to the side, where it lent flickering golden light to the silver-blue moonlight.

For a long time they sat and stared at one another. Willow reached out and tucked a stray curl behind Rowan's ear, smiling, though her eyes were troubled, probably matching Rowan's own eyes. "I've missed you," she said.

Rowan nodded and drew a deep breath of the cold air, suddenly trembling inside and water-eyed.

"What is it?" Willow asked, cupping her hands around Rowan's cold cheeks. "Why does this stranger make you so stormy?"

"He reminds me…" Rowan sucked a breath, loathe to say it out loud. "He reminds me of Aaro."

"My poor dear!" Willow shot a look back toward the house, hidden beyond a thin fringe of trees. "But Aaro is dead! You've said so many times."

"I know," Rowan said miserably. "But every time I look at him… everything about him. His voice, his scent, his eyes…even his hair is the same color. But longer."

"You don't truly think he could be?"

Rowan shook her head, hugging the blanket closer. "No. I don't. But I can't convince my heart of that. Even if I did believe it... he's a different man. He's bitter and wounded—I mean wounded in his soul, not just his body. I don't *want* him to be my Aaro." She groaned. "But I do. I want him back, Willow. It wouldn't matter what he'd become, or what he'd done, or any of it. I just want him back." Her voice hitched up an octave, and she struggled for a moment, hating her need to cry.

Willow scooted closer and wrapped her arms around her shoulders, leaning their heads together. She didn't say anything, and Rowan got herself under control, swiping quickly at her eyes.

"Sorrell's right. Whoever he is, he's blind in his anger. He can't be trusted," Rowan said, pulling away and focusing her burning eyes on the lantern flame.

"No..." Willow answered, hesitating. "No, he can't. You know for sure he isn't your man?"

"If he would take his mask off..." Rowan scowled. "Other than that... Aaro didn't have a scar on his arm. He did have one, an old bullet wound, almost as high as his right hip..."

Willow laughed softly. "I understand your difficulty now. The only thing left that you could do is tell him who you are."

"I can't though!" Rowan wailed. "It's not

him. It couldn't be him. And I can't trust him.
Who knows what Ormand would do if it got back
to him that I'm still alive! He intended me to die
as a wolf. And Mask is going back to Ormand. He
has to. I just miss Aaro, and that's all there is to
it. I know it's silly. We were only together for a
day. I hardly knew him. I never had a chance to
memorize all the little scratches and lines on his
hands, or the way his lips moved when he
talked...but I loved him."

She stopped again and choked back tears,
struggling for control. "I can't move on. Every
time I convince myself it isn't him... the next
minute, I'm right back to hoping. I can't bear to
be around him, but I can't keep myself away. And
once he's strong enough, he'll leave, and I'll never
know..." she whispered, withdrawing into her
blanket.

For a long time, Willow sat with her,
sharing her silence. The deep, bitter silence of a
winter's night. For once, given the opportunity,
Rowan couldn't bring herself to speak.

"You've been with us for three years now,"
Willow said finally. "And we have not found the
way to break your curse for you. You are one of
us, but you were not always. I cannot think of you
leaving, but some day, if you wish to continue
trying to find a cure, you will have to. I can't tell
you where to seek it, but perhaps your journey
will open up possibilities we aren't aware of now."

"What? You're saying I should go with

him?" Rowan looked up at her friend, startled.

"I don't think I can answer that. But I don't want you to remain here forever, if there is a chance you could find your way back to your old life. But that is not quite what I mean either... I wish you could stay here with us forever, but not if it cost you the opportunity to get your human form back. Or your family. Even though you have had happiness here as a wolf, I know your heart longs for more."

After another deep silence, Rowan said, "Thank you. I have a lot to think about now. It's good to have someone who understands, because I don't think I could ever explain it to Sorrell."

"Probably not. He intends good, and he loves you—he just doesn't understand you."

Rowan laughed. "I've never met a man who did. Maybe Aaro did, for the short time we had together. But no one else."

* * * * *

Aaro hadn't been able to keep track of the days very well, especially there at the beginning, but he thought it must be almost a week since the attack. He leaned against the wall of the cabin, gingerly flexing his injured hand, and listened to the bustle of the tiny village outside. Something was happening tonight. He hadn't heard this much activity in the few days he'd been here, and since there was nothing else with which to occupy his mind, he let himself be curious about it. Willow hadn't brought his dinner yet either, and it was late. Already well past sundown.

Finally Red came in, shoving her way past the blanketed doorway, bringing a whirl of snow on her heels and carrying a lit lantern in her teeth. He noted the lantern was classic Talvan styled, with a glass globe in a metal frame, and a sturdy wire handle that made it possible for the wolf to carry it. She set the lantern down, the handle falling and clacking against the side, and grinned a doggy grin at him.

COME WITH ME, she wrote on the sandy floor.

Aaro looked at her incredulously, and then glanced at his crutch. She nudged it from its place leaning against the wall, making it fall in his lap, then wrote, WILLOW SAYS YOU CAN.

"What's happening?"

WINTER SOLSICE.

He gave her a blank look, and she rolled her eyes at him.

JUST COME.

Aaro levered himself off the ground, balancing until he could get his crutch situated. He hobbled to the door and ducked outside, huffing the cold air full of falling snow. The world looked blue in the twilight, but soon it would be dark, with the storm hiding any hint of moon or stars.

Rorren, the village elder's son, if Aaro remembered right, slipped up beside him carrying an armful of extra blankets, flashing his white smile. He beckoned to the nearby trees, and a path leading through them. Several villagers hustled along, disappearing down the path. The younger man waited for Aaro to start, then dogged his footsteps as he minced along on his crutch, pausing several times to let the tremble in his leg subside, while Red followed them with the lantern.

They stepped into a clearing almost as large as the village itself, lit by a roaring bonfire, as well as at least a hundred little bark lanterns suspended in the trees. The entire village was there. Children shrieked as they chased each other between the log benches, and women fussed over a long table laid out with more varieties of food than he'd ever guessed the Shonnowa were capable of. Smells of herbs and sweetbread mingled with roast meat and corn, and danced in the air with the flying snow, tickling his nose.

"What is this?" he asked, stopping to stare.

"It is celebration," Rorren said in Talvan, pronouncing his words carefully, "of lights."

Aaro made it to the nearest bench and sat, joined the next instant by Red, who jumped up beside him. Rorren dumped the armful of blankets in his lap and hurried away. Aaro turned to Red, raising his eyebrows, though she couldn't see his expression beneath the mask. Whatever he might have asked was interrupted by Dinarrel, who stood in front of the fire and raised his hands. He began speaking in Shonnowan.

Sorrell appeared out of the crowd and slid onto the bench on the other side of Red. He looked as sour as usual, but as Dinarrel's speech ended, he deigned to summarize.

"Our village elder says that we gather for yet another year to thank Nawassel, the Giver of Gifts, for giving the gift of light at the darkest time of the year, the winter solstice; after today the days will grow longer, and the spring will come. And for giving hope, which is a different type of light, when the world was swallowed up in the power of curses and darkness. Nawassa, the Gift, what your people ignorantly call magic, was granted to our ancestors at the winter solstice, during the Age of Fear. We have always used it and guarded it—until the Shonno-mara broke their oaths, of course."

"Huh."

Something similar was taught by the priests of Talva, but Aaro had always been a bit blurry on the historical details, and they had long since lost track of the Shonnowan people, allowing the race to fall into legend. But he recalled that the gift of magic—or rather the knowledge of how to use it— had been given to the Shonnowa to counteract the curses and oppression that were rampant in that age.

Sorrell, perhaps guessing his questions, said, "The Nawassa was created at the beginning of the world for wonder and for delight for the children of men. But it was corrupted soon after, and knowledge of it was lost, except in its corrupt form, which brought the Age of Fear to be. Then Nawassel Himself came and showed our people how it can be used for great good. It is not easy, though, and takes much time and knowledge to learn, and some still use it for evil."

Beside Aaro, the red wolf heaved a sigh that sounded pained. Sorrell stood abruptly and walked away, glancing back once at Red with a frown. So there was some kind of friction going on between the two of them. Aaro didn't know what, but he suspected he was a part of it. Not that he was sorry. He would happily ruffle the prickly Shonnowan if he could.

A line was forming around the food table, and Rorren appeared again, silently handing Aaro a battered tin plate heaped with steaming food. "Hurry, before...cold," he said. He offered Red a bowl of food as well, setting it on the bench beside her before he disappeared.

Aaro ate with cold fingers, and when he finished, bent down for a handful of snow to clean the plate with. Then he set it aside and tucked his hands into his coat. Already the others were finishing up, and someone started thumping on a drum. There were shouts and laughter, and people hurried to form a circle around the bonfire.

He glanced once at Red as the circle of

villagers began their coiling, rhythmic dance, and saw that she was as mesmerized as he, her eyes glowing in the firelight. She turned toward him, giving him that doggy grin, and her tail even thumped once on the bench.

How long they watched the dance he didn't know. The patterns changed. Some of the dancers slipped away, to be replaced by others. The cold began to seep through Aaro's coat and blankets as snow collected on his lap. Red shook it out of her fur several times, and sidled closer to him. He tucked a corner of the blanket around her, sharing each other's warmth again.

Aaro was almost ready to give it up and drag himself back to the cabin, when the dance finally came to a stop. The dancers didn't disperse, though. Instead, the villagers who had been resting joined the circle, leaving only Aaro and Red, and one or two older women who sat with the youngest of the children, to occupy the benches. Dinarrel shouted, raising both hands to the sky, and speaking what sounded like it could have been poetry, or a rhyming prayer. The others echoed his shout, and the instruments, the drums, flutes, and guitar, started up again, this time joined by voices. The entire village sang as they danced. As one, they leaned in toward the fire, and each person drew out a branch. He hadn't noticed before, that dozens of thick branches had been chopped into torches, resting with their ends in the flames. Each villager raised their torch toward the sky, dozens of flames swirling with the dance, mingling white smoke with frosty breaths and snowflakes, and the haunting melody of the song.

"Almighty in heaven," Aaro whispered, "that is beautiful,"

* * * * *

After almost three weeks, during which winter had set in fully, turning the world frozen and bitter as stone, Aaro figured it was time to get out. He had no illusions about being ready to travel, especially in the cold, but his strength had come back enough to tempt him into returning to Silver Rock before Kinnly, the innkeeper, sold his horse and the rest of his gear. Maybe he'd even decide to stay there for the rest of the coldest months, although that would make for an expensive winter.

Sorrell, the healer's brother, still held some unspoken grudge against Aaro, though Aaro hadn't yet figured out if it was a matter of mistrust, or whether there was something else there. None of them truly trusted him—that was another thing he bore no illusions about. And they were right not to. Still, when he wanted to borrow a horse for the ride into town, he sought out Dinarrel, the chieftain, and avoided Sorrell.

Dinarrel regarded him with his dark, sharp eyes, his gaze going from Aaro's face to the crutch he still used to get around. "You do not seem ready for this," he said simply.

"Maybe not," Aaro replied, "but there's a man keeping my horse, and I told him he could have it if I didn't come back after three weeks. My time is almost up, and that was a good horse."

"I understand. Would you come back here, after?"

"Yes," he said. And he meant it. Even though it stung his pride, if he was honest, Willow's herbal remedies had him healing faster than he would if left to his own care. He'd be better off returning and wintering with the Shonnowa, grudge or no.

"You may have the horse," Dinarrel said, "if Willow gives you leave to travel."

Aaro left him, returning to the Wolf House for his weapons, and went to the corral without bothering to talk to Willow. He picked a shaggy little black mare and put a halter on her, which was the extent of most of the Shonnowans' tack. They didn't have the money for expensive saddles, and didn't bother with bits and bridles. Between the whole village there were a dozen horses, and only about three saddles, all of which they'd fashioned themselves. He'd seen amazing craftsmanship from Shonnowan merchants, but these particular villagers seemed content to live more simply.

Limping, he led the horse out of the corral and replaced the bars across the gate. Then he faced the problem of how to get on to the animal. Even if he had a saddle, his leg wasn't strong enough for him to mount from the ground. The mare wasn't very tall... He just prayed she was the gentle sort as he heaved himself, belly-first, across her back. From there he dragged his leg over her rump and sat upright, hissing with the pain in his thigh.

The horse sidestepped, tossing her head, and for a moment he realized what an awkward place he was in, bareback, without enough strength to stay on if the animal bucked or took off on him. Falling off would not be pleasant.

But the mare settled, and he pulled the crutch across his lap, steeling himself to move forward. He guided the horse to the east, across the shallow, partly frozen stream and into the hills. The day wasn't as cold as it had been for the past week. The gray-white of the sky matched the dirty white of last week's snow, and the wind had died. Probably it would snow again soon, but he hoped not until he got back.

After an hour's ride his leg commenced throbbing, and his shoulder, which was healing much faster, ached dully. But he reminded himself why he was going to town. He had liked that horse, and his saddle was broken-in and comfortable, and buying new would wipe out the advance payment he'd received from Ormand, leaving him to face the rest of the winter broke, or else make the ten-day trek back in the dead of winter. And that was if he could even find someone willing to sell him a new horse out in this wilderness.

A flash of movement jerked his attention to the sparse forest. He startled, wrenching his leg again, and swore when he saw it was only Red. She came alongside him, her ears perked forward, tongue lolling out as she trotted beside the horse. When she looked up at him, her eyes formed questions.

"Well, what do you want?" he said, picking the crutch off his lap and turning it parallel to the horse as they passed through a stand of white birch. Something about the wolf unnerved him, though she'd been his almost constant companion for the past weeks. He'd never removed his mask, but still had the feeling she could look right through him. "I'm planning on going back, if that's what you're worried about."

Of course, she didn't answer, but he still felt compelled to give an explanation, telling her about his horse, and his bargain with the innkeeper. "You and Willow would have told me to stay, I know. But it's not as if new horses and gear just fall into my path. I might be a murderer, but I'm not a thief."

He nudged his heels into the mare's sides, urging her up a snowy incline. As their path angled upward he leaned forward, gripping with his knees so as not to slide backward off the horse's rump. His leg throbbed, and he swore again softly as he tugged the horse to a stop at the top of the hill to catch his breath. Red gave him an accusing look.

"I never asked you to come," he reminded her. "I appreciate that you saved my life, but despite all that, I'm pretty good at watching out for myself. You can't go on guarding me forever."

She just rolled her eyes at him, which was an odd look for a wolf.

He started the horse again after a moment's rest, heading down into the ravine, but a sharp bark behind him brought him up. He turned to look at Red. She had a paw lifted, pointing north along the ridge. His gaze followed, but he didn't see anything of interest, and said as much.

Again, she huffed and rolled her eyes at him, lowering her paw to scratch something in the snow. He turned the horse around and walked it back until he could read the word she written.

TOWN.

"Oh."

Without waiting for more, she set off in that direction, her ears back, shaking her head. All he could do was follow.

"So what's your story?" he asked. "For all your trying to get at my name and face, you're pretty protective of your own. You're not really a wolf, so what are you? Some Shonnowan experiment? An animal they've made to be able to think and communicate?"

The ears flattened back further on Red's

skull.

"Not an animal then." He softened his tone. "Perhaps a woman?"

The whole wolf tensed up. The tail went down, almost between her legs, and she stopped, falling behind as his horse kept moving. He reined it in and turned to look down at her. He'd never imagined seeing such an exquisite look of pain and loss on a human's face, let alone a wolf's. She had been a woman, then.

She walked on, still not looking at him, leaving him sitting his horse in the snow, watching after her. Somehow, thinking of her as a woman shifted his perception. The way she watched him, the way she had protected him. How she'd even lain at his side to keep him warm. Why?

"Who are you?" he whispered after her.

Chapter 15

By the time he rode into town, Aaro's leg felt like it had been shot all over again. He eased back off the horse and slid to the ground, nearly pitching over onto his face as his good knee threatened to buckle. He gripped the horse's mane and leaned on his crutch, his legs trembling. In his peripheral vision he saw a blue wool skirt stop on the sidewalk. A muddy pair of boots thudded to a halt as the woman's escort stopped with her.

"My lands! Are you alright?" The woman called. The man mumbled something under his breath, and Aaro caught the movement as he tugged her elbow, urging her to move on.

He lifted a hand without looking up. "I'm fine."

"Was that a wolf...?" the woman's voice drifted back to him as the couple continued down the street.

He straitened up finally, gripping the crutch, and glanced around for Red. She sat on the boardwalk, watching and waiting for him. He looped the horse's reins over the hitching rail and limped through the muddy snow to join her.

"I know, I know," he muttered as she continued with the accusing glare. "I'm starting to wonder myself if it was worth it." He leaned against the post for a minute, waiting for the throb in his leg to ease up, and ran a hand over the stubble on his jaw. "If it wasn't looking like snow, I'd figure to head back in the morning. But I guess we get it over with and get back."

She stood up, waiting, and joined him as he limped toward the tavern door.

A wry smile twitched his lips. "You sure you don't want to wait outside? Any kind of decent lady wouldn't walk into a place like this. 'Course, I'm just assuming you were the decent type, before."

The death glare Red gave him as he pushed through the door set him laughing, and her rumbling growl as she followed at his heels didn't help.

It was only a little before noon, and at that time of day the common room remained mostly empty, save a couple of soldiers who must have had the day off. They sat with their boots propped in front of the fire, with tankards of ale in their hands. But they weren't drunk enough to let Aaro go unnoticed. One, a lanky, greasy-haired fellow, turned and elbowed his buddy, looking like he was about to speak, until he saw Red. His mouth snapped shut and he gaped, elbowing hard enough to draw an annoyed curse from the solid, plain man who sat with him.

"Wolf!"

The solid man sat up and took notice, his eyes lighting with greed. He got to his feet, setting his drink on the table and taking a few steps toward them, his eyes going between Red and Aaro. "What's your business, stranger?" he said to Aaro. "We're soldiers of King Ormand, and we don't appreciate masked bandits wandering through town, but we'd be willing to let it go if you hand over that wolf of yours."

Aaro glanced coolly from them to Red. "Oh, she's not mine," he said, leaning against the bar and propping his crutch beside him.

"Then you won't mind us taking her."

He lifted a shoulder in a shrug. "You could try. What kind of bounty has Ormand put on her?"

The two men seemed taken aback that he should know of a bounty on the wolf, and they were in no hurry to state an amount.

"You need to move on, stranger," the lanky one said, "and mind your own business. Better take off that mask before one of us decides to take it off for you. Then you can forget about the wolf, wherever you picked it up. The beast is a menace, and we're commissioned with taking care of menaces."

Aaro actually laughed. If he weren't in pain, he'd enjoy antagonizing these imbeciles. Red didn't seem bothered by them overly either, though her ears tilted back, and a glint of fang showed below her lip. She sat down by his feet and yawned, then broke into a quiet pant.

Kinnly, the innkeeper, appeared in the

doorway to the kitchen, saw Aaro, and grunted his surprise. "You're alive, then," he said. "You certainly took your time coming back, and lucky you are that I'm a man of my word, for I've had half a dozen offers on that horse of yours." He scowled, looking none too pleased about having to return Aaro's belongings, especially when he caught sight of the two soldiers standing awkwardly behind him, fingering their weapons. He jabbed two stubby fingers at the air, one for Aaro, and the other for the soldiers. "I'll thank all of you to keep it civil while you're in my building."

"Just doing our job," the lanky soldier whined. "Keeping you safe, whether or not you appreciate our efforts."

"I've seen your particular style of 'keeping things safe,'" Kinnly retorted, "and again, I'll thank you to save it for out-of-doors. If anyone gets blood on my floors, I'm going to fetch Robbel and he'll have you back here mopping it up yourselves."

The two backed off, watching and waiting, with their hands on their weapons. Aaro settled onto a stool at the bar, massaging his thigh and ignoring them while Kinnly went to retrieve his things. Kinnly's wife brought coffee, offering him a suspicious glance before she ducked back into the kitchen.

One of the soldiers dug a piece of jerky out of his pocket and squatted on his heels, holding it out for Red, calling and coaxing her to come. Aaro glanced down at her. She looked downright offended, with her ears flattened back against her skull, and a good number of teeth showing. He turned away, hiding a grin. Knowing she was a woman tickled his sense of humor even more, as he imagined Rowan in the same situation. She'd blister the man's ears. Of course Red couldn't speak, but if she could, she'd doubtless have a similar response.

Kinnly came back in and hefted Aaro's saddlebags and extra pack onto the bar, then leaned on his elbows. "I've given some thought to this," he said, his eyes sliding away nervously. "I've been feeding that horse of yours for three weeks now..."

Without waiting for him to go on, Aaro slapped two more silver coins onto the counter and stood. "You have a nice day, mister." He took his crutch and headed for the door, figuring the longer he stayed, the greedier Kinnly would work up the nerve to be. The two soldiers followed him and Red out into the courtyard.

"We have business, yet," the stocky one said.

"Good for you." Aaro kept walking. His leg throbbed, and he was ready to be done with the day, dreading the ride back out to the village, even with the benefit of his saddle, once he got it back.

"Business with you, stranger. Bandits ain't

allowed in this town. You bring that wolf here though, and hand her over, and we'll let you go."

Aaro stopped finally and looked down at Red. "Care to go with these donkey-brains? You might have a chance at meeting our esteemed Lesser King."

She snarled.

Aaro started toward the stable again, talking over his shoulder. "Guess you boys aren't lucky today. The lady says no."

"It's a demmed dog! And since you see fit to insult King Ormand in the face of his royal soldiers..." The lanky one caught up with them as they stepped into the stable. Aaro's horse, one of only three in there, whickered a greeting.

"We would've let the mask go," said the other man. "But insults to the royal D'Araines name don't go unpunished."

Aaro barked a laugh, ringing his bitter merriment against the stable walls. He drew and fired his left-hand gun while he was still laughing.

The stocky man stumbled back a step, looking in shock at the blood soaking through his trousers. He stumbled against the wall, fumbling to hold the wound closed while his companion gaped.

"Get out of my sight," Aaro snarled, suddenly furious. His own wounds ached, he was tired, and above all, he hated himself. The men were buffoons, and he'd let them goad him, even if they'd done it unwittingly. Also, he didn't miss Red's yelp of surprise at the gunshot, and the horrified look she gave him. "What? He's not dead." He turned back and picked out his saddle from the lineup of pegs along the wall, and hefted it to his hip, staggering toward his horse's stall, leaning painfully against the crutch to balance out the weight of the saddle.

It took the lanky man that long to react. He drew his sword—Ormand didn't allow his men to carry their pistols while off-duty because ammunition was so expensive—and took a shaky step toward Aaro, stammering for him to stop. Red's low growl set him back for a moment. He gathered his courage and advanced toward them. Aaro swung his crutch up and around, slamming it into the man's wrist, making him drop his sword with a yelp. He jabbed the end of the crutch into the man's stomach, sending him staggering back, trying to breathe. Once recovered he opted to go back to his friend and help him limp outside rather than try his luck with another attack.

Red waited for Aaro, silent as ever, as he struggled to saddle his horse. The wound in his hand had closed up, but the nerves were damaged enough to make him hiss his displeasure as he wrestled the saddle into place. Between that and his shoulder, it almost got the better of him. He could feel Red's disapproval, either for the shooting, or his bullheadedness, or both.

He finished cinching the girth with a final round of oaths, led the horse out, and dragged himself into the saddle. He nudged his stallion over to the hitching rail where he'd left the Shonnowan mare, and went through another round of curses and wrestling as his horse showed his keen interest in the little female. He tugged them in a tight circle, away from the mare and back again, and the stallion showed his annoyance by turning and trying to smash Aaro's leg into the hitching rail. Aaro kicked his foot out of the stirrup in time, and brought them in another circle. Of course he would have to pick the mare that was in heat, and the stallion had been confined so long that he was half-wild anyway.

Finally, Red came to his rescue, tugging the mare's reins free from the rail and leading her out onto the street. The stallion was happy to follow.

By that time the gunshot and the soldiers had roused the garrison, and the sound of boots clomping up the boardwalk could be heard above the rising wind.

Red sniffed the air, the mare's lead still clenched in her jaws, and her hackles rose as a dozen soldiers turned the corner, headed toward them. Nothing could ever be simple. Aaro drew the horse to a stop beside Red and leaned on his saddle horn, waiting for the soldiers.

Robbel, who led the small company of men, stopped in front of Aaro's horse. "You! So, you're still alive." He sneered, and his eyes flicked toward Red. "I take it you found the Shonnowa." He turned to the lanky soldier, who still gripped his wrist. "You imbecile. This is one of the king's pet mercenaries. Next time ask the right questions before you corner and threaten a man." He turned back to Aaro. "And you. If you're done with your mission, then get out. I don't want your kind here, no matter who's paying you."

Aaro straightened in the saddle. "I'm not quite done, actually. But don't concern yourself. You won't be seeing much of me." He twitched the reins, moving around the men and heading on up the street.

"Wait," Robbel called. When Aaro turned in the saddle he waved toward Red. "Better watch your back. King Ormand's just put a hefty bounty on your new friend there. I can't promise my men won't get to feeling greedy and lucky at the same time."

Aaro looked at Red, who was growling around the reins in her mouth. "Red does as she pleases. She's not bound to me. But anyone that wants to try to kidnap her is an idiot." He turned away and nudged his horse on up the street, glancing down at the wolf, who wore an expression he couldn't read.

"What would you have told them, then?" he said as they followed their own set of tracks leading away from town.

Her ears flicked backward briefly, and she shook her head.

* * * * *

"You going to follow me forever now?" Mask said to her as they plodded back toward the Shonnowan village through thickening snowfall.

She flicked her ears at him and kept walking, the muffled crunch of the horses' hooves trailing her. His voice held a rasp that she'd come to recognize meant he was in pain. Not that she could do anything for him besides make sure he didn't get lost again.

"You didn't like my work back there in the barn, and I didn't even kill anyone. I guarantee you won't want to be around me once I leave your village. Almighty knows, even my best friend left me," he continued. "You want to know the real reason I wear this mask, Red? It's 'cause if I took it off, then it wouldn't be some faceless monster that's covered in people's blood. It'd be me."

Rowan didn't look back, glad, for once, that she couldn't speak. Her stranger was even more broken than she'd imagined, and she didn't have a thing to say to him.

Neither of them spoke for the rest of the journey, each navigating their own thoughts. Hers kept wandering back to her conversation with Willow the last time she'd been human, and her friend's suggestion that she wouldn't find a remedy for her curse by staying with the Shonnowa. She'd exhausted their knowledge without gaining anything useful. She could go on living with them, falling further into her new sense of normalcy, or she could go seeking again. See what knowledge she could find beyond the village. Perhaps other Shonnowa, in other villages, would know something. Perhaps she could find Rigall again, if he wasn't still enslaved to Ormand, and see what more he could tell her. Perhaps he would have a good idea how to break the curse, since he was the one who had given it to her.

But how would she ever find him? It wasn't as though she could go around asking. No one was going to sit around long enough for a wolf to spell out a question in the dirt or the snow. No. They'd shoot her. Unless she travelled with someone who could ask for her. A wolf seen in the company of a man might draw surprise, but it would be unlikely anyone would shoot her on sight if it appeared she belonged to someone.

She glanced back at Mask. He was not her Aaro, but perhaps he could be of some use to her.

Chapter 16

It was a little over a week later that Rowan almost put her foot in a trap.

The wind had shifted, bringing yet another gust of snow, and with it the scent of men. Not the men from the village, but her own countrymen. Judging from the amount of sweat, horse, and steel mingled in, they were probably soldiers, and they had been in the area recently. The area to the north and east of the village, just beyond the bonfire clearing, was saturated with their scent, so they must have spent some time wandering, though they hadn't bothered to come into the village.

Rowan had gone sniffing around, trying to fathom what their intentions might have been, when she paused mid-stride, her paw hovering over an irregularity in the expanse of snowy ground. Something else had caught her eye at the same time. A length of black chain looped around a nearby tree. The Shonnowa didn't use chain for anything. Most of them despised it as being artless. So why was there chain here, outside the village?

She backed up a step, and after a few moments of careful sniffing and digging, unearthed a huge, rusted trap, nearly big enough to cripple a bear. She stared at it in horror.

Soldiers had been here. They'd set traps. That could only mean they were hunting her, like Robbel had warned. And it hadn't taken them long, either. Curse Ormand and his meddling! It wasn't enough to turn her into a wolf? Now he had to have his men hunting her like a common beast? She dug around till she found a fallen stick, and used it to set the trap off. The stick shattered. Then she went, carefully, in search of other traps.

She found four more scattered throughout the area, and set them all off so that they were harmless, but she was even more bothered by the hunks of venison that they'd used to bait some of them. It would draw real wolves into the area, and that was the last thing the Shonnowa needed.

* * * * *

That night the skies finally cleared, revealing enough moon for her to shift back to a woman. Willow met her in the clearing, bringing extra blankets and steaming cups of spicy tea sweetened with honey. Rowan wrapped her cold fingers around the mug and buried her face in the steam.

"You spoil me," she told her friend. "It's a good thing I'm *not* human most of the time."

"I don't get nearly enough opportunities, though, and you look as if you need comforting this evening," Willow said, settling down, cross-legged, on the bench next to the snowed-over fire pit. "What bothers you?"

"Everything."

She allowed herself a sigh before she launched into an explanation about her discovery earlier that day. Then she had to back up and explain about her and Mask's trip into Silver Rock, and everything that had happened that she hadn't had a chance to share before, thanks to the constant cloud cover that had hidden the moon.

Willow nodded slowly once she finished, her expression in the moonlight caught between twinkle-eyed mischief and bittersweet sadness. "I will speak with the masked man for you. But now that it comes to a decision, I do not think I can bear to let you go."

"I will come back, I promise," Rowan said. "I'll always come back. Even if everything were restored to me, I'd still come to visit." She paused, staring up at the gibbous moon, thinking suddenly how strange it would be if she had the opportunity to go back to her old life. If given the chance to go back, would she find she'd outgrown it? Would she miss her freedom? She hadn't thought about it in those terms before.

She shook free of the notion and turned back to her friend. "Find out, if you can, how long he thinks it will be before he goes."

"Of course. But winter is here now, in its fullness, and traveling through the mountains will be treacherous until spring. I hope he doesn't plan to leave before then."

"I doubt it." Rowan let a rueful smile stretch her face. "I think perhaps his trip to town taught him something about prudence."

"And did it teach you anything about him?" Willow asked.

Rowan set aside her empty cup of tea and drew her feet up onto the crude bench where they sat, hugging her knees. Her breath left a fog in front of her face as she sighed. "No. Only that he's dangerous, and that I still don't trust him."

"You won't reveal your identity then?"

She shook her head. "I don't dare. I don't know who he is, and I've never seen even a hint of loyalty in him, toward anything. And, now that Ormand has a bounty out on me, how do I know he won't just turn me over to him for the money?"

"He wants to kill your king."

"That's a common sentiment. It doesn't mean I can trust him."

"But you love him?"

"No!" Rowan stared at her friend, taken aback. "I don't love him." She shifted and looked away for a moment. "He's compelling, surely, and mysterious, and dangerous, and all sorts of interesting things, but I don't love him. He drives me mad. Being near him is like having an itch I can't scratch. He reminds me of Aaro, but I couldn't even say exactly what he says or does that is so similar. If I think about it too long it makes me wild. For all those reasons—for Aaro's sake—I have an interest in him. But I don't love him. Or trust him."

Willow didn't respond, and as if her silence had the power to compel the truth, after a moment Rowan went on, but more thoughtfully. "I don't love him," she repeated. "But he makes me feel. I mean, something other than frustration or anger or loss. It's like—I remember that I'm a human, and a woman, when I'm with him. You would think that being a wolf would feel wild and fierce and alive, and sometimes I feel that way. But Aaro—I mean Mask—makes me truly *feel*." She shook her head. "And that's totally ridiculous. My feeling something has no bearing on the truth of it. The truth is, he's dangerous, and I don't trust him."

Willow laughed softly, standing up and rubbing her arms against the cold. I shall tell you what *I* feel. I feel that the temperature must be dropping. The moon is getting low, and there is someone else who wishes to speak with you tonight."

"What?" Rowan dropped her feet to the ground and half stood, looking around for someone who might have been listening to her spilling out all the tangles of her heart.

"It is only Sorrell," Willow said with another laugh. "I will fetch him."

She left, and in a moment Rowan spotted Sorrell working his way toward her, his form black against the snow under the trees. He stepped out into the clearing carrying a blanket, which he offered to her.

"You've been out here a long time. I thought you might be cold." He took Willow's spot on the bench beside her, and she could feel his stare, even as she avoided it, gazing up once again at the moon. She nodded toward it.

"It's become quite like a friend," she said, keeping her tone glib. "I never considered that one could feel any sort of attachment to a celestial body, but I am quite fond of the moon. It's been a good friend to me for the past three years."

"And I am grateful for it as well," Sorrell replied, his eyes still on her, "for revealing your true beauty."

Impatience stirred in her, and she turned, suddenly wanting to have things settled and done, rather than dance around the obvious yet again. She met Sorrell's gaze. "I wish I could return your feelings, but I don't. You know that, don't you? You and Willow have been the best of friends to me, but I'm going to leave, come spring."

He regarded her for several seconds in silence. Then, "Will you come back?"

"To visit, yes. Always. To live?" She shrugged. "I suppose that will depend on the success of my journeys."

"You would return to your own people,

then, if you can break your curse?"

"Yes. For a while, at least. I have to. You can see that, can't you?"

He nodded slowly, and a sad smile dimpled his cheeks, making him resemble Willow. "I cannot help but cling to my fondest hopes, yet I see the way you act around our guest, this Mask. I do not know what draw a stranger in a mask could have for you, but I see that you feel more for him than you ever have for me, so I must let you go."

"Sorrell, that's not true!" Impulsively, she threw her arms around him and hugged him tight. "I do love you. Just not the way you want. Which has made things awkward, but even still, you are the best of friends. You and Willow have replaced the family I lost." She withdrew, searching his expression in the white moonlight to see what he might be thinking, or if she'd gotten through to him. The Shonnowa were aggravatingly hard to read most of the time. He still wore the same sad smile, though now it reached his eyes.

"Your friendship is a treasure, and we never know what the future may bring." His smile turned teasing. "For now, though, I still cannot find any thoughts of friendship toward Mask, for revealing this disappointment."

Rowan laughed. "No, no, I don't love him either. It's just... surely Willow must have told you...?"

"Yes. He puts you into thoughts of your man. I am sorry that his loss still burdens you so greatly. I only hope one day someone can feel the same about me." He shifted on the bench, and Rowan sensed the change of topic coming before he spoke again. "I have in mind to go to the Shonno-mara and find out what this gift that Mask delivered to them does."

"I see."

He watched her for a moment. "That is all you would say? 'I see?' You don't object then? I thought you might, since you were so adamant that I not go to the Shonno-mara to search for a cure for you."

"That was completely different."

"How?" Sorrell looked aggravated and puzzled.

"Either way, it's dangerous, but going in order to answer a question that could involve the safety of both of our people is completely different than risking everything to break my curse. Certainly we both wanted my curse broken, but for entirely different reasons. It would have been a debt of love, and I had no way to repay it."

Sorrell shook his head. "You would not have had to. But I don't plan to risk a great deal. I am Shonnowan, after all. They do not need to know I'm not one of their own."

"I see."

"And I hoped you might come with me."

"What."

"I have long wished to show you our ancestral home. As a friend to the Shonnowa people. And your—ah—wolf's body has unique and useful traits. We might even learn about breaking curses while we are there. But not if there was extra danger involved." He winked.

"I see." Rowan answered a little easier this time. A grin tugged the corner of her mouth. "Well. Who could refuse an offer like that?"

"We cannot go until the thaw begins. The pass through the mountains will be too treacherous until then. But I hope to make the journey and be back before our guest leaves."

She nodded, finally smiling, though her face fell when she remembered the traps in the woods. "I have to tell you," she started, when the clearing grew suddenly dark, and she felt the tingle of her curse along her skin. She looked up and saw that the moon had gone down behind the trees, and huffed in frustration. "I found traps set around the village today," she said in a rush. "By Talvan soldiers from Silver Rock. King Ormand has put a price on my head, and they are trying to trap me. I'm afraid it could put your people in danger."

That was all she got out before she shifted, and found herself sitting awkwardly on her tail, swallowed up by the blanket that had been draped over her shoulders. She fought her way free with a growl and jumped down.

"I will tell Dinarrel of the men hunting you. We will keep you safe."

Rowan shook her head. It wasn't her own safety she was worried about. What if they set more traps, and a child stepped in one of them? Hopefully someone else would think of that as well. She sighed. She would just have to be more vigilant in the future.

The sound of a twig snapping tugged her ears toward the blackness under the trees across the clearing. What might have been a muffled curse followed. She looked toward the sound, feeling the fur along her spine rise, and saw a wink of light. There and gone.

"What is it?" Sorrell crouched down next to her, following her line of sight. Starlight reflected on the snow, not as bright as the moon, but bright enough to illuminate the clearing with its log benches and fire ring buried under a foot of snow. Another moment and a figure stepped out of the trees, carrying a shaded lantern and a naked sword. Rowan rumbled out a low growl, and the man flinched, dropping into a partial crouch.

Sorrell rested his hand on her head briefly before he stood and called out, "I greet you, stranger. What do you seek?"

The man flinched again, but he straightened up slowly and flashed his lantern three times toward the woods before leaving it uncovered. A signal, Rowan guessed. In a moment she heard more twigs snapping and another man's voice called, "Find something, Fin?"

Fin, who she thought might be the lanky soldier they'd encountered in Silver Rock, called back, "She's here."

"Your people are very rude," Sorrell said in an aside to her as Fin waited for his friends and didn't speak. She snorted. She'd long since ceased thinking of Ormand and his followers as being from the same species, let alone the same nation.

"What do you seek," Sorrell asked again as two other men joined Fin in the clearing. They all shifted uncertainly. Rowan had no doubt they were the same ones who had set the traps, and they were coming back to check on them. Given that, they probably weren't sure what to do with this situation, where she was free and facing them down with a Shonnowan man at her side.

"Give us the wolf," one of the men said. "She's a menace, and our king wants her brought to him alive."

"Alive? Interesting. So you set traps that could have killed her?" Sorrell said. "That doesn't seem wise. And why would your king want a wolf brought to him alive if he merely thought she was a menace?"

They shifted uncomfortably, their lanterns casting ugly shadows across their faces.

"And tell me, please, how she is a menace?" her friend went on. "Has she threatened anyone?"

"Who cares?" Fin said. "The king wants her, so he'll have her. Bring her here."

"Very rude," Sorrell grunted in Shonnowan. To the soldiers he said, "Go home, king's men. The wolf is not mine to give any more than she is yours to take, and you are being offensive. Also, do not set your traps here. They are a danger to my people."

"Or what," Fin sneered. "You'll curse us? Everyone knows you vagabonds are too high and mighty for that."

"What is a vagabond?" Sorrell asked her. She couldn't answer, of course, so he just shrugged. Stepping in front of her, he unfastened his belt—a worn leather one with ornamental tracings of silver on it that he always wore—and pulled it free, holding it in a loose loop in his hands. He jerked it taunt suddenly, a motion that should have produced a loud crack. Instead, *boom!* A shockwave reverberated through the clearing. Rowan, standing mostly behind him, was knocked backward off her feet, her ears ringing, but the soldiers in front of him fared far worse. They were thrown backward, smacking into trees or skidding through the snow before they came to a stop.

Shouts rose from the village, though they sounded muffled to Rowan's shocked ears. By the time the soldiers began to stir, picking themselves off the ground, she and Sorrell had been joined by Dinarrel, Jannen, and several other men, including Mask, who had limped out into the snow in his shirtsleeves and without his crutch.

"Who are they?" Dinarrel asked.

"Soldiers from Silver Rock. They set traps trying to catch Red."

Dinarrel stepped forward, peering at the men. "It is best, I think, if you do not come back here," he said.

The trio of soldiers left, casting dirty looks back before they disappeared into the trees. The Shonnowa stood and watched their lanterns bobbing until they disappeared.

"Set a watch tonight," Dinarrel said to Sorrell as he turned back toward the village.

Sorrell nodded. He caught Rowan's eye and grinned. "You like that? Not a very practical weapon, but it is my favorite."

Rowan nodded dumbly, her ears still ringing. She'd been with the Shonnowa for three years, and they lived so simply that sometimes she forgot they could craft with magic.

* * * * *

During the remaining weeks of winter, Mask continued his silent recovery, staying in Rowan's tiny hut. Occasionally, as his leg grew better, he would wander out hunting, or ice fishing. He always cooked his own meat, seasoning it in the fashion Rowan remembered from home, with the stronger flavors of salt, spicy pepper, garlic, or vinegar, rather than the Shonnowa's typical mild herb flavorings. It made her miss her family. Uncle Lance, Dustan, her father—even aunt Rose Marie haunted her as the smells drifted out of the deerskin doorway, calling her inside, where they would share a silent meal.

Each day she wished she could speak to him, to ask the questions that continued to burn her. But even Willow, with her infectious smile, couldn't pull any more information out of him than they already had, so perhaps Rowan wouldn't have done any better with her voice. Mask seemed to prefer her silent company anyway, over any of the others.

When snow still covered the ground beneath the trees, but the breezes blowing up from the valley smelled of dirt and thaw, Sorrell came into her hut, wrinkling his nose at the smell of pickled rabbit, and announced that it was time for their visit to the Shonno-mara. He cast Mask an accusing glance that neither he nor Rowan could miss.

Rowan—who'd long ago given up trying to eat like a human—finished licking her bowl clean, while Mask looked up sharply from his own dinner.

"I'm going with you."

Chapter 17

"No." Sorrell looked at him like he'd grown a second head.

Mask gave a little shrug of impatience. "You think this information is any less important to me than it is to you? The danger from Ormand's schemes is my people's, not yours."

"You should have considered that before you put an unknown power into enemy hands."

"Next time I've got three arrows in me, with a sword at my throat, maybe I will stop and 'consider' it. In the meantime, I'm going with you."

Sorrell turned to Rowan, stiff with anger. "I don't trust him. He lives for nothing but revenge. Surely I am not the only one reluctant to put my life in his hands." He switched to Shonnowan halfway through his tirade. "Even you can't be so soft toward him that you cannot see the danger of this idea. He may remind you of your husband, but this is *not* the same man."

Rowan huffed an annoyed sigh and scratched in the sandy floor, HIS PEOPLE ARE MY PEOPLE, AND I DO NOT HAVE THE MEANS TO WARN THEM.

"He can wait for us to return, and bring word," Sorrell said, still in Shonnowan.

"I will follow on my own, you know," Mask

interrupted. "Which do you fear more, having me with you, or following where you can't see?"

Sorrell growled and flung aside the deerskin door to stomp outside.

Mask watched him disappear, then went back to eating. When he'd finished he went about packing his saddlebags, pausing when Sorrell came back in a short while later, tossing a set of Shonnowan clothes at him.

"If you come with us you'll need to look like one of us. Your mask covers your face, but keep your hands in your gloves. They are not dark enough. And do not show your guns. Or speak."

Mask nodded. He started unbuttoning his shirt, and Rowan figured it was time to take a walk. She followed Sorrell back out into the evening dusk, sniffing the air for the smells she'd come to find comforting, of cookfires, horses, pine, earth, and people.

"You'll want to see Willow before we go," Sorrell said. He nodded toward the bonfire clearing, though the moon was hidden by clouds that night, and would not allow her to say goodbye to her friend.

She found Willow—and most of the rest of the village—seated on benches around a roaring bonfire, and stopped in surprise. Willow rose and welcomed her into the circle. Unable to ask why they had all gathered, Rowan jumped up on the log bench beside her friend and waited, at their mercy for information.

"We've gathered to bid you farewell," Willow said.

Rowan blinked in surprise, scanning the familiar faces around the fire. A heavy, empty feeling opened up in her gut. No. She wasn't leaving yet. Only going with Sorrell and Mask on a small trip...

Dinarrel stepped forward, his arms folded together with his hands tucked into the sleeves of his deerskin coat, making him look like a wizened little sage. "We think it likely that your friend, Mask as he calls himself, will wish to part with us once he finds what he wishes to know about this medallion from his king. He will not return to us here, and if you wish to travel with him, then you must not plan to return either, until the Almighty directs your steps back to us. So we bid you good-bye now. Well met, Red Wolf."

A murmur of approval from the others in the circle wrapped around Rowan like the warmth from the fire. "Good hunting," some of them called, while others just repeated Dinarrel's words, "Well met, friend."

Dinarrel pulled his hands free from his sleeves, and the crowd grew silent again as he held out what looked like a collar, or a circlet, gleaming with a hint of metallic shine in the firelight. He handed it to Willow, who presented it to Rowan. A slender strip of stiff leather had been fused, by the Shonnowan art, with strands of copper to form a glittering band, from which hung a coin-sized copper pendant. As she looked at it closer, Rowan cocked her head in surprise, for it was crafted in the shape of the D'Araines family seal. Not the seal of the kings, but the modified one that Aaro had used to sign his marriage proposal to her, going on four years ago now.

Again, questions jumbled in her mouth as she looked from Willow to Dinarrel for an explanation. Willow undid the little copper clasp, securing the collar around Rowan's neck, and bringing the subtle thrum of magic to her through her fur.

"Our gift to you," Willow said. "For our parting. Dinarrel and the elders have worked on it for many nights and days, infusing it with Nawassa. If you are hurt, it will heal you. It will remain true to its own form whether you are human or wolf, and, like our friend's mask, it can only be removed by the one wearing it."

"And unlike your incomplete curse," Dinarrel added, "it will work in sunlight, moonlight, or darkness."

Rowan bowed to them. She had so many questions that still burned her tongue, but she did her best to convey her gratitude without words. One by one the Shonnowa filed past her, either bowing, or hugging her, or giving her whiskers a friendly tug—which had somehow become one of their favorite signs of affection toward her. At last the clearing emptied, and only Willow remained.

"I wish so many things this night," she said, sighing as she sat beside Rowan. "I wish that we had been able to break your curse, that you didn't have to leave, or that I could go with you."

Rowan nodded, looking up at the cloud cover that obscured the moon and sighing.

Willow laughed softly. "Yes, and I also wish the moon was out to let us have a conversation this last time."

Rowan shook her head.

"No, no, I didn't mean for the *last* time. But the last time for a long while, almost certainly."

With a nod, Rowan touched the pendant on her new collar—not an easy feat with canine forelegs—and swiveled her ears.

"Ah. You wish to know more about your gift." She reached out and fingered the copper pendant. "The elders layered it with many different facets of Nawassa. As Dinarrel said, it is not limited to light, as are some things. It also will not be used up. It draws the Nawassa from the atmosphere and stores it, so it will always renew itself."

Rowan nodded, but tapped the pendant again.

"Oh I see. You mean the seal?"

She nodded again.

"Sorrell and I discussed it at some length, and hopcd it would be the best choice. Married into the D'Araines family, it is legally *your* seal now, even though Aaro is dead, and it might provide protection, especially with the collar. If people see the collar, they will know you belong with someone, and perhaps they will not fear you so. And if they examine it and see the D'Araines seal, they would not dare harm you. So I hope it will protect you in more ways than just the one."

Rowan nodded. The coin-sized seal nestled in her fur, small and inconspicuous. No one would recognize it unless they were close enough to touch it.

"Your collar is unique, you know," Willow said. "I don't know if there is another like it anywhere. Healing spells are the most difficult and complex to render, and require knowledge of how healing works. Dinarrel has tried many times before to infuse some of my tools with the healing gift, but has never been entirely successful until now. Some of them were only good for a single use, or were too weak to heal completely. Every person at any given time has multiple, little things wrong with them. Whether they are overly weary, or have an issue with their digestion or any number of insignificant things, yet as soon as you touch a healing object, it would right all of those things, as well as trying to mend your more grievous ailment, and it would be too much. Your collar has many, many layers of spells. That is what makes it genius."

Rowan bowed her head. They should not have given her something so priceless. It could have been used for the village. But she had no way of saying so, and her paws were too clumsy to undo the buckle and give it back. Not to mention, that would have been offensive to all of them. She sighed.

"Have no fear," Willow said. "Now that we have perfected the spells, we will make other healing objects, though it will take some time." Her eyes twinkled. "And then I shall be unemployed, and my skill will be unappreciated and will diminish without practice." She laughed. "But I suppose one cannot complain about that."

Rowan leaned her head on Willow's shoulder, lifting a paw in an awkward attempt at a hug. Inwardly she raged that it was the best she could do. A paltry, failed gesture to convey all the gratitude and friendship of almost four years, plus much more. But Willow understood. She wrapped her arms around Rowan's shoulders and shed tears onto her furry head.

* * * * *

Three days later, Rowan peered across a valley in the fading light, dimly making out the shape of mountain cliffs and crevasses, where Sorrell assured them there was a city. It took her a few minutes to realize that the mountain *was* the city. Or some of it, anyway. She looked up at Sorrell, though she couldn't read his expression well in the dark. Even Mask grunted his appreciation of the spectacle.

"Impressive, is it not?" Sorrell said, squatting down on his heels, staring across the dark valley. He took off his glove to blow on his fingers. "This should have been our home as well. It would have been, if we had not been cast out for our convictions."

And do you regret your ancestors' choice? Rowan wanted to ask him. Surely not all the generations of Shonnowan children shared their parents' conviction. But did any of the Shonno-mara ever turn back to the ancient laws of their people?

"We should camp down the ridge tonight," Mask said, turning away as a gust of bitter wind swirled snow around them. He started back down their disappearing trail, leading his horse and gathering fallen branches and sticks as he went.

They had climbed further into the mountains during their three days' ride, and spring still seemed mostly like wishful thinking here. It would be a cold, cold night, even for Rowan. She turned and followed Mask, leaving Sorrell to cast a last, wistful look before he reluctantly followed them.

The two men hadn't said more than two dozen words to each other since they'd left the village, and their obstinate silence grated on Rowan. Nor did she blame one over the other. They were both acting like children, as far as she was concerned.

When they had retreated down the ridge a way, they stopped to set up camp. Sorrell worked on starting a fire, while Mask gathered more wood to put up a small shelter. Rowan, meanwhile, walked a circle around the area, sniffing for danger. She picked up several old scent trails, but nothing within the last few days. The Shonno-mara had a different caste to their scents than the Shonnowa. More earthy, complex with tones of mineral and metal, while her friends from the village typically had more woodsy, herbal nuances to their scents.

She lifted her nose to sniff the air, catching the faraway taint of wood smoke and people. Much nearer to their camp were hints of deer. A pack of wolves had been in the area recently, but so far as she could tell, they hadn't lingered. The only sounds were the trees, creaking and snapping in the cold, the whisper of snowflakes, and occasional clacking of tree branches when the breeze kicked up. It all formed a wild, unforgiving sort of peace. A vast, eternal beauty.

"Do not forget, tomorrow you are a wolf, not a woman," Sorrell said as the three of them sat beside the fire, gnawing on jerky and dehydrated berries. She shook her head and twitched her ears at him, which he must have taken for a shrug, because he said, "Yes, they are more familiar with curses of your kind, but it is still not common. The Shonno-mara chieftains discourage their people from turning each other into animals." He snorted. "A wise tradition, since without being curtailed, they would end up ruling a nation of beasts."

Mask watched their exchange, though Sorrell spoke in Shonnowan, so he couldn't have understood. He left the fire and crawled into his shelter a few minutes later. After a moment of rustling around getting his bedroll situated he said, "There's room for two in here. It's going to be a cold night."

Sorrell sneered, switching languages. "Yes. And a perfect opportunity to put one of those daggers through my ribs."

Rowan rolled her eyes and bobbed her head toward the shelter.

"I don't trust him," Sorrell replied.

They had slept in separate shelters for the past two nights, which Rowan considered a deplorable waste of time and body heat. Tonight would be the coldest night yet, and snow continued to fall, swirling around them in ever increasing intensity.

She got up and padded over to Mask's little tent of tree branches, slinking inside, and after a moment Sorrell followed, grumbling. She spent that night sandwiched between the two of them, listening to first one, then the other, snore, and going over in her mind just exactly how inappropriate this would be if she were still a woman. Eventually she dismissed the concern. There were more fearsome things to stay awake worrying over. Like whether the Shonno-mara would kill them all tomorrow.

* * * * *

The next morning Rowan woke from a fitful dream about woodcutters chasing her, to a cavern of white. Snow had piled up around their shelter, encasing them in a blue-white bubble. Sorrell was still snoring, and Mask had somehow rolled so that he was practically hugging her from behind, with one of his arms draped over her shoulder, his curled-up knees cuddled against her tail, and his breath tickling her ear fur. She froze.

He sighed in his sleep and his arm tightened, snuggling her closer with the ghost of a whisper. "So sorry, my love."

Rowan lay there for one blistering moment, wondering who his love was, but then mortification sent her catapulting out of the tent, scrambling over top of Sorrell, who grunted awake, and out into the open. A bitter wind raked through her fur, chasing away the flush of embarrassment. Sorrell crawled out after her, grumbling, and a moment later Mask followed. He leaned against a tree and fished a wolf hair out of his mouth. Rowan gulped and looked away.

It was near noon by the time they hiked down into the valley and began the climb back up the far side. Last night's snow made the footing treacherous, and she wondered if they would not have been better off waiting several more weeks. Eventually they made it to ground though, picking their way across a river spanned only by a single, dilapidated wooden bridge. The hackles rose along her neck as they passed abandoned stone and log buildings in the valley. While the air was already drenched with the smells of the city, these outlying buildings obviously hadn't been used in decades. Maybe centuries. She could smell Sorrell's mounting tension as they picked their way through the ruins.

"Our brothers allow their city to crumble with disregard, while we wander in the wilderness, without a home."

Rowan thought that was a bit unfair. After all, what was stopping the Shonnowa outcasts from building their own city? But then she got a sight of the city proper. She stopped and stared.

"You may be the first of the king's people to ever see the hidden city and still live," Sorrell said, glancing between her and Mask.

Hidden wasn't the word Rowan would have used, although in a way it was hidden—in plain sight. The mountain itself was the city. Walls, ramparts, towers and bridges had all been chiseled into the mountain's rocky face, artfully blended with the contours of the natural stone. Up and up it climbed—level upon level. Rowan's mouth filled with questions she couldn't voice. Above all she wanted to know *how?*

Mask didn't seem inclined to ask questions for her, but after several moments Sorrell spoke in Talvan so both of them could understand.

"Hendella was the capitol of the Shonnowa nation a thousand years ago. There were three mountain cities in the north, and towns across the plains. Our nation was great once, before we divided. The Whonollo in the south were also our people, but they separated from us even before the Shonno-mara broke the ancient laws. And now your people occupy our towns on the plains, and soon, possibly, these cities as well, if your king's ambition is not checked."

He ceased speaking as they passed under a towering archway, pitted with age and spotted with moss. They entered the mountain, and were hailed by two guards that stepped out of the shadows, bows drawn and trained on them.

"What's your business?" They asked in Shonnowan, eyeing Rowan and Mask by turns.

Sorrell performed an exaggerated bow, twisting his words to mimic their accent. "Friends!" He swept his hands out to include them in a gesture of welcome, even though he was the stranger, not they. "We are most honored to set foot in our ancient home! I have recently come from travelling among the king's men, seeking news and learning their ways. My friend and I seek shelter until this cursed snow ceases, when we can return to Tennorra."

"What do you want with a wolf, and why does your friend wear a mask?"

"A beautiful creature, is she not? I acquired her from one of our weaker cousins, who did not appreciate her true value." He lowered his voice conspiratorially. "In truth, I think there may be value of another kind in this beast, but I assure you, she's no danger."

"And your silent friend?"

Sorrell shrugged, all but dismissing Mask. "An assassin. His skills are valuable to the clumsy king's men. He has no professional business here, but he's become so used to silence I believe he's forgotten how to speak." He elbowed Mask in the ribs, and was rewarded with a grunt.

Rowan nearly choked on a snort.

"Keep that wolf contained," the guards warned as they lowered their weapons.

"But of course! She's a perfect lady." Sorrell grinned as he sauntered past them. Mask, for his part, glanced at each of them as he passed, and remained silent. He could not have understood the conversation, yet acted in keeping with the explanation given, and Rowan took a second to appreciate Sorrell's brilliance at telling them what was mostly the truth.

A wide staircase of shallow stone steps led them into the mountain, and into the city proper. They trudged up the grand staircase into a great, cavernous marketplace, then out again into the sunlight, where houses of stone and wood, fused together by Nawassa, lined a flagstone road. Side streets wove in and out of the inside of the mountain. Another broad, winding staircase brought them to the second level, where again, the city spread half inside and half outside the mountain.

The city's second level had another cavernous marketplace, where Sorrell paused beside one of the great bonfires that they must keep burning continuously throughout the winter. Smoke drifted up and swirled around the stalactite-bedecked ceiling, a hundred feet above, where vent shafts had been carved to let it out. A dozen or more of the Shonno-mara formed a circled around the fire, watching them with suspicious glances and whispers.

Rowan sat beside Sorrell, glancing at the milling crowd. Stone pillars, sculpted like giant oak trees, held lanterns in their cold, stony branches. She looked around with equal parts awe and trepidation. She'd never imagined the Shonno-maran city to be an actual *city*. They were only on the second level, and it spread out above, below, and around them like a massive anthill.

"Where'd you find a beast like that?" someone said.

Sorrell dropped his hand to Rowan's head, scratching behind her ears. "I liberated her from one of our weaker cousins." He gave the man an acidic laugh.

"How much for her?" The man asked, his glance shifting between Sorrell and Mask, unsure whom he should address. His glance turned wary as he took in the leather and silver mask.

Rowan studied the man, twitching her ears. He looked like the Shonnowa from her village, yet he didn't. There was something off about him, and the others too, she realized. Though she couldn't pinpoint what it was exactly. An air, perhaps. He wore callous disregard like a coat, but she sensed a hidden savagery in him as well, and it made her cringe.

Instead of immediately refusing, Sorrell shrugged, scratching the dark stubble on his chin. "I hadn't thought of selling her right away—though I might be persuaded. In truth, I wonder if she is not more than an ordinary wolf. It would be rich if our cousins, after all these millennia, turned to cursing their own." He snorted.

The man looked at Red with new appreciation. "She can't understand us, can she?"

"No, although she does have a remarkable intelligence. If she is indeed cursed, then whoever did it must have been a true master. I hoped to find him and hire him myself, which is why I am reluctant to sell her.

Rowan had to work hard not to pin her ears back when the man reached a hand toward her. She backed off, growling. Several people scurried away from the bonfire. But Sorrell just grated out another of his fake laughs. "She's not the friendly sort, but she is quite loyal, once she warms up to you."

"I'll give you silver."

"Talvan currency?" Sorrell said, drawing his brows together.

"Straight from Skybreak. Where have you been, that you haven't heard of the new negotiations with their King Ormand?"

"Eh. Travelling," Sorrell replied, glancing at Rowan and Mask. "I've had no news since the summer."

The man nodded, his eyes flickering away from Rowan only for a moment. "Their king sent a caravan with silver, cloths, and mirrors."

"And what did he require in return?"

The man shrugged. "It is rumor only. They say he wanted a tutor, that he wishes to learn our craft."

Shock turned Rowan's world dark for an instant as her heartbeat exploded in her chest. Ormand with magic? Almighty help them. But that would mean that he no longer had Rigall under his thumb, wouldn't it? Had he defied Ormand and been killed? Or released, as the king promised? Or was Ormand simply greedy for more power than his pet magician could give him?

Sorrell threw his head back and laughed, the sound jarring her out of her panicked thoughts. "That is indeed rich. And how did all of this come about?" he asked.

"A token. Scrying stones, such as we have been seeking to achieve for years. He and the Chieftain are able to communicate directly, as well as our other leaders." The man shifted impatiently, his frown growing into a scowl. "What of your price, stranger? I have not all day to discuss gossip."

Sorrell nodded and grinned, though Rowan could see it was forced. "My apologies. Your hints at this news took me by surprise. But for the price of the wolf—alas! I do not think I could part with her for silver. As I said, I am seeking a skilled Nawassa craftsman myself..."

"Gold then," the man snapped, fumbling in his pockets.

Sorrell shook his head. "I don't know..."

He was interrupted by a shout from the crowd. The three of them tensed, searching the throng. People were already beginning to scatter as several men shoved their way toward the bonfire. "Kingsman!" one of them shouted again, pointing at Mask. "Grab the man in the mask!"

Chapter 18

Mask's lips pressed flat, and in the next fraction of a second he had his gun in hand, and the bellow of it filled the enormous cavern. One of the men running toward them stumbled, a red stain spreading over his heart. His companion went down next, the bullet tearing through his neck. But the damage had already been done. The man Sorrell had been talking to whipped out a sword while the crowd screamed and scattered, some running away, some running toward them.

Sorrell pulled his twin knives in time to block the sword, and Mask shot two more men before they could join the fight. He never missed. Even with his sharpshooting though, they were nearly surrounded within moments. Mask emptied his gun and shoved it back into his belt. The other, she knew, he'd hidden inside his coat, out of sight, but also out of easy reach. He pulled one of his twin daggers, going back-to-back with Sorrell, but everything after that she only caught in flashes as the fight reached her, and she dodged someone's sword.

Another instant of panic nearly blinded her as several men came at her at once. She'd never killed anyone before, let alone with her teeth. She'd ripped the throats out of animals, and hated the feel of hot blood flowing in her mouth, sticking her prey's fur to her tongue. But now it was fight or die—or lose her friends.

She leaped straight into the air as a blade whistled underneath her. Before her opponent could recover she launched herself at his face, claws ripping down his forehead and cheeks, over his eyes. He screamed, dropping the sword, hands going to his slashed eyelid. Another two came for her. She ducked and dodged weapons, biting the back of someone's leg, crippling them, breaking another's arm in her jaws, which was appallingly easy.

Out of nowhere a curling whip snapped across her shoulder, and she yelped. It must have been infused with the Nawassa, for it glowed red, sending out sparks as it struck. She felt the searing burn, then the instant tingle of magic coalescing around the wound, beginning to heal it even as she leaped over the hissing whip toward the man wielding it, driving him back by sheer force, grabbing onto his arm and shaking him like a puppy. She'd had no idea she had the strength for such a thing.

Then, above the blood thundering in her ears she heard Sorrell shouting, and got a glimpse of him and Mask fighting their way toward the merchant's stands, and beyond them, toward the houses built inside the mountain. She plowed over another Shonno-maran and ran after them, aware without consciously taking note that arrows had begun to fly. One hit the ground at her feet and skidded along the floor. She leapt over it.

As she reached them, Sorrell and Mask settled the last man near them, gaining a break from the steadily growing mob. They turned and ran, with Rowan on their heels. An arrow stuck in Sorrell's thick leather coat collar, half an inch from his neck. Mask, meanwhile, had got his daggers back onto his belt as they ran, and dragged his other gun out of its inner pocket. He ran with it in hand, and when they ducked around a corner, he paused and took out three of their pursuers with three shots.

Sorrell touched his shockwave-creating belt, his face scrunched for a moment as he looked up at the distant cavern ceiling with its stalactites. He must have thought better of using it inside the mountain. When Mask quit shooting they ran again, continuing their mad dash until the huge cavern with its stone huts and gardens of stalagmites began to run out. First they passed more pillars, elongated along their bases so that they formed dividers between the roads, then in another moment they entered a broad, open tunnel with more buildings carved out of stone on each side. They must have passed a stable at some point, because Rowan was overwhelmed by the scent of horses, hay, and dung. They kept running, and at the first opportunity turned off, following a smaller road. Then another. Sounds of pursuit faded, along with the shouts and screams of the wounded they'd left in their wake.

Finally they got onto a narrow road between buildings that led away, deeper into the mountain, becoming a tunnel, claustrophobic and only dimly lit. For the first time, Rowan noticed that instead of torches, the road was lined with phosphorescence. Glowing patterns had been painted onto the walls, either some sort of phosphorescent plant-based paint, or else infused with Nawassa to keep the way eternally lit. She could still feel the tingling magic healing her shoulder, numbing it as the muscle and fur knit back together.

Sorrell stopped and leaned against the glowing wall, swearing softy in Shonnowan as he plucked the arrow out of his collar. He switched languages to ask, "Everyone alright?"

"Yeah." Mask's voice sounded harsh and angry in the stillness.

"Red?"

She let out a shaking sigh and nodded. Her legs felt like water, her muscles trembling and threatening to dump her on the floor, while she became aware suddenly of the taste of blood in her mouth. Revulsion shook her, and she heaved, turning away to throw up by the wall. Her mouth tasted sour afterward, but it was better than the blood. Neither of the men said anything.

Still hacking and scraping her tongue against her teeth, Rowan put her nose to the ground and went down the tunnel a bit. The smell of horse manure pervaded, wafting on the air rising from the ground, though they'd passed the stables long ago. She sat down on her haunches, head cocked to one side in thought.

Mask joined her, squatting on his heels, and she noticed his scent had grown stronger, laced with fear and blood, though not his own blood this time.

"What do you smell?" he asked.

But she had no way to tell him. Only a hunch that could be completely wrong. Any turn could bring them back to the growing manhunt they'd left behind. She cast them an anxious look.

"Go on," Sorrell said. "We'll follow."

They tailed her down the tunnel as she tracked the smell of dung through the mountain. The path stayed level, eventually branching off several times. She stuck with the scent trail, and it didn't disappoint. In a few minutes, she could also smell fresh air and pine. A cold draft brushed her whiskers.

"*Darsaw!*" Sorrell exclaimed as they stepped out onto a ledge on the side of the mountain. "You've led us out! Good woman."

A narrow path, not much more than a goat trail covered in snow, wound down the hillside, along the edge of a gorge, till it disappeared between boulders. At their feet they saw evidence of what Rowan had smelled—cartloads of horse manure dumped over the side of the cliff, some of it staining the ground at their feet.

"Did you get any information at all?" Mask asked as they picked their way down the path, reminding Rowan that he hadn't understood any of Sorrell's conversation with the Shonno-maran man who'd wanted to buy her. Sorrell related the gist of it, and Mask grunted, which was his general response to everything. "So this means they can communicate over any amount of distance without travel?"

"So it would seem," Sorrell sounded bitter, now that he'd dropped his act. "A dangerous tool."

"A powerful one," Mask agreed.

"Perhaps not as dangerous as your king, if he learns our ways of using the Nawassa. What would he want with such a thing? He already has one of the Shonno-mara to do his bidding."

Mask shrugged, though the gesture was lost on Sorrell, who walked in front and wasn't watching. He'd become preoccupied enough that he'd forgotten to worry about Mask putting a dagger through his ribs.

After another moment of scrambling down the snowy path, Mask said, "Ormand doesn't like to rely on other people. Either he sees them as incompetent, or he doesn't trust them. Usually both. As much power as he can hold in his own two hands, he will."

Sorrell swore. "He's seeking to become a Wielder, then. He is a fool."

"A Wielder? What's that?"

The Shonnowan man shook his head. "He is a fool. Any man or woman who gives themselves to the Nawassa becomes its slave."

"What are you saying?" Mask's voice had a flat edge.

"Nothing. Go back and warn your people. But it will do no good. We will not welcome them in our mountains, when they flee. Unless you kill this king of yours before his plans are full, you will be lost."

"What do you mean?" he demanded. When Sorrell made no reply, he turned to Rowan, even though she couldn't speak. "What is he saying?"

The only answer she could give was to look up at him and let the fear shine through her eyes. Almighty help them, if Ormand became a sorcerer.

"And what of you?" Sorrell asked. "Why did they recognize you?"

Mask huffed through his nose, but he answered anyway. "The man was one of the ones who attacked me that night. He recognized the mask."

Sorrell grumbled softly. Rowan could almost read his thoughts. That Mask had put them in danger by insisting on coming along. Thankfully, though, neither of them said anything more until they were off the mountain and hiking back to where they'd left the horses and supplies.

"They will search for us, even out here," Sorrell said as the two men packed their gear. "And they will not be loud when they do it, as your own people so foolishly are, so you will not hear them coming. This is where we part ways." He tied the last of his supplies to the light Shonnowan saddle before he added, "And if they do find either of us, they will bring more than swords and bows."

"More magic weapons?" Mask said.

Sorrell nodded.

"Why weren't there more of those in the city? Only the one with the whip seemed to have any special power. I expected worse."

"Do *you* carry your best enchanted weapons to the market on any given day?" Sorrell asked, raising an eyebrow.

"Uh..." Mask exchanged a look with Rowan.

"Contrary to what you seem to believe about us, not every Shonnowan or Shonno-maran can craft the Nawassa. It is a fine art, and even those who have a natural talent for it also need the creativity to make it do anything useful, and the time to practice. Enchanted items are costly, even for us. So no, of course most people don't carry them around every day. Not to worry though, if they catch you, you will get a fine display of what we can do."

He knelt down, eye-to-eye with Rowan,

and switched to Shonnowan, glancing at Mask, who stood watching them. "Please, be careful. Do not trust this man, even though you travel with him."

She nodded, putting a paw on her friend's shoulder.

Sorrell surprised her by wrapping his arms around her shoulders, like Willow had done, and squeezing her close for a moment. Her whiskers brushed his ear as she leaned her head into his neck, wishing she could say goodbye, but glad that she didn't have to find the words. She would have cried, and she hated crying even more than she hated blushing.

He released her, swinging onto his horse. "Ride fast and be silent," he warned Mask. "Ride through the night. They will track us both, but they have to find our tracks first. We are ahead of them for now, and they cannot follow our trails during the night."

"How far will they go?" Mask asked.

Sorrell shrugged. "It depends on how dangerous they think you are to them." With that he clicked his tongue, turning his horse.

Rowan watched him go, her heart sinking. Almost, she ran after him. But Mask mounted up as well, drawing her attention. He looked down at her from his perch in the saddle.

"You should not have stayed with me," he said.

* * * * *

Aaro sat on his horse and stared down at the wolf for a full minute, expecting her to take off after Sorrell. But she didn't. Finally, with a growl, he turned the horse and urged it south, down the slope and away from the Shonno-maran city. Red loped along beside him, her ears swiveling constantly, lifting her nose at times to sniff the wind.

She should not be here.

They fled south, the only sound the rushing of wind past his mask, and the steady, slushy footfalls of the horse as he alternated walking and trotting, landscape permitting.

There were no roads in this wilderness—at least none that he'd dare to follow now. Red corrected their path at times, either giving one of her short barks, or speeding off in a different direction. The part that bothered him about it was that he trusted her, implicitly.

They rested several times during the day, though never for long. Darkness came on, and still he kept going, even though the land in front of him dimmed to black shapes against the blackness, making it dangerous to ride. Finally he got off the horse and walked, leading it.

"Of all the nights not to have a moon," he grumbled. He could just hear the faint crunch of Red's paws in the icy snow up ahead, but could see little more than a shadow as she guided him.

She huffed and snorted at his words, though it was hard to tell the difference sometimes, between when she snorted and when she sneezed. Either way, he got the distinct impression that she disapproved, though he couldn't fathom why. If there had been even a partial moon visible, he'd be able to ride, putting that much more distance between them and the Shonno-mara. But the sky remained overcast.

"You should have gone with your friend," he said after a while, to break up the monotony of crunching snow and creaking trees.

Naturally, she didn't reply.

"What did your friend tell you before he left? Did he say not to trust me?" He saw a faint gleam from her eyes as she turned her head to regard him for a moment as they walked. "You should listen to him. You can't trust me. Go back to your people, Red."

She sighed, but the soft sound of her footsteps went on. At some point, the overcast sky cleared enough to reveal stars through the canopy of trees. By their faint light he could see the wolf's silhouette in front of him, and could make out more clearly the bushes and branches he'd been stumbling over and brushing against for so many hours.

"You know Ormand has a bounty on your head," he told her when he needed another distraction from his weariness. She glanced back at him again, and he thought he saw the starlight gleam on her fangs. "I don't care about the money, but I'm going back to Ormand. I'm going to kill him, one way or another, and if turning you over to him gives me a chance to do it, I will."

His boot struck another rock, and he stumbled to his knees, still clinging to his horse's reins as it halted beside him. He stayed there for a moment, weary enough not to want to get up. Red crunched back to him, extending her cold, wet nose to snuff at his face. He put a gloved hand on her head, stroking back one of her ears. Her eyes gleamed. Probably she could see him much better than he could see her. The thought, along with the cold that worked its way through his clothes, chilling his sweat, made him shiver.

Eye-to-eye in the starlight, he said, "I don't want to betray you, but if you're with me, I will. Go home, Red."

Red's head beneath his hand gave a small, decisive shake *no*.

"Fool."

He stood and tugged his bedroll from behind the saddle. If he needed rest, then so did Red and the horse. Dawn was only an hour away, and then he'd be back riding. He opened the small sack of grain he'd brought for the horse and let him finish off what was left, then settled down on a cleared-off patch of ground with his blankets wrapped around his shoulders to wait for dawn.

Red curled up beside him, lending her warmth, as she always did.

"Fool," he murmured again as he dozed. His head fell against her flank, her soft fur tickling his lips. But he was too far asleep to care.

He woke up, he found himself curled on his side in a cocoon of blankets, his head still pillowed on Red's shoulder. She'd partially rolled over, and he faced toward her head, where he could see one ear and half her whiskers twitching as she slept. For a moment, before he woke fully, he wondered what she had looked like as a woman.

They had stopped, as it turned out, at the edge of a small clearing in a valley. A brook, overflowing with melting snow, rushed nearby, and the horse, who had wandered a little way off, had found a patch of last year's tall, brown grass to eat.

He shifted to sit up, and Red tensed, instantly awake. Her nose quivered, while her ears swiveled in every direction. She must not have sensed any danger, because she relaxed after a few seconds, stretching and yawning.

He watched her, angry at the pang of fondness he felt when she looked up at him with her copper-amber eyes. "Go home, Red."

She gave him one of her sneeze/snorts and stretched again. When she had settled, she reached out and wrote in the muddy snow, ORMAND TOOK MY HOME.

Aaro sat back on his heels, startled. After his months with her and the Shonnowa, it was the most information she'd ever given him.

She swiped out the words, muddying her

paw, and wrote again, I HOPED THE SHONNOWA COULD HELP ME. Swipe. THEY COULD NOT. Swipe. I MUST SEEK ELSEWHERE. She regarded him, her expression unreadable.

Before they left, Willow had spoken to him about guarding Red and being her voice. Her words had seemed cryptic, and made him uncomfortable, and he'd done his best to be angry and show her just what a bad idea that was, but she had been unmoved. As though she could see past his façade of brooding anger and silence, down to the place where he knew that in order to go on being a monster, he had to push them all away. But she couldn't see beyond that, deeper still, where he kept the rage of his burned home and murdered wife. That rage would drive him to commit any treachery, any atrocity he had to, to make sure Ormand died.

Now Willow's words made more sense. Red wanted him to help her search. But for what? To a cure to turn her back into a woman? He shook his head.

"You're better off being a wolf," he said. "You know that? Whatever, or whoever, you were before, you should just let it go. Go back to your friends. Coming with me will only get you killed or caged."

She rumbled a low growl.

"Doesn't matter," he said, as if replying to his conscience, rather than to her. "You saved my

life, but my life's only good for one more thing.
I'll give my last breath to make sure Ormand
gives up his, if I have to. No obligation or loyalty
is going to stop me."

Red rolled her eyes, scratching in the mud,
KILL ORMAND, THEN JOIN THE THEATRE.
YOU HAVE A GIFT FOR DRAMA.

He stared at her for a minute, then broke
out in a laugh that took him completely by
surprise. "I hate the theatre." He sobered,
meeting her eyes again. "Red, I'm going to warn
you for the last time. I don't want to hurt you, but
I will. If you're with me, I'll use you."

She nodded and wrote, I UNDERSTAND,
then took off into the trees. For a moment, Aaro
thought she'd actually decided to go back to the
Shonnowa, and was surprised by the sudden
hollow feeling that opened up in his chest.

But then she reappeared, nose to the
ground, and circled the clearing. When she came
back and sat down next to him, head cocked to
one side he asked, "Smell anything interesting?"

She shook her head no.

"Let's go then." He tossed her a strip of
jerky, which she caught with a snap and a dirty
look in his direction, then stood, checking his
horse over quickly before he swung into the
saddle. He would owe the animal a decent meal
and a rest once they got back to civilization.
Though if he succeeded in killing Ormand, they
probably wouldn't get to rest until they were

dead. For now, he wanted to put more distance between them and the Shonno-maran city. He had no desire to repeat his last encounter with them in the wilderness, when he'd never heard them coming. Though he hadn't had Red with him then.

* * * * *

Three more days without any signs of pursuit brought them out of the mountains and endless, dripping pine forests, and onto the plains, where spring was getting underway in earnest. Aaro slowed their pace, letting his horse crop at the new grass as he rode. He lifted his hat and let the wind ruffle his hair and tease the edges of his mask. The temptation to take it off as well nagged at him, as it usually did, when the wind was in his face as he rode, and for a moment he imagined throwing it away, forgetting his mission, and riding just for the love of it. He squashed the thought. Another four days would bring them to Skybreak. After Ormand was dead, if Aaro wasn't as well, then he would think about what came next.

He glanced down at Red, who was looking over her shoulder to the line of trees they'd left some time ago, her ears perked.

"What's back there?" he asked.

She shook her head, though a line of fur along her spine lifted into a ridge.

"Animal or human?" He asked.

She looked up at him, then back at the

distant forest. Her ridge of fur settled, and she started walking again, only casting occasional glances over her shoulder. Aaro followed her, looking back often now himself. Call him coward, but the back of his neck crawled, and the healed wound in his leg gave him a twinge.

"Wind is from the south," he muttered.

Red looked up at him and nodded. With the wind in their faces, she would never be able to scent someone following them.

That night they took turns keeping watch, though Aaro did most of the sleeping, and Red did most of the watching. Whatever she might have been before, she seemed to have a canine ability to run on naps, and listen while she slept. After three months together, he was just now beginning to realize how valuable a friend he'd found.

Another day passed, then a third, still without incident, and Aaro began to relax again. I would be difficult, even for the Shonno-mara, to sneak up on them on the open prairie. Not that there weren't hidden gullies and folds in the land, but it would be much more difficult now than when they'd travelled through the mountains. And tomorrow they should reach Skybreak.

They made camp that third day as darkness eased across the plains, the light leaking out of the sky and leaving endless stars in its absence, reminding Aaro that he'd missed the open places. The wind, the endless sky. Again, he pushed aside thoughts of riding free.

He had gathered a meager bundle of firewood that day as they travelled past little hidden valleys with trees and low bushes. As soon as they stopped, he set about building the first fire they'd had since before they entered the mountain city.

Red gave him a dubious look as he struck flint.

"Now what's your problem? Can't a man want a hot cup of coffee while he's on the trail?"

The fire didn't light, so he sent another shower of sparks onto the handful of dead grass he'd been hauling around all day so it would dry out.

Of course she didn't say anything, just looked at him blandly then looked around at the deepening dusk. He followed her glance, and saw nothing out of place. The horse, its reins dangling, nipped at the grass a few yards away, while in the distance he could hear the rush of a river, swollen with melted snow.

After another scant meal that he shared with the wolf, he unrolled his bed and crawled in, trusting Red to watch and listen, and wake him if needed. She curled up at his back with her nose in her tail, her ears perked as she watched the night beyond the flames of the campfire. He drifted toward sleep, and at first her low growl wove itself into his dream, where he stood on the edge of a cliff, and the rocks shifted and rolled under him as he tried to scramble back from the edge. In the dream, he slid out over the cliff's edge and fell into darkness.

He startled awake.

Chapter 19

The campfire had burned down, the last of the flames flickering bright orange, and at his back, Red rumbled her low growl. He twisted enough to see her in the flickering firelight, her hackles up, looking out to the side, into the darkness.

Aaro eased his hand toward his gun belt without otherwise moving, and Red rose to her feet with such slow grace she didn't appear to move either. Again, he cursed the useless sliver of moon that did nothing to light their camp. The smooth wood of his pistol grip filled his hand, and he drew it towards himself, bringing the belt with it. He eased the belt around his waist and sat waiting, his eyes going back and forth between Red and the place beyond the fire that held her attention.

He felt rather than saw Red crouch. The second seemed to drag out for an hour as she watched what his eyes couldn't see, and then she pounced on the fire, scattering embers and snuffing the dying flames. At almost the same second he heard the rushing whistle of an arrow, and felt a tug on his sleeve. He threw himself to the side and both felt and heard another arrow pass so close to his head that the fletching stung his ear. He kept rolling, putting distance between himself and the place he'd lain, where they had no doubt been able to see him by the dying firelight.

Laying on his belly several yards from where they'd shot at him, he waited for his eyes to adjust to the starlight, and wondered where Red had gotten off to. He switched gun hands long enough to wipe his palm on his shirt. Across camp, he caught a shadow of movement and raised the gun, drawing back the hammer and straining to see the shape he thought had been creeping toward him.

He jumped and nearly dropped the gun when someone shrieked not ten yards away. Red gave a short bark, followed by another scream from someone else. Then, to his side, he saw a shadow rise out of the dead grass. He turned, bringing his gun to bear, when a flicker of movement turned from a shadow to a fiery flash of light. He had a half second to register the thin line of the fiery whip blurring toward him, when the end of it caught around his wrist and yanked back, pulling him forward while his gun few out of his hand. He drew and fired his left-hand gun with the whip still curled around his other wrist, burning through his coat and shirt sleeves and into his skin. The whip loosened as its wielder let go and dropped to his knees. Aaro shook the coil off and slapped his flaming sleeve, wincing.

He turned his attention back to the commotion that he couldn't quite make out across the campsite as another arrow impaled the grass a few feet away. The instant it struck the grass, it burst into dazzling white light without flames. Aaro blinked and half threw a hand up to guard his eyes, when another arrow landed and illuminated a few yards off to his other side, casting him in glaring light and static electricity that made his hair stand up. He dove backward out of the light a second before lightning arced between the two shining arrows, the instant crash of thunder throwing him off his feet.

He rolled to a stop, stunned. A few seconds passed before he lifted his head off the ground, trying to shake the ringing out of his ears. He peered over the tall prairie grass and saw that the arrows were still glowing, though not as brightly. If he hadn't been all but blinded a second ago, he probably would have been able to see the whole area surrounding his camp by their light.

"What *was* that?" he muttered.

One of the Shonno-mara, their attackers, stepped into the light. He struck Aaro instantly as being different than any other Shonnowan or Shonno-maran he'd ever seen. Not in appearance. But he moved like a tiger, and the air rippled around him. He pinned Aaro with his gaze, then he began to move, dancing in the eerie light of the magic arrows. A low hum filled the air, undulating and rippling like light shining through running water. It took Aaro a full second to realize the Shonno-maran was singing, because it didn't sound like any noise that should come out of a human throat. The air felt like it was thickening, pulling toward the Shonno-maran. Aaro tried to get up, to run, even crawl backward, but moving felt like trying to swim through molasses. Or quicksand. Another figure stepped out of the shadows, his teeth flashing white as he grinned. His sword reflected the white light. Aaro couldn't move.

Then, out of the darkness, Red howled.

* * * * *

Rowan had been uneasy since they left the forest behind, which made no sense at all, because they were far less likely to be attacked in the open, and the closer they got to Skybreak, the less their chances that the Shonno-mara would catch up. Mask must have thought so too when he lit his campfire, but it still made her nervous for some reason. She hadn't seen, heard, or smelled anything since they left Hendella, the Shonno-maran capital, but she felt watched.

Then the night went silent. That was what warned her. No night should be without noise, but it all died away, and she felt the change in the air. The subtle movement of Nawassa.

Almighty protect us! They have a sorcerer! Her mind shrieked at her.

She jumped on the dying fire, scattering it, blotting out the soft light and temporarily scorching her paws. Then she ran. As unnaturally silent as the night, she shot out of the gloom and prairie grass and leaped at one of their attackers. The man had no idea what hit him as her jaws closed over his arm, and his bone gave out with a snap she could feel through the muscle. Blood poured over her tongue, hot and coppery. She let go as he screamed, gagging on his blood. One of them was pulling his bow back, aimed at Mask. She barked to get his attention, then hurtled into his chest. More bones snapped. Another scream. She leapt over him and kept moving.

Their attackers were spread out in a circle. She had no idea how many there were, but she had three of them on the ground clutching broken limbs when the first Nawassa-infused arrow struck the ground and lit up. The second one exploded with light, nearly blinding her night vision, and she could feel the zing of electricity gathering in the air. She crouched in the grass and watched as Mask threw himself backward, out from between the two arrows a bare second before lightning jumped between them. The explosion an instant later plastered her whiskers against her face and rocked her back onto her rump.

It must not have done their enemies any favors either, because none of them moved for several seconds. Then the sorcerer stepped into the light. He started his fluid dance, summoning the Nawassa, and Rowan's stomach bottomed-out. Even with his attention focused on Mask she could feel the tug of the Nawassa, pulling toward him, ready to obey his command. She sank even further into the grass, terrified. She had to stop him...

The blade came out of nowhere and buried itself in her shoulder. Fierce, unnatural pain ripped through her, blotting out her sight, clawing at her heart, lighting her veins on fire. For one choking second she endured, waiting for her collar to heal her. Nothing happened. She howled. It started as a scream, and ended in an eerie wail.

The Nawassa shattered.

The night snapped back into place as though it had been warped, twisted with the sorcerers will, and then wrenched away from him. Her eyes popped opened and she saw that he had stopped his dance. His throaty song strangled out, and he rocked back on his feet. At the same time, her collar tingled, and its magic raced through her, wiping the pain away so fast her breath caught. The knife popped out of her healing shoulder like it had been pushed.

Someone let out a surprised curse in Shonnowan, and another throwing knife zinged toward her. She flinched away, and it just nicked her ear, again bringing a flood of unnatural pain. But this time it receded almost instantly.

The sorcerer turned toward her, his eyes glowing silvery. He stamped his foot and raised his arms, preparing to regather the Nawassa that had been ripped out of his control. The healing tingle went out of Rowan's collar. As if they were in a macabre game of tug-of-war, with the gathered Nawassa pulled between the sorcerer's command and her collar's demand to recharge itself. The atmosphere warped.

A sudden memory whispered to her, of Ormand's magician, Rigall, explaining to her as he prepared her curse. *"This next part involves drawing the Gift out of the air, and sound is one of the things I'll be using. You may think it's a good idea to make some noise of your own to disrupt things..."*

She lifted her nose and howled again.

The sorcerer almost toppled backward, his shock staring at her out of his glowing eyes. Then his head exploded.

* * * * *

Aaro's gunshot cracked across the prairie, leaving silence in its wake. Red stopped howling. The Shonno-maran sorcerer crumpled, and the swordsman who'd been about to run him through lunged.

Aaro, still panting from the release of the spell, jumped back, pulling one of the daggers from his belt and using it to catch the next swipe of the sword. It held for a moment, then there was a sudden release of pressure. The sword continued its arc, narrowly missing Aaro's neck as he stumbled forward, off balance. He still held the dagger hilt, but the blade was gone. Belatedly, he thought of Sorrell's warning about enchanted weapons as he ducked another swipe. He backed up a few more steps, and tripped over the sorcerer's body, sprawling on the ground. From there he finally got his gun up and shot the swordsman. The man stumbled and kept coming, so he shot him again. This time he fell.

Aaro stood back up slowly, half expecting either the swordsman or the sorcerer to get back up and trap him with another spell. He shuddered.

A snarling yelp made him jump. He snapped his gaze from the fallen sorcerer to the shadowy form of Red struggling against another of their attackers. He jammed his gun back into the holster and drew his remaining dagger, grabbing the man from behind, twisting him away from Red before he stabbed him through the heart.

"Was that all of them?" his voice sounded harsh.

Red sniffed the air, turning in a circle to survey their destroyed campsite. Somewhere someone moaned. Aaro followed the sound and put the man out of his misery with a bullet through the head. He moved on and did the same thing with the rest, making sure none of them remained alive to stab him in the back.

The red wolf, who was also a woman, watched him for a moment, then slunk away and retched.

When the night was finally quiet, Aaro examined his destroyed dagger by the light of the still-glowing enchanted arrows, and saw that the blade had been melted clean off it. He found his bedroll and saddlebags and the gun he'd dropped, and sat down, his fingers going through the automatic motions of reloading his pistol and cleaning his dagger.

"Red?" he called. She hadn't wandered back yet. "Red, you hurt?"

Still no answer. He got up and wandered through the remains of the Shonno-mara, careful not to trip over their bodies. "Red?"

Finally, he caught the gleam of her eyes, watching him from a crouch. He paused and approached her slowly, with his hand held out, as he would with a frightened animal. When his fingers finally brushed her head, he felt her tremors. They only became stronger as he ran his hand down across her flank, feeling for blood.

"Shh, it's alright. They're dead," he tried to sooth. But was it fear, or revulsion that shook her? When she shrank away from his touch he felt his guts twist, first in sorrow, then in anger. He sat back on his heels. "Well, maybe now you'll believe me when I say I'm a monster."

* * * * *

Rowan gave him a whimpering whine. She was still trying to process everything; the night's attack, Mask's slaughter of the wounded Shonno-mara, and the blood that was congealing on her muzzle and down her chest. She'd already thrown up once, but her stomach was still rolling with the leftover taste of blood that she couldn't spit out.

Mask sighed. "I heard you cry before. You're hurt. At least let me take care of it." He rose and walked back to the campsite. Rowan followed him slowly. Her collar had healed all her wounds faster than ever, thanks to the extra Nawassa the sorcerer had gathered. It was still flooding her with energy, in fact. Mask lit a stump of candle, even though the enchanted arrows still shone. He turned and faced her, taking in her blood-saturated fur, and his eyes softened behind his mask. He reached a hand out to her.

"You saved my life again." His voice had gone soft, and sounded natural, for once. Not the rough, bitter tone that he always used, and he smiled a little. "Thanks, Red."

It was the way he said her name at that moment. His smile. The scent of strength and fear that invaded her quivering nose. The way he watched her as though he could see through her. All that on top of months of wondering.

Rowan turned and fled into the night, leaving him to swear in surprise.

Aaro! No, no, no! Almighty, don't let that *be my Aaro!*

Her sides heaved, cracking the drying blood caked in her fur, and she let out a wail to reach the heavens.

Aaro is dead. That is not him. But which would be worse? To have him back and know that he was a monster, or to have him dead?

She shuddered.

When she came upon Mask's (or was it Aaro's?) horse, grazing under the stars, she stopped.

The other animal picked up his head and perked his ears at her. She flopped into the wet grass beside him, and wiggled around, trying to wipe away some of the blood that clung to her. The stallion shied at the blood, and wandered off a few yards to find grass that wasn't ruined.

Aaro, what have you done?

But not Aaro. Because Aaro was dead.

But what if he wasn't?

She stayed with the horse that night, and when the sky began to brighten, took its dangling reins in her teeth and led it back toward Mask's camp. *Mask*, she said his assumed name again in her mind to convince herself.

The man sat hunched beside the scattered remains of the fire, head bowed, with a blanket wrapped around his shoulders. But he turned when he heard the horse's hooves. He looked Rowan over, studying the dried blood smeared through her fur, no doubt trying to decipher where she'd been hurt.

"Thanks," he mumbled when she placed the reins in his hand. His voice sounded shadowed, and for once the constant stubble on the visible portion of his face made him look haggard rather than roguishly handsome.

When he'd packed his gear, including the enchanted weapons of the dead Shonno-mara, and mounted up, he sat still for a moment, staring at the horizon, then sighed. "You should have stayed away, Red. I owe you my life, twice over, but Ormand owes me more."

He flicked the reins, sending the horse into an easy trot, and Rowan followed. What else could she do? She had little to no doubt that *Mask* would carry through with his threat of betraying her. But she needed him—in more ways than one. And she also knew, without a lick of doubt, that at some point he had been an honorable man. It was some twisted version of that honor that drove him now. She just hoped he would come to himself before it was too late for both of them. And there wasn't much more time. They would reach Skybreak that day.

* * * * *

By midmorning they could make out Skybreak as a blot on the prairie. They approached it from the north and a little west, and could see the towers of Ormand's palace, the polished slate roof tiles gleaming blackish in the sun. Rowan rumbled out a growl as they drew nearer.

"Couldn't have said it better," Mask said.

Rowan remembered Ormand's home in

flashes. The manicured grounds, the sculpted gardens. Now it looked like a military compound. Rows of barracks blocked any view of the gardens, if they still remained, interspersed with muddy training grounds. A stockade surrounded the whole thing, blocking the view entirely as they trotted down a knoll, skirting the perimeter and giving it a wide berth. Mask made no move to go in through the gate, instead heading toward town and leaving Ormand's compound behind.

Rowan's stomach rolled as they reached the outlying estates. She guessed Mask must be intending to get supplies and be ready to flee, if it happened that he was actually able to kill Ormand and live through it. But she couldn't calm the conflict that raged through her, making her heart pound as waves of nausea hit her. If she were a human she'd be sweating. As a wolf, she panted like she'd just run a three-mile race in the desert.

Mask didn't notice her discomfort, fortunately, as they rode through Old Town. Its elegant stone mansions, gardens, and fountains felt both familiar and strange to her, with a mix of fondness and fear and bitter separation. They passed the chapel where she and Aaro had been married, and soon after that her uncle's house, though it looked more run-down than she remembered. Her heart leaped at the prospect of seeing Uncle Lance, Dustan, or some face she might recognize. But no one stirred outside, and they passed across the little creek into New Town, leaving it behind, which was both a relief and a sorrow to her.

Every place her gaze landed brought back memories. Especially of her last day, when she and Aaro had had lunch in the hotel dining room, and afterward walked the market. How the ladies had stared at them, whispering behind their fans. They gathered even more stares this day, she and her stranger. A masked man on a horse and a huge red wolf walking the street at high noon. More than one man they passed dropped his hand to his belt, whether he wore a gun or a sword or no weapon at all. Rowan could feel her hackles rising, which surely wouldn't help their reception, but she couldn't stop it. Mask tugged the horse to a stop in front of the general store and left the reins dangling when he went in, apparently trusting Rowan to keep an eye on him.

She sat by the stallion's reins and watched the street, her apprehension rising as the stares continued, from both women and men. People who passed went a long way around to avoid walking near her, some even crossing the street.

Her gaze snagged on a young couple, obviously in the throes of courtship, walking so close together that their hips brushed. The young lady clung to her beau's arm with two hands and had her adoring eyes fixed on his face. The young man... Rowan's breath snagged in her throat, and her jaws closed with a snap loud enough to make several passerby cringe. *Dustan.* Unwittingly her hind end left the ground, and her tail, rebellious organ that it always was, twitched a wag.

The four years had been good to her cousin. He looked taller and broader, glowing with health and affection for his young lady. His glance strayed to her, as everyone's was, and he paused, making his lady break her concentrated adoration to see what he was staring at. She gave a delicate little yip of surprise. A frown creased Dustan's forehead between his eyebrows.

"What is that thing?" the girl said, tugging backward on his arm.

"A wolf, I think," he replied. "I've never seen one like that before.

See me, cousin. Please. See me.

"How fearful! Is it safe?"

Dustan shrugged, peering closer, taking a step nearer. Then he drew back, muttering under his breath, and Rowan remembered last night's dried blood matted in her fur.

"Not sure we want to meet whoever that belongs to," her cousin said, drawing his sweetheart across the street and continuing their walk, just like the others.

Rowan sat back down, a tide of bitter heat rising in her chest. So that was it. The one person in the whole world who stood a chance of looking closer and maybe, just maybe, seeing the woman behind the wolf, was walking up the street making wedding plans without looking back.

"What's got you spooked?" Mask said behind her, his boots clomping over the boardwalk. He came around the end of the hitching rail and squatted down beside her, resting a hand on her head between her flattened ears.

She met his intense blue eyes and suddenly felt like the ground had been ripped out from under her all over again.

How many times had she looked into those same eyes over the last couple of months and unconsciously her imagination had formed Aaro's face under the mask? How many times had she caught his scent and had her heart break because she suddenly remembered one perfect night of being *one* with her man? How many times had his voice, even in its broken bitterness, haunted her dreams?

But now he was here in this town, where she'd looked into his eyes the first time and wondered what mysteries their sparkling blue concealed. His lips quirked into half a grin.

"Almost there, Red. And once I'm done with our Lesser King... maybe then I can be free."

Rowan's hide shuddered under his touch as he brushed a hand across her blood-caked shoulder. He packed the few supplies he'd bought into his saddlebags, and offered the stallion a small sack of grain, holding it while he ate. He'd replaced his ruined dagger as well.

She stared at him.

Aaro?

But then the vicious circle of her thoughts turned again, and she remembered his cold detachment as he murdered every single one of the Shonno-mara that had attacked their camp. Not that his actions didn't have reason behind them. But there were other ways the problem could have been handled. This man was a monster.

Not Aaro, she tried to convince herself, even as she followed him down the street, back toward Ormand's palace, where he'd warned her he would betray her if it meant an opportunity to kill the king. This was her last chance to run.

If he was Mask, the faceless assassin, she should leave now, wait to see if he was killed, and rejoin him later.

If he was Aaro—her ears flattened again as she trotted at his horse's heels—if he was Aaro, then she would follow him to the ends of the earth if it meant not losing him again.

And if he was Aaro and he still betrayed her? What then? Would she risk a broken heart, plus whatever Ormand had planned for her? Should she stop him and try to tell him the truth?

They were passing through Old Town again, and tremors wracked Rowan's body. She should leave now. This man was not her husband. He owed her his life, but she owed him nothing. Nothing whatsoever.

She couldn't do it.

Chapter 20

Aaro admired Red more than he'd admired anyone since Rowan, as she followed him through the gate into Ormand's courtyard. What on earth could drive someone—for she was a person, not a wolf—to display that much loyalty to someone she knew almost nothing about? What was she thinking?

He was surprised by a sudden tremor of anxiety as he dismounted and looped his reins over the hitching rail just inside the front gates. The two gate guards left their post and stood watch over him and Red with their hands on their gun butts.

"Captain Fernand will be here shortly to escort you in to see the king," one of the guards informed him, though his eyes never left Red. "You better put a rope on that animal."

Aaro shrugged. "Red, I'd be insulted."

She looked up at him, panting and visibly trembling. She was afraid.

He swore under his breath. He'd threatened her, warned her, practically begged her to leave so he wouldn't have to betray her. Why hadn't she left?

"So you're still alive after all."

Aaro turned to see Captain Alonso Fernand striding toward them, grinning broadly under his moustache. He looked like he was relieved and trying to hide it under brash swagger.

"I thought for sure you weren't coming back to claim your silver. And you brought the king a new pet."

Red's hackles rose.

Alonso halted in front of them, eyeing Red, and whistled. "Can't imagine what he wants with such a creature, but he'll be pleased." He turned and waved for them to follow. When they passed through the second gate and stood alone in the inner courtyard he stopped and faced Aaro. "Don't do it," he said flatly.

"You're going to stop me?"

Alonso shrugged impatiently. "This country *needs* you. Not an assassin. *You.* Someone they can rally behind."

"They need Ormand gone."

"And who's going to take his place?" the captain's sharp brown eyes glared at him.

"Whoever Heymish appoints." Aaro returned his glare, while Red watched, her head cocked to one side.

"Yes. Someone these people don't know or respect. And who knows if his second choice would be as bad as his first one. King Ormand needs to be brought to justice, but not at the expense of making yourself a villain. He's plotting something, and it's not good. Something Heymish isn't going to be able to stop. I'll beg you, if I have to, not to do this."

Aaro brushed past him. "Take me to see Ormand. He owes me money. Especially since I almost died for it."

With a growl Alonso spun on his heel and led the way up to the same ornate double doors that they'd entered before, passing two guards on the outside, and facing four more once they were in the vestibule.

The lit fireplaces at either end of the narrow room put off heat that slapped into Aaro like a wall. After over a week of travel, and living in little more than a hut made of saplings all winter, the heat threatened to suffocate him as two of the guards stepped forward and waited for him to remove his weapons belt. One of the other guards rummaged through a closet until he came up with a length of rope, which he handed to Aaro.

"Tie your animal," he said.

Aaro looked at the panting Red as he took the rope, running it through his hands, considering. After a moment he handed it back. "She'd get offended. Believe me, you don't want to see Red offended."

The guard thrust the rope back into his hands. "Tie her, or she doesn't go in. You want to get paid, don't you?" He sneered.

Aaro shrugged. Kneeling beside Red, he fastened a quick sliding knot and dropped the loop over her head, taking a moment to scratch her ears. She was shaking worse now than she'd been before.

The loop of rope hung loose. All she would have to do to get away would be to duck out of it. Unless she pulled on the rope and made it tighten. But she could always loosen it up with her paws if she had to. On her, the rope was little more than a decoration, though the guards didn't know that, and Red didn't let on, dutifully flattening her ears and backing away growling. She even took a snap at his hand, conveniently missing, of course.

One of the guards patted him down for hidden weapons, then sent them on their way.

Neither Aaro nor Alonso spoke until they neared Ormand's receiving hall. But before they were in earshot of the guards Alonso whispered, "If you must sacrifice something today, let it be your bloodlust, not your life."

Aaro ignored him.

He was searched for weapons again by the next set of guards, and then they were in the king's hall. Aaro felt as though a block of ice had settled in his stomach.

Ormand stood slowly from his throne as they approached, stopping a dozen yards from the dais. "You brought her." He breathed a laugh. "I can hardly believe it." He turned to Red. "Hello, my dear."

The red wolf stared at him, all the fur standing up along her back as she rumbled out a growl so low it was barely audible. Aaro heard it. His hands twitched on the rope.

"If I had known you would fare so well as a wolf, I would have chosen something else for Rigall to turn you into," Ormand said. There were three steps leading up onto his dais, and he stepped down one.

Aaro's eyes flickered over him, noting the sword and dagger he still wore on either hip, along with the medallion now draped around his neck. There was something else about Ormand now though. Something he couldn't pinpoint. A different air, perhaps.

"What would you give to be a woman again?" Ormand asked Red, still perched on the second stair.

She growled at him. Loud enough so the whole room could hear this time.

Ormand laughed. "In that case, I have no use for you either." He beckoned to Aaro. "Mask. Come. Leave the beast."

Aaro handed Red's rope to Alonso and walked forward. His vision had tunneled down until the only thing he could see clearly was Ormand's dagger, and his fingers twitched. Killing the king was going to be the easy part, and it was looking easier by the second. Red would back him against the guards, and hopefully Alonso as well.

"I congratulate you on a successful mission," the king said as Aaro drew nearer. "And also for living through it. I had heard a rumor that you were dead. Since you are not, the rest of your payment is at this moment being counted."

Aaro stopped when he was a pace away from Ormand. A lunge was all it would take. He could have Ormand's dagger out of its sheath and into his heart in under three seconds. His muscles tightened.

"But I would ask one more small thing of you first," the king continued.

Aaro's heart faltered as Ormand reached for and drew his own dagger, holding it out to Aaro, hilt first. Aaro's hand came up of its own volition, slowly, to grasp the hilt.

One of the guards appeared suddenly at his elbow, standing so close he brushed Aaro's arm as he drew his sword and pressed it into his side, cheerfully ensuring his king's safety.

At the same time Ormand voiced the rest of his command. "Cut out her heart." He nodded toward Red.

Time froze for Aaro as his hand closed around the dagger hilt.

In one second his plan had gone from perfect to nightmarish.

Ormand held his hands up to the guard, cautioning. "Let him prove his loyalty to me. I insist. He will need it for his next mission."

Aaro kept himself from swaying on his feet, but he could feel the color leave his face beneath the mask. Light reflected off the polished blade and into his eyes as he hesitated. The guard's sword stayed at his ribs. He could still kill Ormand, maybe, but he would in turn be killed. Could he deliver a fatal blow with the guard standing at his elbow, holding a sword to his ribs? Dare he try?

"I have great plans, my friend," Ormand was saying, with the oil in his voice that he used for killing people. "And I can make you a wealthy man."

"Oh? With a sword at my ribs?" Aaro growled.

Ormand waved him off. "Prove your loyalty. I see you are fond of the she-wolf. Kill her, and I will consider you my right-hand man." He laughed. "No more swords in your ribs. If it makes you feel better, I'll tell them not to take your weapons when you enter my hall."

How could this go so wrong?

Aaro met Ormand's gaze, and wondered what was behind those calculating blue eyes.

"You're wondering why I would trust you?" Ormand said. He shrugged. "I don't. and I won't. But you won't get paid if I'm dead, and I'll be paying enough to make keeping me alive a worthy goal."

"I see." *Which would be good reasoning, if money was my motive.*

So, after everything, all he had to do was kill Red, and Ormand was as good as his.

He turned slowly, and found Red and

Alonso watching him. Alonso gave a barely perceptible shake of his head, while Red met his gaze without blinking. He took a step forward. She had stopped shaking, though her ears were flattened back. Another step. Who was she?

It took him an eternity to reach them. He knelt in front of Red, bowing his head before the force of her gaze, her eyes their indefinable shade of copper, amber, and brown. The king's dagger shook in his hand.

Above him he heard a hiss of breath from Alonso.

With the only guards up near the dais, Aaro faced his two friends, and beyond them, an empty room. He reached up with his free hand and grasped his mask. The magic tingled for a second and then released, and fresh air swept over his face. He would hate himself after today. The best outcome he could hope for was to kill Red, kill Ormand, and then die by the guards' hands.

"I'm sorry, Red," he whispered.

The razor-edged dagger slid between her ribs, just behind her shoulder.

* * * * *

Rowan flinched.

Not at the dagger through her lung, but at the face of her husband.

Aaro.

His hand dropped from the dagger before he'd pushed it to the hilt, his gaze snagging on the little pendant hanging from her collar, half hidden in her fur. Recognition flashed in his eyes. "What..." he whispered. "...what...?"

Then the pain hit her. Along with a wave of blinding fury.

She lunged at Aaro, snapping her jaws open. She drove him over backward onto the floor, while his hand came up at the same time and slapped the mask back onto his face, and then she clamped her teeth around his shoulder, tasting the salty tang of blood, and gave him a shake. The movement tore at the dagger in her side, and she let go of him, both of them yelping in pain. For a bare instant she stood over him, drooling blood, and they stared at the mutual horror reflected in each other's eyes.

"Who are you?" he whispered hoarsely.

She snarled, baring bloody fangs at him, and his eyes widened as though he expected her to rip his throat out. She considered it. But then she was yanked backward, gagging, as Captain Fernand, who had seemed to already know Aaro's identity, snapped out of his shock and hauled on the rope tied around her neck.

Aaro scrambled to his knees and lunged forward after her, grabbing the hilt of the dagger and jerking it free. Blood poured after it, and dizziness assaulted her. He reached for her, dagger in hand, and she thought he would slit her throat. Instead he grappled for a second with the knot, and the rope slid free. Rowan bolted.

She snarled at one of the guards who tried to intercept her, and he faltered long enough for her to rush past him, through a side door and into a deserted hallway. She ran in the direction of the kitchens while magic swarmed her wound, buzzing unbearably. She could feel it tickling inside her chest, along with the blood that gurgled with every breath and coated the back of her tongue.

Racing down another corridor, she burst into the kitchens to the sounds of shattering crockery and screaming cooks. Somewhere there would be a door open. There was always a door open in the kitchen, unless it was the dead of winter. There. She got a whiff of fresh air and barreled toward it, with shrieking servants diving out of her way. She burst out into the herb garden, leapt over three rows of lettuce and newly sprouted pea plants, and followed her nose toward the stables.

In the shadow of the stable she collapsed, coughing and panting. Her lung felt like it was filling up faster than the magic could heal it, thanks to her pounding heart. She coughed up more blood, gagging on it, then forced herself to stay still, to slow her breathing and wait for the magic to heal her lung. Another coughing, retching fit helped to clear it out, and her panic subsided a bit. She was still alive. Still breathing. It was coming easier now, though the tingling, crawling feeling of the magic made her squirm.

As soon as she could draw a decent breath again she slunk away from the shadows of the building. She had to find a way out.

The old portion of the grounds was not as heavily fortified as the new. Sunken sod walls, shoulder high to a man, protected the immense gardens from the open prairie. Willing strength into her legs, she leapt to the top of the wall, teetered, for a second, then dropped down to the other side, taking off at a loping run.

* * * * *

The pain in her side grew less as she put miles between her and Ormand and Aaro and the rest of her cursed former life. She should never have left the Shonnowa. She would always be a wolf there, but at least she had friends who knew her. Who wouldn't betray her.

Aaro.

Aaro.

His name and his face pounded through her mind with each drum of her paws. She had no coherent thoughts, let alone words, for the volcano of pain welling inside her, and she alternated between fiery fury and ice-cold loss. Dustan had hardly looked at her twice. Aaro, her husband, had *stabbed* her. Though now, she realized, his actions made sense. He'd become a monster. But a monster of Ormand's making. He'd taken everything. From both of them.

When she became too winded to run, she walked for a while. Then ran again. Then walked.

She didn't stop until the sliver of a moon had come up, barely enough to activate her curse. She sat down when she felt the magic tingle across her skin, bringing with it the change in form, then picked herself up and continued north on two legs rather than four, striding along in the moonlight as her tears poured. Finally, when the night was almost spent, she curled up in a ball in the grass and cried herself to sleep.

* * * * *

Aaro flinched when the knot came loose, still more than half expecting Red to rip his throat out. Instead, she ran, disappearing through a side door that had been left open, and leaving a wide blood trail. He stared, his heart thudding heavily, and pressed a hand against his throbbing shoulder. He didn't know what else to do at the moment.

"Go after her," Ormand barked, snapping him out of his shock. He glanced around. Alonso still held the dangling rope in his hands, his mouth ajar. The guards weren't in much better shape.

"Go after her, Mask," Ormand repeated.

Aaro took a step, stumbled, and then he was running, turning into the corridor where she had fled, following her blood trail through the kitchen, which was in mayhem, and out toward the stables. He was just in time to see her furry hind end take a leap off the top of the sod wall, headed for open prairie. He scrambled over after her, but she was gone. Like an arrow shot from a bow, she sped across the prairie, becoming little more than a glint of copper in the evening sunlight. Even her blood trail thinned out and vanished.

He had wondered if the collar she wore had some healing magic in it. Obviously, he had been right. But a better question was, why did the pendant attached to the collar bear his own family seal? Who was Red?

He trailed her for more than an hour, though there was no more blood to follow. She had beaten a path through the long, brown grass. When the sun rested on the horizon he stopped, looking off toward the north, where she'd gone. Back toward the Shonnowa. Kneeling on the damp ground, alone, he took his mask off and dropped it beside him, next to Ormand's dagger. The horizon blazed red. Aaro threw his head back and yelled. He emptied his lungs, then yelled again, wordlessly releasing his pain. Not the pain from the bite in his shoulder, but that of having his hands covered in his friend's blood.

When his throat was raw from screaming, he let himself slump forward and covered his face with his hands, for once, instead of his mask.

"Almighty, what have I done?" His chest heaved with a dry sob. "Gah! What have I done?"

My sins against You have become too great a burden.

The dagger beside him gleamed red in the

dying sunlight, and he fingered the blade, considering driving it through his own heart in payment for his guilt. He'd tried to kill his friend. Not a wolf, a woman. An innocent one, who'd saved his life. Had she known all along who he was? How else could she have known to put his seal on her collar? She'd graciously let him keep his anonymity, protected him, guided him, kept him warm. Who was she? And how could he have been so damn blind? Heaping guilt on top of guilt until there was no going back.

A low growl sounded off to his left, and he froze, terrified that he would turn and face Red. When the growl came again, he realized the tone was all wrong. He glanced to the side and spotted a normal gray wolf hunkered in the grass, eyeing him. It looked small compared to Red, and he almost laughed at it. Then a thought occurred to him. He grabbed Ormand's dagger, his only weapon at the moment, and sat waiting.

The wolf yapped at him, edging closer. It must smell the blood on him. He stayed still, not moving until it sprang. He caught it by the throat, mid-leap, and ran the dagger through its ribs. The same place he'd stabbed Red.

The animal yelped and jumped back. It ran, but not far. Aaro followed, giving it time to die before he drew near. Without ceremony he gutted it, cut its heart free, and pulled it out.

"Not so sure I deserve life more than you did," he muttered. "But if the Almighty saw fit to send you, then I thank you for your sacrifice. It's always innocent blood that covers the sins of the guilty. Guess because ours isn't worth anything anymore." He snorted.

He went back to where he'd been sitting and replaced his mask, smearing wolf's blood across it, then headed back to Ormand with the dripping heart in his hand.

* * * * *

Alonso met him at the gate, and led him, without a word, back to Ormand's hall.

"Did you know who she was?" Aaro asked.

The captain merely shook his head, his lips pressed flat, dark eyebrows drawn together. All he said was, "The king asked if I recognized you when you had your mask off. He still doesn't know who you are."

He didn't try to take the dagger from Aaro before they came into the presence of the king. None of them did.

Ormand broke into a sly smile when Aaro threw the wolf's heart down at his feet. He held the bloody dagger out to him, hilt-first, and trembling only slightly. Ormand stared at him for a long moment.

"Wise choice," he said finally as he took the dagger and handed it off to one of the guards to clean. "What took you so long?"

"She was strong. She ran farther than I expected. And I didn't hurry."

"Your next mission then," Ormand said,

settling onto his carved wooden throne, inlaid with silver. "You're going east. Kill King Heymish. It's high time for my brother to die."

Hey there, faithful readers! Thanks so much for picking up my book. If you liked what you read, please consider leaving a review on Amazon or Goodreads. Reviews are SO important for authors! And of course, spread the word to your bookworm friends. It would mean the world to me!

You can find out more about me, check out some of my other writing, and find out when the next book is coming out by following me on Goodreads or Facebook (www.facebook.com/shari.branning/), or going to my blog sharibranning.blogspot.com. Feel free to leave a message or comment. I would love to hear from you!